D1744859

OCEANS

A DARK DRABBLES ANTHOLOGY

Compiled & Edited by D Kershaw

Also available from Black Hare Press

DARK DRABBLE ANTHOLOGIES

WORLDS
ANGELS
MONSTERS
BEYOND
UNRAVEL
APOCALYPSE
LOVE
HATE
OCEANS
ANCIENTS

Twitter: @BlackHarePress
Facebook: BlackHarePress
Website: www.BlackHarePress.com

Oceans, A Dark Drabbles Anthology title is
Copyright © 2020 Black Hare Press
First published in Australia in April 2020 by Black Hare Press

The authors of the individual stories retain the copyright of the works
featured in this anthology.

*All characters and events in this publication, other than those clearly in the
public domain, are fictitious and any resemblance to real persons, living or
dead, is purely coincidental.*

All rights reserved. No part of this production may be reproduced, stored in a
retrieval system, or transmitted, in any form or by any means, electronic,
mechanical, photocopying, recording or otherwise, without the prior
permission of the publisher and copyright owner.

Paperback: ISBN 978-1-925809-62-6
Hard Cover: ISBN 978-1-925809-63-3

Cover Design by Dawn Burdett
Book Formatting by Ben Thomas

wade
through black jade.
    Of the crow-blue mussel-shells, one
keeps
        adjusting the ash-heaps;
            opening and shutting itself like
an
injured fan.
    The barnacles which encrust the side
    of the wave, cannot hide
        there for the submerged shafts of
the
sun,
split like spun
    glass, move themselves with spotlight
swiftness
    into the crevices—
        in and out, illuminating
the
turquoise sea
    of bodies. The water drives a wedge
    of iron through the iron edge
        of the cliff; whereupon the stars,

pink
rice-grains, ink-
     bespattered jelly fish, crabs like green
     lilies, and submarine
        toadstools, slide each on the other.

All
external
     marks of abuse are present on this
     defiant edifice—
        all the physical features of

ac-
cident—lack
     of cornice, dynamite grooves, burns,
and
     hatchet strokes, these things stand
        out on it; the chasm-side is

dead.
Repeated
     evidence has proved that it can live
     on what can not revive
        its youth. The sea grows old in it.

Marianne Moore - 1918, *The Fish*

Table of Contents

Foreword

They cover seventy percent of the Earth's surface, yet we've barely explored the oceans—even though we've sailed these waters for thousands of years.

We have little concept of the undiscovered mysteries and magic of the watery depths, or of the grotesque monsters that lurk there, but myths and fairy tales have been borne from long-ago stories of returning sailors, some of which we are sharing here with you; sirens and selkies; drowned cities; tentacled serpents and hideous sea creatures; the tainted treasure of plundering pirates; the gentle, summoning whispers of the ancients.

Will you dare venture into the depths?

Love and kisses
D. Kershaw & Ben Thomas
Black Hare Press

BLACK HARE PRESS

Dead Man's Chest
by Nicola Currie

I knew the captain was superstitious. Still, I was surprised when he raised his rum to Neptune as we hauled up our bounty from the depths.

I was further surprised when I saw the case of tarnished iron, chained to a wreck of a ship that belonged to the Crown several kings ago. Perhaps its ruined appearance belied its contents. Surely, gold and gemstones beyond imagination lay inside, after the perils of our journey.

"Why is it called the Dead Man's Chest?" I asked.

The captain shot me in the heart.

"It's where we offer the dead man," he said.

Nicola Currie is from Cambridge, UK where she works in educational publishing. She has published poetry in literary magazines, including Mslexia and Sarasvati, and short stories in various anthologies. She has also completed her first novel, which was longlisted for the Bath Children's Novel Award. Website: writeitandweep.home.blog

The Full Moon and the Sea
by P.C. Darkcliff

The moon reflects on the surface. It creates a silvery corridor that runs from the surf toward the black horizon.

I see two figures walking down the beach. Is that Mommy dragging my sister Ronnie?

I hear a childish voice. "Mommy, I'm scared!"

Yes, it's them!

They wade in. Ronnie cries, but Mommy holds her tight. The water reaches Mommy's waist. A roaring wave rolls over Ronnie's head.

Mommy's eyes shine in the moonlight. She drags Ronnie behind a clump of rocks that stick out of the sea—to the place where she drowned me on the last full moon.

P.C. Darkcliff is the author of two novels, Deception of the Damned and The Priest of Orpagus. In September 2020, he's going to launch Celts and the Mad Goddess, the first installment of The Deathless Chronicle.
Social Media: plu.us/p.c.darkcliff
Reader List: mailchi.mp/c5550d315607/pcdarkcliff

Unexpected Laughter
by K.B. Elijah

The wave of seawater towers above the coastal town, the threat clear in its unavoidable anticipation. Gravity conspires with the ocean to bring ruin to our slice of civilisation.

Is it revenge, I wonder, as my family scream and flounder around me, that brings the ocean to our door? All that rubbish and toxic waste humanity dumps into the seas?

The screams die as the tsunami tears our house apart with relish, and I giggle as I'm swept away, pushed down under metres of turbulent seawater.

It's good to be a goldfish, I think. And I've forgotten my humans already.

K.B. Elijah is a fantasy author living in Brisbane, Australia with her husband and three cockatiels. A lawyer by day, and a writer by...also day, because she needs her solid nine hours of sleep per night (not that the cockatiels let her sleep past 6am). K.B. writes for various international anthologies, and her work features in dozens of collections about the mysterious, the magical and the macabre. Her own books of short fantasy novellas with twists, The Empty Sky and Out of the Nowhere, are available on paperback and Kindle now.
Website: www.kbelijah.com
Instagram: k.b.elijah

Reef Head
by Jasmine Jarvis

It was my first dive on the Great Barrier Reef.

Stepping off the end of the yacht, I let my weighted belt pull me under.

A piece of electric blue coral had caught my eye, and despite my better judgement (and the conservation rules), I broke it off its rock to bring it home.

I didn't realise I had cut my finger in the process.

It's been a week now since that dive and I am in a horror of my own making—pieces of electric blue coral protrude from my head with more sprouting with each passing day…

Jasmine Jarvis is a teller of tales and scribbler of scribbles. She lives in Brisbane, Australia with her husband Michael, their two children, Tilly and Mish; Ripley, their German Shepherd, and indoor fat cat, Dwight K. Shrute.

Planet Killer
by Steven Lord

The creature crawled onto the beach, eyes burning red above the black horned ridges of its maw. Tourists fled in terror, leaving their beach towels and mewling children behind as they sprinted for their lives. It towered over them all, looming as high as the skyscrapers in the city centre just a mile or so back from the shore.

With a mighty roar, it started to shuffle towards the financial district, wreaking havoc in its path. Then, after three steps, it collapsed with a ground-shaking thud.

When they cut it open, they found sixteen tonnes of plastic in its stomach.

Steven Lord is a debut author based in the south of England. He is currently attempting to cram writing in alongside a busy day job, with varying levels of success. While his long-term aspiration is to get a novel published, at present he would be pretty pleased with a drabble or two.

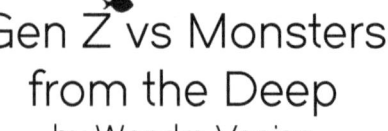

Gen Z vs Monsters from the Deep
by Wondra Vanian

People were watching the sky when invaders came from the sea.

The creatures had tentacles, sharp teeth, and old grudges when they squelched onto the beaches that Fourth of July. Battle ready, they carried weapons made from the sharpened bones of whales.

It had been countless lifetimes since they'd encountered humans, but they were finally ready. Only…things had changed.

They came expecting war.

They got Generation Z.

"Are those *tentacles*? That's lit, fam! Selfie?"

It took hours to realise humanity was no longer worth conquering.

The verdict that humanity was too stupid to live, however, was reached within minutes.

Wondra Vanian is an American living in the United Kingdom with her Welsh husband and their army of fur babies. A writer first, Wondra is also an avid gamer, photographer, cinephile, and blogger. She has music in her blood, sleeps with the lights on, and has been known to dance naked in the moonlight. Wondra was a multiple Top-Ten finisher in the 2017 and 2018 Preditors and Editors Reader's Poll, including the Best Author category. Her story, "Halloween Night," was named a Notable Contender for the Bristol Short Story Prize in 2015.
Website: www.wondravanian.com

Seoltóir

by J.M. Meyer

I pray for mercy to the Sea God, Ler, while the raging waves dwarf our ship. My unheard prayer is a whisper compared to the deafening wind, explosions of thunder and the splintering of helpless wood. I hear the wailing of the Fairy, Bean Sídhe, preparing our sorry band of men that all will soon be lost. Man is no match for the wrath of the Gods. Other sailors say the sea is their one true love, but I long for the warmth of my bride's embrace and fear for the fate of our child, whom I will never see.

J.M. Meyer is a writer, artist and small business owner living in New York, where she received her master's degree from Teachers College, Columbia University. Jacqueline enjoys writing speculative fiction and mysteries. Her favorite author is Alice Munro and her favorite film…is…anything horror related. Jacqueline also enjoys hiking with her dog Molly and the company of her husband Bruce and daughters; Julia, Emma and Lauren. Jacqueline's Mantra lately; there's no such thing as failing, it's called learning.
Website: jmoranmeyer.net
Amazon: www.amazon.com/author/jacquelinemoranmeyer

Flotsam
by Raven Corinn Carluk

"Leave it alone," Anne yelled.

Travis laughed, poked the dead fish again. "See if I care." He left his younger sister, raced to the tide pool waiting amidst the seaweed-strewn rocks. He hoped there were plenty of treasures to be found. Maybe something to leave in Anne's bed.

While she ran off to report him to their mom, he scaled the jagged barrier. The brackish smell grew stronger, and he climbed faster.

"Just seaweed?" he complained at the top. Nothing worth his effort.

A maw opened, revealing sharp teeth. Travis barely had time to scream before he was pulled in.

Raven Corinn Carluk *writes dark fantasy, paranormal romance, and anything else that catches her interest. She's authored five novels, where she explores themes of love and acceptance. Her shorter pieces, usually from her darker side, can be found in Black Hare Press anthologies, at Detritus Online, and through Alban Lake Publishers.*
Twitter: @ravencorinn
Website: www.ravencorinncarluk.com

When Confronted by the Big Bull Seal

by Hannah Retallick

She holds its stare. It's what she wants. They bob in the waves, a black swimsuit and a mound of grey.

He once told her his ocean elephants story. "Imagine if I hadn't been wearing flippers!" he'd said. "Yes, imagine that," she'd echoed, honeymoon hands trailing through the salty sea. He pulled her into deeper water, spouting yarns of great adventure.

How much he'd experienced; how much he knew!

The seal disappears. Its shadow moves closer. She waits, hopeful for a ripping growl, a searing pain in her foot, and a rising cloud of red.

This will make him listen.

Hannah Retallick is a twenty-six-year-old from Anglesey, North Wales. She was home educated and then studied with the Open University, graduating with a First-class honours degree, BA in Humanities with Creative Writing and Music, and is studying for an MA in Creative Writing. She is working on her second novel and writes short stories and a blog. She was shortlisted in the Writing Awards at the Scottish Mental Health Arts Festival 2019, the Cambridge Short Story Prize, and the Henshaw Short Story Competition June 2019.
Website: ihaveanideablog.wordpress.com

The End of a Hard Day
by Michael D. Davis

It's been years or even decades now for all I know. I lost track of time after the first few months on this God-forsaken island. It's the picture postcard view from hell, nothing but sand and ocean. Except for today, there was something in the distance, moving in the water, something big. It made waves in the usually tepid waters that nearly sunk the island. It's the end of everything.

Carl had a hard day. He was going to end it right. He stripped nude and splashed down in the tub. Sitting quietly in the water, tiny screams were heard.

Michael D. Davis was born and raised in a small town in the heart of Iowa. Having written over thirty short stories, ranging in genre from comedy to horror from flash fiction to novella he continues in his accursed pursuit of a career in the written word.

No More Stars
by Caroline S. Kent

There was war. What wasn't destroyed by the nuclear blasts was made barren by the radiation that followed. The surface was rendered unfit for life. So, we survivors found shelter in the caves under the oceans.

Genetic engineers modified our bodies, and within two generations we are now all aquatic men and women. Our children will never know any different.

I am the last of the surface dwellers. I remember being able to look up and see a night sky full of stars. Now, with a watery ceiling to our world, there are no more stars for me to see…

Caroline S. Kent is a lady of distinction. She likes wine, women and chocolate. Probably in that order.
Facebook: caroline.s.kent

Cleon's Stone Figurehead
by McKenzie Richardson

The detail of the figurehead was so precise it appeared it may climb down off the bow at any moment. How Cleon had obtained it was just as fascinating.

The storm that claimed his brother's life marooned Cleon and a few survivors on an island, its lone inhabitant a sculptor perpetually shrouded in an opaque black mourning veil.

After making repairs, she'd given Cleon a sculpture to replace his smashed figurehead. "For luck."

The figurehead, which bore a striking resemblance to his lost brother, proved her promise true.

Although he wished the face wasn't carved into such a terrified expression.

McKenzie Richardson lives in Milwaukee, WI. Her horror stories have been featured in various anthologies including Evil Lurks, Pandemic, and After: Undead Wars. She has also published a variety of poems and flash fiction pieces.
Facebook: mckenzielrichardson
Blog: www.craft-cycle.com

Stranded
by R.J. Meldrum

He'd been stranded for five days. He cursed his stupidity. He'd pointed his jet ski out towards the open ocean, not thinking about what might happen. His fuel had run out, and the currents had pushed him further away from shore. There was no cellphone signal, no sign of any boats or ships. He was stuck. He was going to die. He considered his options. Thirst, sunstroke? He thought about slipping into the water to drown, but he wasn't really serious. He needed something faster.

A grey shape appeared. A fin emerged from the water. His prayer had been answered.

R.J. Meldrum is an author and academic. Born in Scotland, he moved to Ontario, Canada in 2010. He has had stories published by Horrified Press, the Infernal Clock, Trembling with Fear, Darkhouse Books, Smoking Pen Press, and James Ward Kirk Fiction. He also has had stories published in The Sirens Call e-zine, the Horror Zine and Drabblez Magazine. He is an Affiliate Member of the Horror Writers Association.
Twitter: @RichardJMeldru1
Facebook: richard.meldrum.79

The Edge
by Nicola Currie

Of all the people to prove me wrong, of all the conspiracy theorists who turned out to be right, I never thought it would be the flat-earthers.

I shouldn't have goaded their number one vlogger, should never have argued that no matter what route he dictated to my crew, it was impossible to fall off the edge of the earth.

Because we fell. A sudden full ninety-degree downturn. We're still falling, in fact, days, weeks later, somehow still breathing, in this liminal perpendicular place between earth and space as a waterfall sea gushes not underneath but alongside us.

Falling.

Falling.

Nicola Currie is from Cambridge, UK where she works in educational publishing. She has published poetry in literary magazines, including Mslexia and Sarasvati, and short stories in various anthologies. She has also completed her first novel, which was longlisted for the Bath Children's Novel Award. Website: writeitandweep.home.blog

New World
by Sara A. Mosier

The water mocked the dark inky nature of the sky. Each star seemed like a knife in her already bleeding body. But all she could do was focus, float, breath. As her consciousness faded in and out as frequently as the lapping waves, a hand, then two, gripped her tightly. They pulled her into the cold depths. For a moment the stars were simply dimming glitter and she no longer needed or cared to draw breath.

The world fell around her, lungs burning but no more fight left.

She was greeted by dazzling topaz eyes and an icy, toothy grin.

Sara A. Mosier is a Nebraska author, poet, and recent graduate from the University of Nebraska-Lincoln where she received a BA in English. Her writing focus is fiction and poetry of which she enjoys typing on an old 1950's typewriter. She has poetry published in several issues of Laurus Magazine, Cocky-Tales anthology, and University of Nebraska Press's 75th Anniversary edition of "Voices of Nebraska". Her romantic short stories "Sparkling Human Conundrum" and "Summer Dilemma" can be found in the anthologies Love Dust and Salty Tales on Amazon.

Family Bonding
by N.M. Brown

Papaw and I love fishing. Mama won't let me go anymore on account of what happened the last time we were on his boat.

The sun had just set. Papaw liked fishing after nightfall due to calmer waters. He'd taught me how to cast a net the month before, so I eagerly threw it out.

After asking repeatedly, Papaw finally let me start pulling it up. Only, it was too heavy for me. I screamed when I saw what we pulled in; a bloated, human torso.

"Papaw's getting lazy I guess," he said, ruefully dropping it back into the ocean.

*Since **N.M. Brown** made her first post to a popular Internet forum, she's taken the horror community by storm. Her ability to create, terrify, and drive home her stories is insurmountable. N.M. Brown's published works can be found in multiple anthologies for all to read, but be forewarned, if you do... you may want to call your therapist after, her stories are terrifying, disturbing and devilishly unsettling. She is not only a fright visually, but also has a creepy tentacle in horror podcasting as well. Sinister Sweetheart writes, voice acts and is the media director of the Scarecrow Tales podcast.*
Website: Sinistersweetheart.wixsite.com/sinistersweetheart
Facebook: NMBrownStories

With the Morning Dawn
by J.W. Garrett

Colours of dawn peeked above the horizon in the early morning. Whose idea was it to get married now?

The crowd gathered, smiled at him and his wife to be, their eyes fixed on the sunrise above. He waited for the minister's words and the ceremony to begin.

A roar sounded. He squeezed his love's fingers tight within his own. The crowd heaved a collective groan.

An alarm thundered. Chaos ensued.

A wall of water approached the small island. Terror made him move. Dragging his bride, he ran inland.

But nowhere was safe from the gigantic wave coming for them.

J.W. Garrett has been writing in one form or another since she was a teenager. She currently lives in Florida with her family but loves the mountains of Virginia where she was born. Her writings include YA fantasy as well as short stories. Since completing Remeon's Quest-Earth Year 1930, the prequel in her YA fantasy series, Realms of Chaos, she has been hard at work on the next in the series, scheduled to release August 2020. When she's not hanging out with her characters, her favourite activities are reading, running and spending time with family.
Website: www.jwgarrett.com
BHC Press: www.bhcpress.com/Author_JW_Garrett.html

Destiny
by Jennifer Hatfield

Jeremy manoeuvred his mini sub around the rusticle-covered hull of Titanic, awed by the anemones, crabs, and coral that called the enormous wreckage home. His eyes widened at the sight of shoes, in pairs, resting on the ocean floor alongside china bowls and a megaphone.

Upon resurfacing, Jeremy watched the video. A rhythmic discord of unknown vibrations was heard throughout. After equalising sound frequencies, and filtering background noise, his jaw dropped. Shivers travelled down his spine.

"Destiny Waltz" played through his speakers. A song the bravest staff members aboard played, moments before plunging beneath the surface to perish for eternity.

Jennifer Hatfield spent a large portion of her life being a dedicated mother and wife. She managed her epilepsy diagnosis, and handled the loss of her husband. Grateful to find comfort in the ability to write in an effort to express her feelings, thoughts, and struggles. She's published 5 poems.

Beckon me to Waters Sweet
by Shelly Jarvis

There's a man at my window.

It's creepy to see him there, not just because I don't know him and he's staring at me, but also because we're at depths no human can survive in open water, and he's not wearing a suit.

He beckons me to join him and I want to, desperately. Something in my gut pulls me towards the hatch. But I can't. I shouldn't. I can. I will.

I input my passcode and hear the blaring alarm, a symphony. Override engaged. The water rushes in, the pressure squeezes, and I join him in his watery grave.

Shelly Jarvis is a speculative fiction author from West Virginia, US. She found a life-long love of sci-fi and fantasy in the 3rd grade when she found Madeleine L'Engle's "A Wrinkle in Time." Shelly is an avid reader, a Whovian, the ideal viewer of dog rescue videos, and undoubtedly Ravenclaw. She currently has three YA sci-fi books available for purchase on Amazon. Website: www.ShellyJarvis.com

Expedition of One
by F.J. Bergmann

When the lifeboat began to dissolve, he knew that he was doomed. The shuttle had hit some airborne entity on the way down, made an emergency landing in the vast wine-red ocean. A breathable atmosphere, but analysis of the water, or whatever fluid he floated in, was incomplete. Not that it would matter. On the horizon, vast stormclouds veined with lightning were rising. Overhead, vast avian forms spiralled slowly; beneath him, immense shadows circled. If he put his pressure suit back on and sank, for how long might he walk on the ocean floor? What was waiting for him there?

F.J. Bergmann edits poetry for Mobius: The Journal of Social Change, serves as vice president of the Science Fiction & Fantasy Poetry Association, and imagines tragedies on or near exoplanets. She has competed at National Poetry Slam as a member of the Madison, WI, Urban Spoken Word team. Her work appears irregularly in Abyss & Apex, Alcyone, Analog, Anti-Heroin Chic, Asimov's SF, and venues elsewhere in the alphabet. Her dystopian collection of first-contact expedition reports, A Catalogue of the Further Suns, won the 2017 Gold Line Press poetry chapbook contest and the 2018 SFPA Elgin Chapbook Award.
Website: mobiusmagazine.com
Website: sfpoetry.com

A Beautiful Place for a Bad End
by G. Allen Wilbanks

A beautiful place for a bad end, thought Will as he gazed out over the crystalline blue ocean waters below him. He stood at the railing of the cruise ship, gripping the upper bar in his hands.

It was cold, almost freezing, and that was fine with Will. The colder the better. Maybe the ship would even hit an iceberg and save him some trouble.

No, that was too much to hope for, he knew. When had things ever been easy for him?

Resigned, he climbed the railing and jumped; arms outstretched to welcome the frozen embrace of the sea.

G. Allen Wilbanks is a member of the Horror Writers Association (HWA) and has published over 100 short stories in various magazines and on-line venues. He is the author of two short story collections, and the novel, When Darkness Comes. Website: www.gallenwilbanks.com Blog: DeepDarkThoughts.com

Everlasting Life Theory 1520
by D.J. Elton

"Fact!" Roderick adjusts his telescope. "Humans expire, then their subtle form goes into the waters, from where it originally came. Returning to the unbounded oceans."

"What madness," says Terrence. "All that time with astronomers, priests and marine scientists. You can't come up with a better theory?"

Roderick implored, "You can see them in any stretch of the ocean water. I've seen thousands."

"Definitely crazy," snorted Terrence. "I've never seen one. Ever. A person dies and goes up to the heavens."

"Ha! Not so!" Roderick is passionate. "And have you ever seen one rise up to the heavens?"

Terrence is silent.

D.J. Elton is a writer living in Melbourne's west. As a child she came from England to Australia, on the last boat down the Suez Canal, where she underwent a sacrificial dunking ritual in the court of King Neptune, and has never looked back. She likes creating speculative micro fiction and short stories, as well as random essays. Her work has been published in several anthologies, and she has written a historical fantasy novella, 'The Merlin Girl.' When not playing with a pen, she likes most of all to go to the green country.

More Plastic for the Ocean
by Andrew Anderson

"Let's go zorbing lads," the drunken bachelor had said.

Idiot.

Inebriated, I'd lost my balance on the hill and veered off-course. My orb emulated James's peach by going over the cliffs and rapidly being swept out to sea—it escalated quickly.

I'm sweltering inside this oversized beach-ball, and I'm parched. Worse still, I can't swim, so I'm in a translucent prison where all my options mean death.

Drowning; dehydration; heatstroke; s*hark*.

I can make out their ominous silhouettes moving around in the inky depths beneath my feet.

A thin wet spray hits the back of my neck—it's a puncture.

Andrew Anderson is a spare-time writer of microfiction, flash fiction and short stories, from Bathgate, Scotland. His work has been published on FlashFlood and Re:Written, and published in Black Hare Press anthologies.
Twitter: _soorploom_

The Shallows
by Anika Claire

I keep pace as she walks along the beach, the sky black above her, speckled with infinite stars.

Her face is brooding, her voice angry as she shouts out to the dark ocean. She turns to walk back the other way, tracking down to the wet sand near the lapping water.

I wait, patient.

What care I why she's upset? Why she chooses to walk alone on the shore at night? I care only that she steps closer to the water until the waves wash over her feet.

I grab her ankle; pull her down. Her screams turn to bubbles.

Anika Claire lives in Brisbane, Australia with her young family, where she alternates between making maps and escaping to other worlds, through either reading or creating them. You can find her reviewing and podcasting about books at;
Website: teainthetreetops.com
Instagram: @anni.treetops

Finite

by Sara A. Mosier

Above the sun-soaked sky, there was a massive cloud; it enveloped the entirety of the heavens. They could feel the heat rising from the mountain top, in such a way that nature told them to flee. Their gazes locked forever, their hands entwined, as the thunder enveloped everything around them. As the air grew thin, they plunged into the ocean hand in hand, cheek to cheek, grasping at one another as the world closed around them in a vastness of heat and darkness. Their limbs tangled, their lips joined, as they became stone, sinking to the bottom of the ocean.

Sara A. Mosier *is a Nebraska author, poet, and recent graduate from the University of Nebraska-Lincoln where she received a BA in English. Her writing focus is fiction and poetry of which she enjoys typing on an old 1950's typewriter. She has poetry published in several issues of Laurus Magazine, Cocky-Tales anthology, and University of Nebraska Press's 75th Anniversary edition of "Voices of Nebraska". Her romantic short stories "Sparkling Human Conundrum" and "Summer Dilemma" can be found in the anthologies Love Dust and Salty Tales on Amazon.*

Encircled
by Radar DeBoard

Michael watched the sharks continue their encirclement of the ship debris that he and Tom sat upon. The sharks had been circling them since they had finished off the rest of the crew.

Michael looked away from the monsters in the water and out over the waves. He noticed something static far in the distance, something that wasn't moving with the waves. A rush of hope filled him as he realised it was land.

He knew he could swim to it if he wasn't being pursued by the sharks. *I need a distraction,* he thought as he looked at Tom.

Radar DeBoard is a horror movie and novel enthusiast who resides in the small town of Goddard, Kansas. He occasionally dabbles in writing, and enjoys to make dark tales for people to enjoy. He has had drabbles and short stories published in various electronic magazines and anthologies.
Facebook: WriterRadarDeBoard

Bound for the Sea
by Crystal L. Kirkham

Bad luck, a woman on a ship, but mostly for the girl who's found.

Tied up, thrown overboard, seawater fills her lungs, and the coldness seeps in. It fills her heart and soul. Transforms her. She becomes a creature born of anger, seeking revenge on those that tried to take her life.

To her, every ship is the same as the one that sent her to a watery grave. When they sail by, she sings the siren's song. It calls and they cannot resist. Willingly to death they go, their ship sacrificed upon the rocks. Blood bound for the sea.

Crystal L. Kirkham is a multi-genre speculative fiction author. She has published novels across several genres including her fantasy adventure Feathers and Fae (October 2019 from Kyanite Publishing) and her self-published urban fantasy series, Saints & Sinners. She is also a contributing author to multiple best-selling anthologies. Hailing from the wilds of Canada, she is an avid outdoors person, unrepentant coffee addict, part-time foodie, servant to a wonderful feline, and companion to three delightfully hilarious canines - Treble and Freddie the Standard Poodles, and Nahni the Australian Shepherd.
Website: www.crystallkirkham.com

Then and Now
by Brian Rosenberger

Then.

Patiently, we waited as they returned from the sea, the distant sailors. We waited for them to lay their eggs in the sand. Their eggs still a delicacy. We were one of many hunters—sea birds, dogs, raccoons, foxes, and crabs. Competition was fierce. Their eggs were mouth-watering delicious.

Now.

After the world wars, the bombs and the radiation fallout, and generations after generations of genetic mutations, the seas have dried. When they return from the sludge to bury their eggs, we flee in terror.

Once we hunted their eggs for food. Now the turtles hunt us as food.

Brian Rosenberger lives in a cellar in Marietta, GA (USA) and writes by the light of captured fireflies. He is the author of As the Worms Turns and three poetry collections. He is also a featured contributor to the Pro-Wrestling literary collection, Three-Way Dance, available from Gimmick Press.
Facebook: HeWhoSuffers

Unsuitable Home
by Paula R.C. Readman

The sand tickled the child's toes as she bent to pluck a tiny shell from the rock pool.

"Hold it to your ear, and you'll hear the sea?" her mother said.

A hermit crab within felt it was time to move on. With a hurried squelch, he slipped into his new home.

"I hear nothing, Mummy," the child said, dropping the shell.

The crab moved much deeper into his new home, enjoying the taste of it.

"Mummy, I see nothing." The child staggered before falling face down in the sand, twitching.

"Unsuitable home," the crab said, slipping from her nose.

Paula R.C. Readman *learnt 'How to Write' from books which her husband purchased from eBay. After 250 purchases, he finally told her 'just to get on with the writing'. Since 2010, she's had 34 stories published.*
Blog: paulareadman1.wordpress.com

D'eye
by Catherine Kenwell

At 30 feet, it's murky. As we descend to 50 feet, I lose my dive partner—at least I think I do. I hold my hand in front of my face. It's faintly grey in the dim light.

That's when I knock up against something. Head first. I push out with my hands as the water blackens, and the faded sunlight from the surface disappears. Frantically, I attempt to swim around the thing, but it's moving alongside me. Panicking, I check my air gauge. 300 PSI. *Fuck*.

I glance up. An eye, the size of a dinner plate, stares back.

Catherine Kenwell is a Barrie, Ontario, mediator and author. After 30 successful years in corporate communications, she sustained a brain injury, lost her job, and joined the circus. She writes both horror/dark fiction and inspirational non-fiction. Her works have been published in Chicken Soup for the Soul, Trembling with Fear, Siren's Call, and HellBound Books. Website: www.catherinekenwell.com

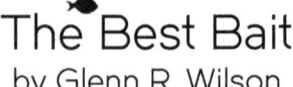

The Best Bait
by Glenn R. Wilson

You laughed when I told you I wouldn't go to your mum's.

You said that if I didn't go, it was over between us.

Well, you got it half right.

As I soak in the morning sun rising far away on the watery horizon, I tend my line miles offshore. The marlin are jumping, and with your help, I'll finally catch one. This time, I'm prepared for success. I pat the bucket of cold ones at my side and send a wink to the larger one filled with bits of you.

I have all the time in the world now.

Glenn R. Wilson has come full circle. Making a point to mature, like fine wine, before diving head-first into his long list of writing projects, he's approaching them with a plan. That strategy is to build with one brick at a time. He's accumulated a few bricks already and is adding more. Over time, with persistence and determination, he'll have a home. But for now, a solid foundation is the goal. Please, enjoy the process with him.

Mayday
by Galina Trefil

All throughout her childhood, instinct had told her, "Never trust the ocean." And she hadn't. But today, she accepted an invitation from a fisherman friend of hers to finally conquer her fear.

"Hey!" he called, leaning over the side of his boat when they were far out in the sea. "Come look at this! I can't beli—"

And then the vessel had been hit, hit hard, by something below the surface. Overboard, he toppled, to be yanked down into the murky void.

Now water was leaking fast through the floor. What had taken him?

Soon, she would find out.

Galina Trefil is a novelist specializing in women's, minority, and disabled rights. Her favorite genres are horror, thriller, and historical fiction. Her short stories and articles have appeared in Neurology Now, UnBound Emagazine, The Guardian, Tikkun, Romea.CZ, Jewcy, Jewrotica, Telegram Magazine, Ink Drift Magazine, The Dissident Voice, Open Road Review, and the anthologies "Flock: The Journey," "First Love," "Sea of Secrets," "Coffins and Dragons," "Organic Ink volume One," "Winds of Despair," "Waters of Destruction," "Curses & Cauldrons," "Unravel," "Hate," "Love," "Oceans," "Forgotten Ones," "Dark Valentine Holiday Horror Collection," and "Suspense Unimagined."
Website: galinatrefil.wordpress.com
Facebook: Rabbi-Galina-Trefil-535886443115467

Peace

by Chris Bannor

The ocean is my calming place, my respite against the world. It washes away the plethora of stains on my weary soul.

The clash of waves against the sand, so much like the thoughts circling around in my head, gives me solace. Each foamy wave that laps against my toes reminds me that I am not alone.

There is nothing more serene, nothing more fulfilling to me than coming to the beach at night to confess my sins and try to start anew.

As I send my beloved to rest in the depths, I hope he finds peace as well.

Chris Bannor is a science fiction and fantasy writer who lives in Southern California. Chris learned her love of genre stories from her mother at an early age and has never veered far from that path. She also enjoys musical theater and road trips with her family but is a general homebody otherwise.
Facebook: chrisbannorauthor
Website: ChrisBannor.com

Maritime Mayhem
by John H. Dromey

"You're a regular passenger on the ferry. Maybe you can bring me up to date. I noticed there's a new captain. What happened to the old one?"

"Lost at sea. A Bermuda Triangle victim."

"Wait a minute! That theory has been thoroughly debunked. Ships and planes disappeared over long stretches of open water, but nothing supernatural was proven."

"Let me explain. The late Captain Blaubart was a bigamist. He had one wife in Hamilton and a second wife in Warwick Parish. Rumour has it, when his spouses found out about each other, they went fifty-fifty and hired a hit man."

John H. Dromey was born in northeast Missouri, USA. He enjoys reading—mysteries in particular—and writing in a variety of genres. In addition to contributing to the Black Hare Press series of Dark Drabbles anthologies, he's had short fiction published in Alfred Hitchcock's Mystery Magazine, Martian Magazine, Mystery Weekly, Stupefying Stories Showcase, Thriller Magazine, Unfit Magazine, and elsewhere, as well as in numerous anthologies, including Chilling Horror Short Stories (Flame Tree Publishing, 2015).

A Queen is Born
by Ximena Escobar

Long embedded in the ocean floor, the blue diamond woke, releasing a stream of light through the water; lighting the passing eyes, shimmering on fins and scales and in all the gazes aboard the *Night Queen*, whose presence the diamond had sensed. One set of eyes shone the brightest on deck; her black hair lifting, separating into live eels.

The diamond broke through the water and into the night sky, glowing suspended before shooting directly into the woman. The crew's flesh evaporated; their screams lost with their throats as her studded chest dripped her beautiful blood—immortal, blue, and desolate.

Ximena Escobar is writing stories and poetry. Originally from Chile, she is the author of a translation into Spanish of the Broadway Musical "The Wizard of Oz", and of an original adaptation of the same, "Navidad en Oz", both produced in her home country. Since 2018 she has published several short stories in various anthologies and online platforms, and is now slowly working on her own collection. Ximena has a degree in Arts & Communication Science and lives in Nottingham with her family.
Facebook: Ximenautora
Twitter: @laximenin

His Last Day at Sea
by Stuart Conover

The old captain knew his time had come.

This would be his last day at sea.

It had been foretold in his youth.

No one would believe him…

But the captain had once met a mermaid.

Long after, he would claim his first love was the sea.

But it was her.

It was always Alisa.

No human woman could compare.

Their tryst had changed him.

Yet, all good things must end.

In parting, she shared that they would reunite once more.

On the day he would draw his last breath.

And in the distance, her tail shimmered in the sun.

Stuart Conover is a father, husband, rescue dog owner, published author, blogger, journalist, horror enthusiast, comic book geek, science fiction junkie, and IT professional. With all of that to cram in daily, we have no idea if or when he sleeps or how he gets writing done! (We suspect it has to do with having evil clones.) Stuart is a Chicago native and runs the author resource Horror Tree.

Yo Ho Ho

by Joachim Heijndermans

Mutineers. They took me ship and me gold. Shot me thrice in the belly, cut me throat, then threw me overboard. Bastards. Should've cut me to pieces.

Dunno how I still walk, as I'm nothing but bones. No matter. I got me cutlass and me legs. And I know where they'll be docking me ship.

I'll walk across this wet desert till I reach the buccaneer harbour in Crescent Cove, hidden from the royals and Spanish, where their homes, their wives and their children be. I will have me fun, then wait till those bastards come home.

Yo ho ho.

Joachim Heijndermans writes, draws, and paints nearly every waking hour. Originally from the Netherlands, he's been all over the world, boring people by spouting random trivia. His work has been featured in a number of anthologies and publications, such as Mad Scientist Journal, Asymmetry Fiction, Hinnom Magazine, Ahoy Comics's Edgar Allan Poe's Snifter of Terror, Metaphorosis and The Gallery of Curiosities, and he's currently in the midst of completing his first children's book.
Website: www.joachimheijndermans.com
Twitter: @jheijndermans

The Last Resort
by Stuart Conover

The tentacles splintered the deck of the *Warrior Poet.*

Jash swore as her ship was attacked.

Her women hacked at the creature with their cutlasses. To no avail.

If the hull broke, it would be too late.

Another crack tore through the air.

"Abandon ship," she yelled, rushing to her cabin.

Her crew would never make it with the creature there.

She had one final trick.

Her ship had a failsafe.

One she likely wouldn't survive.

Jash lit the fuse, ran.

Reaching the top deck, the world went white.

The explosion tore her ship apart and ended the beast below.

Stuart Conover is a father, husband, rescue dog owner, published author, blogger, journalist, horror enthusiast, comic book geek, science fiction junkie, and IT professional. With all of that to cram in daily, we have no idea if or when he sleeps or how he gets writing done! (We suspect it has to do with having evil clones.) Stuart is a Chicago native and runs the author resource Horror Tree.

We Didn't Listen
by Matthew A. Clarke

It came from the Pacific Ocean, just off the coast of Japan, all tentacles and sharp claws.

Somehow, it hadn't shown up on radar, theorised to be composed of otherworldly substances. Even if we'd seen it coming though, could we really have been better prepared?

It shrugs off each and every thing we can throw at it; armour-piercing rounds, missiles, there's even talk of a nuke. I don't think it'll work.

Two more appeared this morning, woken from deep slumber. Heading for North America and Australia respectively.

He tried to warn us. We didn't listen.

The Old Gods have returned.

Matthew A. Clarke is a new face in the world of horror. He has been writing short fiction as a hobby for two years and has decided to share his passion with likeminded people. Matthew loves all things that go bump in the night, having been introduced to slasher movies at a young age. He lives on the South Coast of England with his fiancé, Isabelle, and a little dachshund called Frank.
Facebook: matthewaclarkeauthor

Creatures of the Deep
by Kaitlyn Arnett

No one knew what was down there, and if they happened to discover it, it was doubtful that they'd want to.

The dark waters were truly something out of a horror story, inhabited by creatures with glowing scales, sharp fangs, and mysteries never seen before.

Some would call it a nightmare, others an illusion. It was an unnatural world, one that'd never see daylight in one hundred years, a world trapped in twilight. It was a forgotten place, left for monsters to prosper.

They were a disaster waiting to happen, a ticking time bomb, the so-called creatures of the deep.

Kaitlyn Arnett is a teen author who has been writing for five years. She focuses on the fantasy and thriller genres, specifically drabbles and short stories.

Glitters in the Shallows
by Matthew Wilson

I will not swim in the sea where gold glitters in the shallows. The fanged sirens' songs have lost their beauty since my brother dared go out to them one midnight…since we buried what was left of him in a matchbox.

How lovely that gold from sunken pirate ships glows, invading my dreams, but my cowardice is stronger than my greed, but not the siren's hunger.

Their laughter outside my window makes me tremble as they throw gold against the glass. I will not swim in the deep and deadly sea.

I do not have my dead brother's courage.

Matthew Wilson has been published over 200 times in such places as star*line, horrorzine, zimbell house publishing and many more. He is currently editing his first novel.

Blue Ringed Octopus
by J.M. Meyer

Panic set in when I realised I had five minutes to live.

I didn't see the tiny octopus with the sapphire stripes fall into the boat while hauling in my catch. The venomous bites that could kill twenty men were mere pinpricks on my toes.

So many mistakes today. I should have had my boots on. I should have brought my satellite phone. I should have told someone I was going fishing. But 'shoulding' over myself has not stopped the toxins from paralysing me.

I lie on my boat watching the gulls fly above me, waiting for my heart to...

J.M. Meyer is a writer, artist and small business owner living in New York, where she received her master's degree from Teachers College, Columbia University. Jacqueline enjoys writing speculative fiction and mysteries. Her favorite author is Alice Munro and her favorite film… is… anything horror related. Jacqueline also enjoys hiking with her dog Molly and the company of her husband Bruce and daughters; Julia, Emma and Lauren. Jacqueline's Mantra lately; there's no such thing as failing, it's called learning.
Website: jmoranmeyer.net
Amazon: www.amazon.com/author/jacquelinemoranmeyer

Plastic Texas
by Owen Morgan

"Thank you for coming." She turned and pointed to a computer projection of a map of the Pacific Ocean where a giant blob of trash twice the size of Texas floated between North America and Hawaii. "I have solved our problem by making use of genetically modified organisms which feed on plastics. The blob should be eradicated within three months. Let's go to a live feed." The screen changed to the California coastline. A mass of white crab-like creatures erupted from the waves and spread inland, where an aghast reporter said they were feeding on all plastics, including his car.

Owen Morgan writes science fiction, fantasy, and alternate history, and lives in the fishing port of Steveston, British Columbia.
Website: httpwwwkingauthor.wordpress.com
Twitter: @owen_morgan1066

The Lost Isles
by Stuart Conover

"The fabled lost Isles of Gold," Captain Dermuta muttered.

He didn't expect a response.

His crew still manned the ship, but the curse has taken their lives.

Husks of men, they were bound to him in life and death.

As long as he kept to the sea.

Finally, he'd found it.

Tales of these Isles had been told since his childhood.

Only he would never see it.

Not really.

Lifting the remnants of his hand to shield his eyes, the undead pirate king sighed.

He was as cursed at his crew.

Trapped at sea.

Never to walk on land again.

Stuart Conover *is a father, husband, rescue dog owner, published author, blogger, journalist, horror enthusiast, comic book geek, science fiction junkie, and IT professional. With all of that to cram in daily, we have no idea if or when he sleeps or how he gets writing done! (We suspect it has to do with having evil clones.) Stuart is a Chicago native and runs the author resource Horror Tree.*

The Wrong Type of Angel
by Lyndsey Ellis-Holloway

Something moved beneath the waves, figures flickering beneath the boat.

They looked like angels. Beautiful slender frames, flowing golden hair, beautiful faces.

But their wings were wrong. Dark and sleek, oily and short.

Perfect for the water.

These angels brought no hope, their songs no joy.

A siren's only gift is her song, and the inevitable despairing death that comes from it.

Ethereal melodies paralysed the men, making them easy prey.

The sirens reached up to the enraptured sailors, pulling them into the water.

Angels no more, their faces changed, dark and terrible and full of teeth.

Death was welcomed.

Lyndsey Ellis-Holloway is a writer from Knaresborough, UK. She writes fantasy, sci-fi, horror and dystopian stories, focussing on compelling characters and layering in myth and legend at every opportunity. Her mind is somewhat dark and twisted, and she lives in perpetual hope of owning her own Dragon someday, but for now she writes about them to fill the void... and to stop her from murdering people who annoy her. When she's not writing she spends time with her husband, her dogs and her friends enjoying activities such as walking, movies, conventions and of course writing for fun as well! *Website:* theprose.com/LyndseyEH

On the Hunt
by Susanne Thomas

T'eri felt the water swell beneath her. The ebb and flow of the ocean lifted her and then dropped her. She bobbed up and down with all the other junk on the water's surface.

A sound alerted her to a motion under the surface. Sharks were on the hunt, circling a nearby seal colony. T'eri shook herself, and adrenaline surged through her body. She could smell the tang of the sharks below.

T'eri fought through the waves of the ocean and smiled, exposing her sharp, razored teeth. She'd have to be fast to catch her dinner. She loved shark meat.

Susanne Thomas reads, writes, parents, and teaches from the windy west in Wyoming. She's an MFA graduate of the University of Arkansas at Monticello Creative Writing Program and she loves fantasy, science fiction, speculative fiction, poetry, children's books, science, coffee, and puns.
Website: www.themightierpenn.com

Ghostly Galleon
by Zoey Xolton

The clouds parted, and the moon shone down upon the sea, illuminating the pale sails of the *Caleuche*. Children upon the island of Chiloé watched in awe from the beach as the galleon sailed by.

Warm light and music spilled into the night, its deck full to bursting with dancing, drinking, song and laughter.

The legend of the *Caleuche* was well-known in South America. It was a living, sentient entity that rescued the drowned and lost at sea—so that they might live again, aboard.

The *Caleuche* disappeared into the darkness…and the children took comfort, knowing they had family there.

Zoey Xolton is an Australian Speculative Fiction writer, primarily of Dark Fantasy, Paranormal Romance and Horror. She is also a proud mother of two and is married to her soul mate. Outside of her family, writing is her greatest passion. She is especially fond of short fiction and is working on releasing her own themed collections in future.
Website: www.zoeyxolton.com

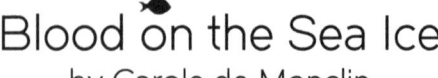

Blood on the Sea Ice
by Carole de Monclin

We swim from one empty chunk of drifting ice to the next.

I've spent days on the hunt for seals. My cub is starving.

In the distance, I glimpse a shape emerging. Much bigger than me. A male.

Our eyes meet across the white expanse. His hunger and desperation mirror my own.

He growls, sending my heart into a frenzy.

Alone, I'd outrun him, but right now, fighting's my only hope.

His formidable claws slash out. I tumble away, helpless.

He pounces, and his jaw closes over my baby's neck.

I howl my despair as red sprays on the ice.

Carole de Monclin travels both the real world and imaginary ones. She's lived in France, Australia, and the USA; visited 25+ countries; and explored Mars, Ceres, and many distant planets. She writes to invite people on a journey. Her stories can be found in The Arcanist, The Deep Space Anthology, and every volume of the Dark Drabbles series.
Website: CaroledeMonclin.com
Twitter: @CaroledeMonclin

Wreckage
by Maxine Churchman

Geoff winked and blew Vicky a kiss before falling backwards off the boat to follow his dive buddy, Ron.

The clear waters enveloped him, and the only sound came from his breathing apparatus. Ron was already entering the wreck through a hatch.

As Geoff followed, a blow to the back of his head dislodged his mouthpiece and stunned him momentarily. Before he could retrieve the mouthpiece, Ron kicked him hard in his stomach making him lose the last breath he held. Another blow and his last thought before blacking out was; *I guess Ron knows I've been shagging his wife.*

Maxine Churchman lives in Essex UK and has recently started writing poetry and short stories to share. Her interests include learning to improve her writing, reading, knitting, walking and teaching yoga. She is also planning a novel.

Fog Between Worlds
by Matthew M. Montelione

Catherine relaxed on the beach all morning, listening to her family bicker about what to do for the day. Bored, she got up. "I'm taking the kayak out."

"Don't go too far, Cathy," her father said.

Catherine smiled as her oars cut through the ocean, a strong breeze cooling her hot face.

Suddenly, thick fog encircled her. She panicked, unsure what to do. She breathed a sigh of relief as the fog dissipated. *Weird.*

Her heart dropped. Two suns hovered above her in a pink sky. It was unbearably hot.

Catherine screamed, bobbing on the ocean in a strange world.

Matthew M. Montelione is a horror writer born and raised on Long Island in New York. His work has been published in many titles, including MONSTERS: A Horror Microfiction Anthology, Mother Ghost's Grimm, and Quoth the Raven: A Contemporary Reimagining of the Works of Edgar Allan Poe. Matthew lives with his wife in New York.
Website: maybeevils.com
Facebook: maybeevils

The Seasteaders
by Daniel Purcell

The boy had sidled through the putrid and polluted waters on his kayak, body scarcely clothed. His flooded city had become sweltering, uninhabitable. The world had ended, but not for everyone. The others were relics in the opaque waters, along with their nation's rusted vessels. They'd been employed and then terminated over time.

He eventually scoped them out: the Seasteaders. He drifted towards the ocean metropolis. Above, it looked like a vast butterfly, metallic and viridescent. The bustling aqua-city mesmerised; so pristine. Yet, before the sunset, it was washed in crimson.

Then the pods emerged from the bio-reefs.

Daniel Purcell lives with his girlfriend in Glasgow, Scotland. He studied English at the University of Liverpool—where he was born—and has travelled extensively around the world, living in America for six months along the way. He has upcoming short-fiction being—or already—published with Farther Stars Than These, two Black Hare Press anthologies (Dark Drabbles: 'Oceans' and 'Ancients'), 101 Words, a Rogue Planet Press anthology ('Unexpected Turbulence,' in the Halloween 2020 edition) and Eerie River Publishing (The Beast in the Black Isle in 'It Calls From the Forest: Volume 2').

Nix in Line
by Peter J. Foote

The gorgeous woman peers around the seaweed-covered boulder and beckons young Lewis.

"Hi, are you in our tour group? I would have noticed you," Lewis says.

In reply, the woman wets her lips and winks before withdrawing behind the boulder.

Lewis grins and chases after her, only to discover the woman draped in nothing but her long tresses. She motions for a kiss. When her tongue slides into his mouth, she pours the ocean into him.

Once the male has stopped thrashing and is still in death, the Nix water spirit returns to the boulder, hunting for her next victim.

Peter J. Foote is a bestselling speculative fiction writer from Nova Scotia. Outside of writing, he runs a used bookstore specialising in fantasy & sci-fi, cosplays, and alternates between red wine and coffee as the mood demands. His short stories can be found in both print and in ebook form, with his story "Sea Monkeys" winning the inaugural "Engen Books/Kit Sora, Flash Fiction/Flash Photography" contest in March of 2018. As the founder of the group "Genre Writers of Atlantic Canada", Peter believes that the writing community is stronger when it works together.
Twitter: @PeterJFoote1
Website: peterjfooteauthor.wordpress.com

Deep

by Lynne Lumsden Green

The highwaters keep sending me gifts; strange metal tubes full of delicious morsels of food. I receive their gifts with pleasure, seeing them as a subtle compliment to my Queenship of The Deep. It is a charming wooing for my favours.

I've sent them several messages through the water, to create elegant sculptures of enormous waves. They responded with a confetti of assorted edibles, of both vegetables and animals, along with a strange mixture of bits from the overworld.

I have accepted their invitation. When I get to the surface, I am sure I will find everything in exquisite taste.

Lynne Lumsden Green is enjoying the aging process, contrary to all expectations. She completed a Bachelors' Degree in Science, and after her midlife crisis went back and completed a B.A. in Creative Writing. She writes both fiction and nonfiction and owns more books than bookshelves.

Flotsam
by Evan Baughfman

Everyone was gone but me.

Drowned.

Captain suspected someone hadn't wanted our mysterious cargo to reach mainland. He said a spy had been on board, lighting a fire below deck.

Thankfully, the perpetrator went down with the ship.

I floated away from the wreckage, clinging to a hunk of wood that wouldn't hold me for long.

In the moonlight, I found a larger piece adrift. Swam for it.

A crate?

I held fast to its side.

A casket…?

Its lid threw open. Claws yanked me upward.

The cargo inside had red eyes, fangs, a pale complexion.

A thirst for blood.

Evan Baughfman works in a very scary place: a middle school! He writes all genres, but horror is where he's most comfortable. Much of his writing success has been as a playwright. He's had many different plays produced across the globe. Heuer Publishing has published his Poe adaptation, "A Taste of Amontillado". Additionally, Evan has adapted a number of his short stories into screenplays, of which "The Emaciated Man" and "The Creaky Door" have won awards in various film festival competitions. Evan's "Just Plants" was recently published in Soteira Press's horror anthology, *The Monsters We Forgot - Volume 1*.

Myst
by T.E. Dziadura

The fog crept up the shore, its tendrils wrapping around her legs. Pain wracked her body, dropping her to her knees. Her back arched, a scream caught in her throat and her fingers dug deep into the sand.

Through the pain, she felt a tug. Movement. Her skirt pulled above her waist as she was dragged towards the cold Atlantic. Waves washed over her.

She floated, wrapped in a wreath of blue and white sparkles of electricity that danced over her form. The watery sun receded as she sank beneath the waves.

T.E. Dziadura is a bestselling speculative fiction writer from Newfoundland, Canada, with a focus on science-fiction, horror and fantasy. Her short story "Beyond No Man's Land" can be found in Chillers from the Rock and "Flight 520 to London" in Flights from the Rock. Her writing is inspired by her love of science and history, and the sense of wonder they can inspire. You can follow her writing, and adventures with her husband, kids, cats and rescue beagles on social media or her weekly blog.

Sea Glass Souls
by Jasmine Jarvis

Along the beach they wash up—little pieces of iridescent sea glass of greens, blues, pinks, and opaque. Within each piece of glass is the soul of a poor and unfortunate sailor who had fallen for a siren's wicked deceit. The siren takes the soul and encases it in sea glass. Sometimes a storm so violent will strike, the undercurrent of the ocean steals the siren's collection of souls, bringing them to shore where I will collect as many as possible before I set sail.

For you see, sirens cannot harm you if you too hold the Sea Glass Souls.

Jasmine Jarvis is a teller of tales and scribbler of scribbles. She lives in Brisbane, Australia with her husband Michael, their two children, Tilly and Mish; Ripley, their German Shepherd, and indoor fat cat, Dwight K. Shrute.

Eternal
by Kaitlyn Arnett

Most people called them lost. Soldiers gone to waste in a war that never should have been fought, dragged into the deep sea only to be forever taken by it.

Those people couldn't have been more wrong.

Their bodies never died, never put to rest, nor sentenced to decay.

They worked effortlessly because tiring was no longer an option, their submarine carrying them all across the ocean. It had been years, maybe even decades, since they had seen the light of day, but most of them hardly noticed.

For they were still on patrol, and this was their eternal oath.

Kaitlyn Arnett is a teen author who has been writing for five years. She focuses on the fantasy and thriller genres, specifically drabbles and short stories.

Rebirth
by Kimberly Rei

The cliff has called to me for as long as I can remember. As a child, it taunted hours; both waking and sleeping. Mother forbade playing near the edge, but she didn't need to. I was too afraid of the endless water below.

I am still afraid, as I stand at the rocky lip, staring down. But it is time. And so I leap, arms like wings.

As the ocean embraces me in her loving grip, I am reborn. Webbing links fingers, gills bring air. My eyes glow. My jaw unhinges to accommodate rows of razor fangs.

I am home.

Kimberly Rei has been writing for as long as she can remember. At five years old, her parents gifted her with a set of Children's Classics that she had no hope of reading. Yet. The potential alone sparked a love of words that has never wavered. Kim has taught writing workshops and edited novels for Authors You May Recognize. She has published several short stories and now can't stop chasing paper dragons. She currently lives in Tampa Bay, Florida with her wife and an abundance of gorgeous beaches to explore.

Bubbling Up
by Dawn Knox

The stream of silver bubbles pouring from my mouth descend to the depths of the ocean.

But that's not possible.

Bubbles always rise to the surface.

For an instant, I'm confused; doubting myself.

But realisation comes quickly. I'm disorientated in the water, and I'm not moving upwards towards the light, but down, down into the inky blackness.

When my diving buddy took my hand, I assumed he was saving me. But he's dragging me deeper and deeper, with hateful determination burning in his eyes.

My silent scream is captured in the silver bubbles which surge up towards the distant surface.

Dawn Knox enjoys writing in different genres and has had romances, speculative fiction, sci-fi, humorous and women's fiction published in magazines, anthologies and books. She's also had two plays about World War One performed internationally. Her current work in progress is a story set in Bletchley Park during World War Two.
Website: dawnknox.com
Twitter: SunriseCalls

Silence is the Sound of Freedom
by Terri A. Arnold

I sit down on the edge of the dock with my pant legs rolled up and sandals off. Putting my legs in the cold ocean water and fluttering my feet, I let go of all the pent up stress and anger.

So this is what freedom feels like. What it smells like, sounds like.

It's so peaceful; no husband to nag me, no kids to pester me, no one to worry about but myself. Oh, the things I'll be able to do!

With a contemplative gaze, I take in the floating bodies of my husband and two children, I'm free.

Terri A. Arnold is an avid reader turned writer from a small town in Nova Scotia, who has spent her life reading and wishing she was writing. Although she has written a lot in those years, she has only recently begun to submit pieces for publication. With ongoing encouragement from family and writing challenges with friends, Arnold felt the urge to try her hand at publishing.

The isle of carcasses
by E.L. Giles

The old man's eyes were fatigued from gazing at the horizon. No land appeared before him, only a floating isle of carcasses. He let his heavy body fall back, caring neither about the absence of wind nor if his patched-up pirogue was drifting north or south.

Nothing, thought the dying old man. Nothing remains but the putrescent essences of the decaying great whales and the mighty albatrosses.

Over him, reigned a stoic silence. The sea was flat and oily and poisonous, the pale sun cold. His bag empty, the old man was to join the grotesque congregation of decaying flesh.

E.L. Giles is a dreamer, passionate about art, a restless worker and a bit of a weird human. He started his artistic journey as a music composer until the need to put his thoughts and stories down on paper grew too strong for him to resist it any longer. He lives in the French Province of Quebec, Canada, with his girlfriend and two boys.
Facebook: elgilesauthor
Website: www.elgilesauthor.com

Lover Astray
by Ximena Escobar

A hot breath on the glass, and she saw the cracks extend over her reflection. She saw the waves too, coming for her; breaking, lashing with salt and sand and coldness, everything in their wake. The mirror shattered onto the squeaking floorboards, whining like broken dogs as the tide constricted and rocked the vessel.

Running up to the deck, her hair and dress lifted like sails; lips cracking in the cold, ominous air. As the wood fractured underneath her soles, she whispered farewell to the distant shore.

Blue water dressed her in sequin scales… Ready for the Sea King's bed.

Ximena Escobar is writing stories and poetry. Originally from Chile, she is the author of a translation into Spanish of the Broadway Musical "The Wizard of Oz", and of an original adaptation of the same, "Navidad en Oz", both produced in her home country. Since 2018 she has published several short stories in various anthologies and online platforms, and is now slowly working on her own collection. Ximena has a degree in Arts & Communication Science and lives in Nottingham with her family.
Facebook: Ximenautora
Twitter: @laximenin

There is Such a Thing as Fate
by M.J. Christie

"Ship ahoy!"

Rising, I wiped at a porthole. How had he seen through the fog? Sails stowed to avoid mishap; we'd drifted for days.

Shrugging on my captain's jacket, I climbed on deck.

What greeted me has plagued me these last twenty years. How I survived, I know not.

My crew lay butchered. Their blood frozen by freezing fog. First Mate Jenkins hung from the mast; his eyeglass rested at my feet. Eerie creaking from the starboard side. A ship swaying in and out of view.

Deliver me from evil.

Fate carried me home.

Eyeless sockets now disturbed my sleep.

A writer of novel-length fiction, short fiction and poetry. **M.J. Christie** *recently became addicted to writing shorter fiction— the shorter the better - and poetry. The UK's Lincolnshire Coast provides the backdrop and inspiration for M.J.'s writing, giving focus and meaning to everyday life. M.J. has had 100 word drabbles and one poem published (so far) in online magazines. Website: www.mjchristie.com*

Amazed
by Cassandra Angler

It's staring at me through the glass, eyes glowing yellow. Tentacles waving in the current of the sea. I can see the fangs hidden beneath its scales as they pulse. We stare at one another as it wraps its limbs around my vessel. The metal groans underneath the beast's grip. It isn't long before I can hear the trickle of water splashing against the floor. The centre gives way, a gush of sea sucks me into its mass. Face to face now, it watches me as I gasp in panic, water filling my lungs. Mouth wide, it shoves me inside.

Cassandra Angler is a married mother of four who lives in the State of Ohio in the USA. When she isn't busy caring for her family, Cassandra works on her upcoming novel due out in November of 2020 titled Contaminated. Cassandra has three short story publications as well as several flash fiction and drabble publications.

The Survivor
by Patrick J. Gallagher

When the torpedo hit the ship, I thought I was one of the lucky ones, making it to an air pocket deep in the bowels of the vessel. I survived as the wreck sank to the bottom of the ocean.

Now I sit, surrounded by the bloated bodies of my friends and shipmates. Three days… I know that rescue isn't coming. I recoil as clammy white flesh bumps against me. So many dead.

The meagre yellow light from my flashlight finally flickered and died an hour ago. I can hear them moving in the darkness, wanting me to join them…

Patrick J. Gallagher is a television cameraman and photographer, working in Canberra for the Australian Parliament. He has a life-long fascination with mysteries, the paranormal, and things generally horrific and unknown. He has self-published several books on various topics related to those interests, including the Loch Ness Monster, and an almost-forgotten serial killer operating in London at the same time as the infamous Ripper. All this folklore and history becomes grist for the mill of his imagination.
Facebook: PatJGallagher

The Endless Song
by Paula R.C. Readman

From beneath the waves, she rose up. As a child, she would panic when the salty taste reached her mouth. It created a siren in her mind.

Yet she found comfort in her watery grave, a kind of a release. Visions haunt her mind on stormy nights. Recalling her parents struggling as their expensive yacht faulted in a storm.

The horror on their despairing faces. With open mouths they're caught in silent screams as the yacht capsized and sank beneath the waves.

Obviously, money can't buy you everything.

With her sisters, she sings from their rocky perches, driving ships ashore.

Paula R.C. Readman learnt 'How to Write' from books which her husband purchased from eBay. After 250 purchases, he finally told her 'just to get on with the writing'. Since 2010, she's had 34 stories published.
Blog: *paulareadman1.wordpress.com*

Sanity is Blue
by Joshua Gessner

I am not insane. I am surviving. Stranded in the deep blue of waters, that too. I must resort to the facts to survive. The water is blue, my crew is gone, my knife is missing. Where has it gone? A question, it is a danger to me. There are so many dangers now. I refer once more on the things I know: bad men do bad things, nature is against man, mind against itself, sanity is blue. I fear to think of the rest, wherever it may lie. Is that another's voice I hear? No, it is my own.

Joshua Gessner is a full-time college student, enrolled under the English major at his local community college. He is nineteen years old, and lives with his family in Manchester. Joshua Gessner has been published for the first time ever in January of 2020, and was published again one month later in February of 2020! He now continues working diligently on his craft, hoping to enter literary contests. In the near future he also hopes to publish: novels, novellas, short stories, and poetry!
Facebook: joshua.gessner.98
Twitter: @joshuagessner41

The Indianapolis
by Stephen Herczeg

It was dark and quiet. Just after midnight. The great ocean was black and still.

I was on watch on the top deck.

Then they hit. Two torps into the starboard side. The explosions lit up the night. Turned my world upside down.

I hit the water and watched the rain of my shipmates as they dived in to join me.

The huge ship lurched and died, sliding beneath the waves and taking hundreds with her.

We survivors bobbed in the still night.

I gasped as the first grey triangle cut the glassy surface.

Then the screams rocked the night.

Stephen Herczeg is an IT Geek based in Canberra Australia. He has been writing for over twenty years and has completed a couple of dodgy novels, sixteen feature length screenplays and numerous short stories and scripts. His horror work has featured in Sproutlings, Hells Bells, Below the Stairs, Trickster's Treats #1 and #2, Shades of Santa, Behind the Mask, Beyond the Infinite; The Body Horror Book, Anemone Enemy, Petrified Punks and Beginnings. He has also had numerous Sherlock Holmes stories published through the Belanger Books - Sherlock Holmes anthologies.
Amazon: amazon.com/-/e/B07916SQQS
Facebook: stephenherczegauthor

There Below
by Radar DeBoard

Mary leaned over the boat's railing and looked down into the swirling waters of the ocean. She was amazed at the calm beauty of the waves as they continued to move up and down.

She stood there wondering what it would be like to look up from beneath the waves at the world. Mary wished that she could see that sight.

Little did Mary know that a tentacled creature was just below the surface. It was looking right at her, wondering what she tasted like. In one quick motion, it whipped its tentacle up and pulled Mary beneath the waves.

Radar DeBoard is a horror movie and novel enthusiast who resides in the small town of Goddard, Kansas. He occasionally dabbles in writing, and enjoys to make dark tales for people to enjoy. He has had drabbles and short stories published in various electronic magazines and anthologies.
Facebook: WriterRadarDeBoard

Bad Luck
by Ali House

She hit the water hard, slamming into the churning waves. Her hands reached out, grabbing only air, as the dark waters dragged her down.

All she wanted was to escape her horrible life, but when the crew discovered the new deckhand was actually a woman, they tossed her over the side. "Bad luck having a woman on board."

The frigid water enveloped her, filling her lungs. Closing her eyes, she gave in, accepting fate. Suddenly, a surge of magical power rushed through her. Her eyes opened, searching out her former ship. A wicked smile crossed her face. "Bad luck indeed..."

Ali House is the author of sci-fi/fantasy novels The Six Elemental and The Fifth Queen, along with various short stories in the "From the Rock" series published by Engen Books. She is a traveller, baker, and fan of the Oxford comma.
Website: engenbooks.com/tag/house-blog/

Bait

by Jodi Jensen

Brian couldn't stop smiling. Months ago, he'd entered a contest for a deep-sea fishing trip and won. Now, here he was, zooming across the ocean, after a new species of fish and a heap of prize money.

He readied his pole, then turned to his crewmate, Alan. "What are we using for bait?"

Alan drew a wicked long fishing knife with a curved blade and pointed to a trapdoor. "It's in the hatch."

Brian bent and yanked the door open.

He never saw it coming.

A sharp stab in the back and a slice across the throat.

"You're the bait."

Jodi Jensen, *author of time travel romances and speculative fiction short stories, grew up moving from California, to Massachusetts, and a few other places in between, before finally settling in Utah at the ripe old age of nine. The nomadic life fed her sense of adventure as a child and the wanderlust continues to this day. With a passion for old cemeteries, historical buildings and sweeping sagas of days gone by, it was only natural she'd dream of time traveling to all the places that sparked her imagination.*
Twitter: @WritesJodi
Facebook: jodijensenwrites

Necessity
by Carole de Monclin

Your lips are cracked. Your eyes closed against the blistering sun. Your injured leg throbs.

Five days. Floating on this miserable raft, with no water or food.

Five days. Since that blasted thunderstorm sank your ship.

Five days. Alternating between hopes of rescue and certitude exposure will kill you.

Or dehydration.

Or worse.

The way your four companions have been looking at you since yesterday unsettles you.

With nothing else to do, you force yourself back to sleep, only to be awakened by a sharp pain in your neck.

"Sorry. You've no wife or kids, and we need to eat."

Carole de Monclin travels both the real world and imaginary ones. She's lived in France, Australia, and the USA; visited 25+ countries; and explored Mars, Ceres, and many distant planets. She writes to invite people on a journey. Her stories can be found in The Arcanist, The Deep Space Anthology, and every volume of the Dark Drabbles series.
Website: CaroledeMonclin.com
Twitter: @CaroledeMonclin

Deep Revenge
by Olivia Arieti

The hollow glitter of the ice cloaked the merciless whaler in a ghastly shroud as it struggled through the waves.

Although well acquainted with storms, an unfamiliar fear crawled upon the captain and the sailors for the many hearts their harpoons had struck.

Now the animals' consuming dirges kept resounding in their ears as a warning of pending doom.

When the fury of the ocean capsized the ship, the enraged creatures expelled their deadly spout and with a diabolic light in the eyes advanced towards the drowning crew.

This time no escamotage could ever make them open their famished jaws.

Olivia Arieti has a degree from the University of Pisa and lives in Torre del Lago Puccini, Italy, with her family. Besides being a published playwright, she loves writing retellings of fairy tales, and at the same time is intrigued by supernatural and horror themes. Her stories appeared in several magazines and anthologies like Enchanted Conversations, Enchanted Tales Literary Magazine, Fantasia Divinity Magazine, Cliterature, Medieval Nightmares, Static Movement, 100 Doors To Madness Forgotten Tomb Press, Black Cats Horrified Press, Bloody Ghost Stories Full Moon Books, Death And Decorations Thirteen O'Clock Press, Infective Ink, Pandemonium Press, Pussy Magic Magazine.

They Float Too
by Nicola Currie

The last man on Earth was dragged into the crushing depths, wondering how he hadn't noticed. But as his alien doppelganger floated up past him from the glowing portal beneath the Marianas Trench, he realised the cleverness of the trick.

How long had his wife been gone? His children? They must have been taken already.

The portal beneath him closed as the invisible energy that carried, sustained him, completed its mission and he passed through.

Scientists had never fathomed the possibility that humans might be taken down, debating what creatures could come out instead of what mattered: What lay beyond?

Nicola Currie is from Cambridge, UK where she works in educational publishing. She has published poetry in literary magazines, including Mslexia and Sarasvati, and short stories in various anthologies. She has also completed her first novel, which was longlisted for the Bath Children's Novel Award. Website: writeitandweep.home.blog

Songs to Sing
by A.R. Johnston

"What shall I sing today? Who shall sink to the bottom of the sea?" the siren sang out to the great ocean.

Triton appeared upon the waves. "And who will hear your song today, my dearest? There are no ships upon the seas."

Her eyes got wide as she looked at the sea god. "My liege. I wish only to serve and do as is in my nature."

"The waters will cover the earth soon. There will be many ships for you to pick from. Everything shall be ours."

She smiled. "Then I shall sing them to the depths below."

A.R. Johnston is a small-town girl from Nova Scotia, Canada. She is known to write mostly urban fantasy, though she goes where the muses lead her and you never know where that may be. She is a lover of coffee, good tv shows, horror flicks, and a reader of good books. She pretends to be a writer when real life doesn't get in the way. Pesky full-time job and adulting!
Facebook: arjohnstonauthor
Website: arjohnstonauthor.wordpress.com

Drowning not Waving
by Paula R.C. Readman

Olaf's dream was coming true; the cup was within his grasp. He swung his yacht around to catch the wind. No doubts in his mind; he would be the first to cross the winning line.

Then he saw her, a maiden in the water. Her beauty was captivating. Her long hair eddied around her bare shoulders as she waved madly to him.

It's a miracle, Gressa believed as the boat came into sight. All night, she had clung to the wreckage of her yacht.

"Mermaids don't exist! Such foolish tales won't dupe me." Olaf laughed as he crashed into Gressa.

Paula R.C. Readman *learnt 'How to Write' from books which her husband purchased from eBay. After 250 purchases, he finally told her 'just to get on with the writing'. Since 2010, she's had 34 stories published.*
Blog: paulareadman1.wordpress.com

Ocean Piranhas
by C.L. Williams

Jay and Dustin take a trip to an island in the middle of the Indian Ocean. On the way there, Jay was telling Dustin about piranhas that live in the ocean instead of the freshwater habitats that we all know about.

"It's just a tale to keep people out of the water," Dustin exclaims.

"It's real, I promise!" Jay says in self-defence.

"Really?" Dustin questions him, "How would you know?"

A demonic grin now covers Jay's face, "This is where I take all of the bodies!"

He then pushes Dustin into the Indian Ocean and watches the piranhas devour Dustin.

C.L. Williams is an international best-selling author currently living in central Virginia. He has written eight poetry books, four novellas, one novel, and a contributor to a multitude of anthologies and magazines. His most recent anthology appearance ANGELS: Dark Drabbles #2 from Black Hare Press became a number one in hot new releases. C.L. Williams is currently working on his second novel and a new poetry book.
Facebook: writer434
Twitter: @writer_434

Baptism
by Jeff Slade

The moon's reflection wobbled and wavered upon the water. Shifting like my stomach's contents.

This ceremony was necessary to join the war effort. That knowledge didn't make it comfortable.

The chaplain approached, sacred tablets clutched in one hand and a holy relic in the other. It was time.

He lifted the relic, bathing it in pale moonlight before pressing it upon me. Unintelligible words followed, then he lifted my head, breaching the surface.

I opened my mouth, took a painful breath, then re-submerged.

It was done.

I swam back into the depths with the others, part of the dark tide.

Jeff Slade resides in Salmon Cove, Newfoundland and Labrador, with his wife and two cats. He enjoys reading, writing, and making horrible puns, not necessarily in that order. You can find other short stories by him in Chillers From The Rock, Dystopia From The Rock, and Flights From The Rock, published by Engen Books.

That Sinking Feeling
by Steven Lord

Nigel was holidaying when the event happened. He had spent his life as luck's beggar, kicked in the knackers by fate at every turn. Winning a trip to the Maldives surely meant his fortunes were changing.

That morning, after 45 minutes slathering on his factor 50, he grabbed his snorkel and sprinted out to the shoreline. He splashed out, ooh-ing at the coral, aah-ing at the bright parrotfish.

As he swam further, the seabed plunged away like a cliff edge. Even in the warm water, he shivered as he looked down. That moment, seawater across the planet lost its buoyancy.

Steven Lord is a debut author based in the south of England. He is currently attempting to cram writing in alongside a busy day job, with varying levels of success. While his long-term aspiration is to get a novel published, at present he would be pretty pleased with a drabble or two.

Scuba
by J.M. Meyer

After forty-years, to see them on the cruise was shocking. Harry's grey hair suited him. Kathy's tanned, toned arms highlighted the rock on her ring finger.

Henry and I were to be married, until he met Kathy. Per Harry's style, they always arrived late to dinner. They looked through me; just an older, heavy woman dining alone.

On the last day, I followed them onto the crowded, disorganised scuba diving boat. When everyone dived in, I remained and hid their wallets and sandals in my bag.

Late, as usual, they weren't missed with the returning divers and were left forever.

J.M. Meyer is a writer, artist and small business owner living in New York, where she received her master's degree from Teachers College, Columbia University. Jacqueline enjoys writing speculative fiction and mysteries. Her favorite author is Alice Munro and her favorite film…is…anything horror related. Jacqueline also enjoys hiking with her dog Molly and the company of her husband Bruce and daughters; Julia, Emma and Lauren. Jacqueline's Mantra lately; there's no such thing as failing, it's called learning.
Website: jmoranmeyer.net
Amazon: www.amazon.com/author/jacquelinemoranmeyer

Sally Stole Seashells

by J.B. Wocoski

Sally slaughtered Sheila Seal to steal her ship, the Seashell, by the seashore in Singapore. Sally sliced up Sheila's six sailors when she stole the said ship.

Sally sailed the seven seas for seven years, slicing up strangers. Soldiers spotted the Seashell, they secured and incarcerate Sally in the slammer saying, "Sunday, Sally shall swing from the scaffold seven times."

Sally escaped the scaffold. Stealing the ship, Insidious, to sail the seven seas. A storm sank the ship, which Sally stole as she slipped out to sea. Sally's spectre haunts that shipwreck silently slicing up any skin divers swimming there.

J.B. Wocoski is the author and narrator of the shortstorypodcast.com with three flash fiction short story books published in the last three years. He is currently working on book 4 "Short Story Podcast 2019." He writes mostly science fiction, fantasy, and horror stories. He won the 2016 Little Tokyo Short Story Writing Contest with his short story "The Last Master of Go"
Website: shortstorypodcast.com

Nemo, God of the Seas
by Joshua E. Borgmann

Captain Nemo could not give up the sea. Free of flesh his spirit became one with the waters. Slowly, he learned to control entire oceans. And he watched humanity wage its terrible wars. Thousands of their dead rotting, forgotten, on the ocean floor. He didn't pity them. Their spilled oil dirtied everything. Their excessive fishing and endless trash strangled life in the deep. Nemo couldn't accept dolphins dead in abandoned nets, the radioactive wastes of Fukushima, or dead sharks floating finless. He summoned the great waves and terrible storms. He would make the world an ocean world, devoid of man.

Joshua E. Borgmann holds degrees from Drake University, Iowa State University, and the University of South Carolina. He grew up on horror and science-fiction and had long intended to become a great master of the art form before he was sucked into the bottomless pit of academia. He toils away his days as an English instructor at a small community college and dreams of being able to escape into a world of fantasy and terror where there are no student papers to grade. He and his wife reside in a nameless rural Iowa town surrounded by terrible cornfields where he is terrorized by several felines who have taken refuge in his home.

Join the Crew
by Umair Mirxa

Javier lay shivering on the deck, coughing water out of his lungs.

Heavy footstep on the wood, followed by a dull thud. A large shadow across him. The sunlight muted, he dared open his eyes. Silently, he cursed his luck.

Pirates!

"Here, lad," said the captain. "What be yer name?"

"J-Javier, sir."

"Spaniard, eh? Here be yer first choice: swear fealty."

"I would *never!* What's the second choice?"

The captain chuckled, and his crew fell to raucous laughter.

"Aye, brave lad. Now, we shall keelhaul ye, and you'll walk the plank. Once yer dead, why, then you'll join the crew."

Umair Mirxa lives and writes in Karachi, Pakistan. His first published story, 'Awareness', appeared on Spillwords Press. He has since had stories accepted for publication in anthologies from Zombie Pirate Publishing, Blood Song Books, Black Hare Press, Iron Faerie Publishing, Clarendon House Publications, Fantasia Divinity Magazine & Publishing, and The ReAnimated Writers Press. He is a massive J.R.R. Tolkien fan, loves everything to do with mythology, fantasy, and history, and wishes with all his heart that dragons were real. When he's not writing, he enjoys reading novels and comic books, playing video games, listening to music, and watching movies, TV shows, and football as an Arsenal FC fan.
Website: *umairmirxa.com*

The Consequences of Climate Change for the Merpeople
by Heather Ewings

The whole school of bright coloured fish darted out of reach.

They were deeper than they ought've been, harder to catch, sent into cooler waters by warming coastal currents.

Ineska had fed from the generosity of other merfolk until they threatened her with starvation if she didn't pull her own weight.

Colour stood out in the gloom, and Ineska launched her net. It caught, snagged.

Pulling it loose, her finger sliced along a sharp rock.

She'd never seen her own blood.

Her catch spilled free, a shadow loomed, and she remembered, too late, the danger in this patch of sea.

Heather Ewings is an Australian author of speculative fiction. Her work has appeared at Asymmetry Fiction, Lite Lit One, and Flash in a Flash.
Website: www.heatherewings.com

The Right Bait
by Andrew Kurtz

Joseph's motto was: "You can catch any fish with the right bait."

One day he saw a suitcase filled with money floating in the deep water at the beach. Heart pounding, he rapidly swam to retrieve it. To his surprise, it was attached to a tremendous tentacle.

Suddenly a monstrous tentacled creature rose out of the water.

One of the tentacles punctured Joseph's neck and decapitated him, another ripped his chest open, allowing his internal organs to spill out.

As the creature was returning to the deep, it said to itself, "You can catch any human with the right bait."

Andrew Kurtz is an emerging writer of horror, influenced by Stephen King, H.P. Lovecraft and Wells. He has stories published by Black Hare Press, Eleanor Merry, Renaimted Writers' and R.J. Roles.

Unbroken Wave
by Peter J. Foote

Water horses pranced within the waves as the tide turned, manes of white cap brushing against the shore, hooves crashing against rocks.

The beach was their domain until one foolhardy human arrived and thought he could tame wild waves with a surfboard.

They played with the fragile human, letting it believe that it was master of the waves as he rode through their watery manes. Eventually, they tired of the game and dashed his body against the rocks; bones and board broken to wash up on the beach as the water horses go back to their prancing within the waves.

Peter J. Foote is a bestselling speculative fiction writer from Nova Scotia. Outside of writing, he runs a used bookstore specialising in fantasy & sci-fi, cosplays, and alternates between red wine and coffee as the mood demands. His short stories can be found in both print and in ebook form, with his story "Sea Monkeys" winning the inaugural "Engen Books/Kit Sora, Flash Fiction/Flash Photography" contest in March of 2018. As the founder of the group "Genre Writers of Atlantic Canada", Peter believes that the writing community is stronger when it works together.
Twitter: @PeterJFoote1
Website: peterjfooteauthor.wordpress.com

The Dinner Call
by Patricia Elliott

He's here—the great white. I'm in a cave on the ocean floor, twisted like a pretzel to fit. He's hungry. The bleeding cut on my knee beckons him. My heart pounds erratically. Body shaking. Oxygen depleting. Five minutes left. An image of Mara, my baby daughter, pops in my head. Blond hair. Blue eyes. My chest tightens. I have to survive.

"Rachel, my wife," I whisper. "It can't end here."

The shark's shadow disappears. I race out of the cave, swimming hard. My head breaches the surface. His fin follows, and then comes pain. Death calls my name.

Joshua.

Patricia Elliott lives in beautiful British Columbia with her family. Now that her lovely kids are all teenagers, she has decided to actively pursue her passion for the written word. When she was a youngster, she spent the majority of her time writing fan-fiction and poetry to avoid the harsh reality of bullying. Writing allowed her to escape into another world, even if temporarily; a world in which she could be anyone or anything, even a mermaid. Dreams really can come true. If you believe it, you can achieve it!
Website: patriciaelliottromance.com

Red Calling
by Shelly Jarvis

When the island formed from thin air, everyone thought it was weird. When it kept getting bigger, crazy theories about aliens, Illuminati, and Atlantis started cropping up. But when we received the S.O.S., they called me.

I'm not saying I'm the best for the job, but, well, I am. Or at least I thought I was. But now that I'm here, I don't know what to think.

The land is ordinary all the way across, except for the strange bloody hole in the centre. I haven't seen a living creature, but I hear their whispers. Tomorrow I'll follow the blood.

Shelly Jarvis is a speculative fiction author from West Virginia, US. She found a life-long love of sci-fi and fantasy in the 3rd grade when she found Madeleine L'Engle's "A Wrinkle in Time." Shelly is an avid reader, a Whovian, the ideal viewer of dog rescue videos, and undoubtedly Ravenclaw. She currently has three YA sci-fi books available for purchase on Amazon. Website: www.ShellyJarvis.com

Maybe Not Such a Bargain?
by Nikki DeKeuster

Three hundred nautical miles from civilization, the Milky Way is a stairway to heaven in the pitch of night. Night the way it's meant to be, looming and silent.

Perfect.

I'm an empath, and I don't just *feel* everyone's emotions, I *drown* in them. Anger, fear, anxiety, lust, all as fathomless as the ocean and equally unpredictable.

So I traded people for sheepshead. Not a bad bargain.

Except now, as malice so thick it chokes me rises from the depths, encircling my sailboat.

Ladder rungs clang.

An unyielding hand silences my scream.

And I'm three hundred nautical miles from civilization.

Nikki DeKeuster devours souls. She spits them onto her glowing screen and toys with their lives for your amusement. Reading this story makes you an accomplice to their suffering. You're welcome. A storyteller with decades of experience crafting tales with her friends, she's bound some of them to bring into the wider world. The stories, not her friends. She enjoys throwing stones into Lake Michigan with her daughter and keeping her husband up past his bedtime with her ramblings. The first novel in her horror series will claw its way out of the earth in 2020.
Website: NJDeKeuster.com

Ancient Desires
by K.R. Nox

The virgin sacrifice was strung from the cliff overhanging the ocean; her flimsy, diaphanous gown billowed in the turbulent coastal breeze. *She was going to die.* It was her destiny to appease the gods of the deep— her death would ensure her small fishing village a bountiful winter.

She watched in awe-struck terror as tentacles rose up from the crashing waves. They slithered up her thighs, encircled her waist, and explored her tender flesh. She shivered against their touch, and the old god was pleased.

Breaking her bonds, he drew the beauty below.

He was not hungry…he had *other* desires.

K.R. Nox *is a Western Australian poet and short story writer. Being a consummate lover of ancient myths and legends, the occult, and all things dark and erotic, means there is always something deliciously creative brewing on the horizon… Website: www.krnox.com*

Lost City
by A.R. Johnston

This wasn't how it had always been. Once they had lived above the ocean where the skies were blue as the seas. Oh, how she longed for it.

She tilted her head back to look at the dome above, watching all the creatures of the depths gliding past it. Some creatures that people thought were extinct. There was a megalodon staring down at her right now.

It hadn't been an accident or a great tsunami that had taken this place. They had chosen to leave the world above behind. She missed it. But this was her home.

This was Atlantis.

A.R. Johnston is a small-town girl from Nova Scotia, Canada. She is known to write mostly urban fantasy, though she goes where the muses lead her and you never know where that may be. She is a lover of coffee, good tv shows, horror flicks, and a reader of good books. She pretends to be a writer when real life doesn't get in the way. Pesky full-time job and adulting!
Facebook: arjohnstonauthor
Website: arjohnstonauthor.wordpress.com

The Pinata
by J.B. Wocoski

The research vessel's sea crane lowered three oceanographers in their yellow diving bell into the deep-sea trench. Its captain reported, "Surface, we are making oceanographic history. This is incredible. We have never seen a giant squid this size before. Will you look at the size of that eye?"

The young giant squid slowly approached the small yellow sphere covered with bright lights. The creature's eye stared through the sphere's glass porthole, spotting treats moving inside. With an enormous tentacle, the squid playfully slapped the sphere like a pinata. The sphere burst open, spilling yummy treats for the squid to eat.

J.B. Wocoski is the author and narrator of the shortstorypodcast.com with three flash fiction short story books published in the last three years. He is currently working on book 4 "Short Story Podcast 2019." He writes mostly science fiction, fantasy, and horror stories. He won the 2016 Little Tokyo Short Story Writing Contest with his short story "The Last Master of Go"
Website: shortstorypodcast.com

Trapped
by Carole de Monclin

Salt and screaming have made my throat raw. My hands must be bleeding from the frantic banging.

I was sipping wine on a sunset cruise when chaos erupted, and obscurity swallowed me.

Will my air pocket last long enough for rescue to come?

The normal world lies beyond the upturned hull. So close, yet it could be a different universe.

My hopes dissolve in the frigid water.

I should dive to try to find my way out, but the boat's unfamiliar. What if, in the darkness, I go the wrong way?

I whimper when I feel the water creep higher.

Carole de Monclin travels both the real world and imaginary ones. She's lived in France, Australia, and the USA; visited 25+ countries; and explored Mars, Ceres, and many distant planets. She writes to invite people on a journey. Her stories can be found in The Arcanist, The Deep Space Anthology, and every volume of the Dark Drabbles series.
Website: CaroledeMonclin.com
Twitter: @CaroledeMonclin

Where the Light Cannot Go

by Crystal L. Kirkham

Deep, deep down they go.

Where no man had dared before.

Black like ink, pressure in the deep.

What could survive down here?

They shouldn't have gone, for now they know.

Monsters never seen before.

They lie in wait deep within the seas.

Hungry for what lived in the light they cannot reach.

And those poor brave souls who dared to explore?

Now they call this darkness their home.

Never to see the sky again.

Forgotten bones on an ocean floor.

Those that live in the light will never know

What waits deep down below.

Where the light cannot go.

Crystal L. Kirkham is a multi-genre speculative fiction author. She has published novels across several genres including her fantasy adventure Feathers and Fae (October 2019 from Kyanite Publishing) and her self-published urban fantasy series, Saints & Sinners. She is also a contributing author to multiple best-selling anthologies. Hailing from the wilds of Canada, she is an avid outdoors person, unrepentant coffee addict, part-time foodie, servant to a wonderful feline, and companion to three delightfully hilarious canines - Treble and Freddie the Standard Poodles, and Nahni the Australian Shepherd.
Website: www.crystallkirkham.com

Where Once Whales Wandered
by Clint Foster

Our oceans thrived in a manner we cannot imagine, when the most primitive humans dared not lust for a land beyond their own, when the stars were their guidelines and the wind their motor. Once, before us, whales wandered here in pods as big as islands. They frolicked and fished, singing to the deep, which sang not back with machinery, engines, and nets. Through the oceans so dark and deep, the whales once ruled gently, and did not exact a price from the world for their station. There is much we could learn from the world in which whales wandered.

Clint Foster lives with his herd of four cats, beloved Basset, Zero, and wonderful wife, Nik. He loves to tell stories just as much as he loves to read them and is excited to share his work. A long-time consumer of media of all kinds, he enjoys giving back what he hopes everyone else thinks are good stories.
Facebook: ClintFosterAuthor

Sea Waste
by Derek Dunn

The waves rise and fall to a steady rhythm, washing ashore a mishmash of waste. What man once tossed to the sea returns in unsightly heaps of ruin. Plastic bottles, bags, and cigarette butts line the beach. Scavenging birds search the debris, hoping to find remnants of food.

But something else has washed ashore. Something far more sinister than piles of foam lurks beneath, weaving its way to the prey above. The fowl make a tasty treat, but what it really wants is human flesh. The cloaked creature lies in waiting. It won't be long before another do-gooder shows up.

Derek Dunn is a film enthusiast and musician who writes primarily horror and mystery stories. After obtaining a degree in Media Arts Studies and dabbling in film production, he's turned his efforts to writing fiction. Several of his works have appeared in recent anthologies. He lives in the American northwest with his family, dog, and fish.
Twitter: DerekTDunn

Selkie

by Stacey Jaine McIntosh

The ocean was a dangerous place. Seals roamed these waters. Not just ordinary seals either. Selkies. Mythological shapeshifters capable of shedding their skin and becoming human. Few did out of fear of having their skin stolen, but Isla was certain she would share the same fate as so many other selkies had.

Of course, she couldn't have been more wrong. Now she paced up and down the length of the beach staring wistfully out at the ocean. Mourning her old life. And dreaming of the day she would be able to swim freely in the ocean as her true self.

Stacey Jaine McIntosh was born in Perth, Western Australia where she still resides with her husband and their four children. Although her first love has always been writing, she once toyed with being a Cartographer and subsequently holds a Diploma in Spatial Information Services. Since 2011, she has had a vast number of stories and a few poems published online as well as in various anthologies. Stacey is also the author of Solstice, Morrighan, Lost and Le Fay and she is currently working on several other projects simultaneously. When not with her family or writing she enjoys reading, photography, genealogy, history, Arthurian myths and witchcraft.
Website: www.staceyjainemcintosh.com

It's So Quiet
by Stephen Herczeg

Surfing was my life, right up until my death.

I should have known not to go out that day. It was rough. The waves dumped me; the board's fin split my skull open. All went dark for a while, but then I became aware.

The waves stole my board. The tide dragged me away from the shore.

I can't feel the cold. I should; I've been down here for ages, but I can't.

The fish took my eyes and my ears, but I can hear, and I can see.

It's light above, dark below; but down here it's so quiet.

Stephen Herczeg is an IT Geek based in Canberra Australia. He has been writing for over twenty years and has completed a couple of dodgy novels, sixteen feature length screenplays and numerous short stories and scripts. His horror work has featured in Sproutlings, Hells Bells, Below the Stairs, Trickster's Treats #1 and #2, Shades of Santa, Behind the Mask, Beyond the Infinite; The Body Horror Book, Anemone Enemy, Petrified Punks and Beginnings. He has also had numerous Sherlock Holmes stories published through the Belanger Books - Sherlock Holmes anthologies.
Amazon: amazon.com/-/e/B07916SQQS
Facebook: stephenherczegauthor

Falling into Deep Blue
by Cindar Harrell

The ocean always calmed me. The soothing coolness, the weightlessness. The never ending blue.

It took my breath away. I wished to stay on the ocean forever.

Now I am encased in it, falling. Cold. Weightless.

My eyes were closed against the salty sting, but now I force them open, I want to see.

The blue. The dying light.

My red hair flares around me like a fiery halo. I see a figure standing in the middle of the fading circle of light above my world of blue.

Was he a genie come to grant my wish?

Or a murderer?

Cindar Harrell loves fairy tales, especially ones with a dark twist. Her writing is often fairy tale inspired, but she also loves mystery and horror. Her stories can be found in various. Traveling is a passion for her as it inspires her imagination to run wild, especially in places that have a mystic presence in the air. She regularly moonlights as another human, but no matter who she is, she is always writing. Her novella inspired by The Snow Queen is set to release in 2020 as well as her debut novel, Lithium, and short story collection, Perchance to Dream.
Facebook: <u>*CindarHarrell*</u>

Night Dive
by J.M. Meyer

The hotel concierge suggested my brother Joe and I go for a night-time scuba dive.

As suggested, we floated deep below the surface and turned off our headlamps; vigorously stirring up the water with our arms and fins.

When the water glowed from the millions of neon coloured bioluminescent algae, I froze, realising we were not alone.

A bloated man, wearing only tattered swim trunks, smiled menacingly at us.

I turned on my headlamp, bolting toward the surface. Below, I watched Joe struggle; reaching for me in betrayal and disbelief as the demon dragged him deeper to his watery grave.

J.M. Meyer is a writer, artist and small business owner living in New York, where she received her master's degree from Teachers College, Columbia University. Jacqueline enjoys writing speculative fiction and mysteries. Her favorite author is Alice Munro and her favorite film…is…anything horror related. Jacqueline also enjoys hiking with her dog Molly and the company of her husband Bruce and daughters; Julia, Emma and Lauren. Jacqueline's Mantra lately; there's no such thing as failing, it's called learning.
Website: jmoranmeyer.net
Amazon: www.amazon.com/author/jacquelinemoranmeyer

Inside My World
by Umair Mirxa

Isabela sank slowly to the depths and felt the last of her breath escape her lungs. Cold water rushed to replace it.

A moment lapsed. Eternity flowed.

She opened her eyes to light. To life. To a face more beautiful than any she had seen before.

"Am I dead?"

"Inside my world, darling," came the soft reply, "such ideas hold no meaning."

Isabela realised then she was lying deep underwater, and not drowning. Yet.

"Wh-where am I?" she asked. "Who are you?"

"I am Amphitrite, Queen of the Sea, and you, little one…why, you belong to me now."

Umair Mirxa *lives and writes in Karachi, Pakistan. His first published story, 'Awareness', appeared on Spillwords Press. He has since had stories accepted for publication in anthologies from Zombie Pirate Publishing, Blood Song Books, Black Hare Press, Iron Faerie Publishing, Clarendon House Publications, Fantasia Divinity Magazine & Publishing, and The ReAnimated Writers Press. He is a massive J.R.R. Tolkien fan, loves everything to do with mythology, fantasy, and history, and wishes with all his heart that dragons were real. When he's not writing, he enjoys reading novels and comic books, playing video games, listening to music, and watching movies, TV shows, and football as an Arsenal FC fan.*
Website: <u>umairmirxa.com</u>

Almanack
by Anika Claire

By the light of the sun, find the rock pools where children play, where the waves crash over the rocks and rush down the other side in glittering waterfalls. Where the sun beats down on the white sand, but the turquoise water stays cold.

Return after dark to the luminescent shore. Place your bare feet on the smooth rocks and draw the ocean's energy in. Feel it fill your bones and the hollows in your lungs.

Draw it all in, but make sure to return it to the water once you've completed your working. The ocean can hold a grudge.

Anika Claire lives in Brisbane, Australia with her young family, where she alternates between making maps and escaping to other worlds, through either reading or creating them. You can find her reviewing and podcasting about books at;
Website: teainthetreetops.com
Instagram: @anni.treetops

Siren
by Susanne Thomas

It had seemed like such a good idea to dive into the sea to reach the beautiful mermaid that beckoned Sam. Her hands and smile had invited him. He'd considered the empty winter beach he'd been hiking as he searched for inspiration. Here, in front of him, was all the wonder Sam could want, and she wanted him to join her.

So he had swam towards her, stroke after freezing stroke bringing him further out. The vicious riptide came out of nowhere and pulled him away. He heard her song drifting on the salty breeze before he knew nothing more.

Susanne Thomas reads, writes, parents, and teaches from the windy west in Wyoming. She's an MFA graduate of the University of Arkansas at Monticello Creative Writing Program and she loves fantasy, science fiction, speculative fiction, poetry, children's books, science, coffee, and puns.
Website: www.themightierpenn.com

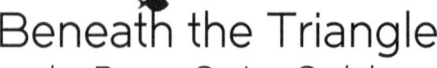

Beneath the Triangle
by Raven Corinn Carluk

Charles sighed, slumped in the crystal chair, eyes drifting toward the display board to his left. The purple gems glowed the same Atlantean glyph they had for what felt like three hours.

For the millionth time since the boat had capsized, Charles cursed his friends for taking him to the Bermuda Triangle.

He'd thought himself the lucky one for surviving and arriving in sunken Atlantis. Charles just had to go through refugee processing.

The interminable waiting and questions sapped his appreciation of the marvel until he began to realise the fabled land had drowned beneath a sea of red tape.

Raven Corinn Carluk writes dark fantasy, paranormal romance, and anything else that catches her interest. She's authored five novels, where she explores themes of love and acceptance. Her shorter pieces, usually from her darker side, can be found in Black Hare Press anthologies, at Detritus Online, and through Alban Lake Publishers.
Twitter: @ravencorinn
Website: www.ravencorinncarluk.com

From the Fog
by Radar DeBoard

The men of the ship all stood in complete silence. Each one terrified of what might be coming. They all knew the old legends and could tell that all the warning signs had occurred.

The ocean's waters had become almost completely still. There were no sounds coming from the sea. Yet, more than anything else, the men were terrified of the fog.

The smothering fog that had just creeped over the ship. It was impossible to see anything. Though it was easy to hear the scraping of a hook against metal as the ghosts of the sea descended upon them.

Radar DeBoard is a horror movie and novel enthusiast who resides in the small town of Goddard, Kansas. He occasionally dabbles in writing, and enjoys to make dark tales for people to enjoy. He has had drabbles and short stories published in various electronic magazines and anthologies.
Facebook: WriterRadarDeBoard

False Memory
by Sara A. Mosier

As he fell from the boat, the blood bloomed around him like bleeding roses; it was a funny thing to admire as he sank to the bottom of the ocean. The taste of salt was on his tongue, his eyes burned, his limbs ached, but nothing else mattered. The sun looming made him think of the prairies of the Midwest, a concept of something so far away. He wished he could take a breath, but then the orange exploded around him. As the ocean pushed him onto the shore, he gripped the sand tightly, and then he heard the scream.

Sara A. Mosier is a Nebraska author, poet, and recent graduate from the University of Nebraska-Lincoln where she received a BA in English. Her writing focus is fiction and poetry of which she enjoys typing on an old 1950's typewriter. She has poetry published in several issues of Laurus Magazine, Cocky-Tales anthology, and University of Nebraska Press's 75th Anniversary edition of "Voices of Nebraska". Her romantic short stories "Sparkling Human Conundrum" and "Summer Dilemma" can be found in the anthologies Love Dust and Salty Tales on Amazon.

No Escape
by Cindar Harrell

The plague spread quickly and with no cure, there were few options left. What people remained unaffected fled beneath the oceans.

The city we built was a technological marvel. I loved looking out the thick windows and watching the ocean life swim by. It was like living inside a giant aquarium.

However, things changed quickly. Some people just don't know how to be happy.

A radical group went insane. Longing to see the sun again, they started killing and taking hostages. It turns out; the plague was hiding in their brains.

Now we are stuck here. There is no escape.

Cindar Harrell loves fairy tales, especially ones with a dark twist. Her writing is often fairy tale inspired, but she also loves mystery and horror. Her stories can be found in various. Traveling is a passion for her as it inspires her imagination to run wild, especially in places that have a mystic presence in the air. She regularly moonlights as another human, but no matter who she is, she is always writing. Her novella inspired by The Snow Queen is set to release in 2020 as well as her debut novel, Lithium, and short story collection, Perchance to Dream.
Facebook: *CindarHarrell*

Keep off the Beach
by Maxine Churchman

The beach was deserted, even though the day was warm. The children hunted through the rock pools for crabs while the adults sat on blankets drinking beer.

Billy saw it first: a grey shapeless blob half-buried in the sand, glistening wetly in the sunshine.

"Cor! Look at this" he said, prodding the leathery surface with his toe.

The others ran over to look. Jenny screwed up her face. "Yuck! What is it?"

Quick as a flash, it reared up; tentacles pulling the children into its gaping maw before disappearing back under the sand again.

"Where are the children?" screamed Lily.

Maxine Churchman lives in Essex UK and has recently started writing poetry and short stories to share. Her interests include learning to improve her writing, reading, knitting, walking and teaching yoga. She is also planning a novel.

In Utero
by Rich Rurshell

She panicked as the salt water rushed into her lungs, unable to hold her breath any longer. She kicked her legs, knowing she was too far away from the surface, but it felt like the right thing to do. After a moment, the pain in her lungs went away and she stopped moving.

Quiet.

Ebony could make out groups of curious fish in her blurred vision. Their beautiful colours. The shades of green and blue around her.

As the darkness closed in, Ebony felt great peace. Safety. At one with her environment. A sense of belonging deep within Mother Earth.

Rich Rurshell is a short story writer from Suffolk, England. Rich writes Horror, Sci-Fi, and Fantasy, and his stories can be found in various short story anthologies and magazines. Most recently, his story "Subject: Galilee" was published in World War Four from Zombie Pirate Publishing, and "Life Choices" was published in Salty Tales from Stormy Island Publishing. When Rich is not writing stories, he likes to write and perform music.
Facebook: richrurshellauthor

Beachfront Days
by Robin Braid

Alex waded into the water, searching for movement beneath the surface. Had nobody else seen the child go under? A group of teenagers splashed past, laughing as they raced towards an incoming wave.

Then he saw her, reaching out. He had a rush of relief as her little hand slipped into his, but it felt strange.

Her long, blonde hair seemed to drift away, debris in a retreating tide, and a cold, grey eye stared up at him. The little hand wound around his, and as a crimson cloud stirred shapes in the water, Alex fell into the ocean's embrace.

Robin Braid writes stories of the mysterious and macabre. A resident of Fife, Scotland, he graduated from Dundee University with a degree in English Literature. When not working in his regular job he can often be found rambling over hills and glens in search of inspiration for further tales.
Twitter: @robinbraid

Cold

by Ximena Escobar

The day came that Ocean decided to be fire. The sun through the ripples; she envisioned grasping it in her hands like a pearl of everything she wasn't; everything she wanted consuming her, lighting her. She'd burn, fly like the shooting stars fly and she doesn't, trapped always in dark cold craters.

Rising like a mountain, she walked to the shore on legs of dream, dragging the planet's water like a wedding dress to the edge.

She jumped, but no wings opened. The unreachable sun dimmed as she floated away shapelessly, missed by the shooting stars around her. Unlit. Unburnt.

Ximena Escobar is writing stories and poetry. Originally from Chile, she is the author of a translation into Spanish of the Broadway Musical "The Wizard of Oz", and of an original adaptation of the same, "Navidad en Oz", both produced in her home country. Since 2018 she has published several short stories in various anthologies and online platforms, and is now slowly working on her own collection. Ximena has a degree in Arts & Communication Science and lives in Nottingham with her family.
Facebook: Ximenautora
Twitter: @laximenin

The Blood Red Sea
by Lyndsey Ellis-Holloway

Hi ho, hi ho, a pirate's life for me.
You can run, you can't hide,
As we sail the high tide,
Upon the Blood Red Sea.

Hi ho, hi ho, a pirate's life for me.
With a swish of my sword,
I'll never get bored,
Upon the Blood Red Sea.

Hi ho, hi ho, a pirate's life for me.
I chop off his head,
And he joins the dead,
Upon the Blood Red Sea.

Hi ho, hi ho, a pirate's life for me.
The rolling waves,
A hundred new graves,
Upon the Blood Red Sea.

A pirate's life for me.

Lyndsey Ellis-Holloway *is a writer from Knaresborough, UK. She writes fantasy, sci-fi, horror and dystopian stories, focussing on compelling characters and layering in myth and legend at every opportunity. Her mind is somewhat dark and twisted, and she lives in perpetual hope of owning her own Dragon someday, but for now she writes about them to fill the void... and to stop her from murdering people who annoy her. When she's not writing she spends time with her husband, her dogs and her friends enjoying activities such as walking, movies, conventions and of course writing for fun as well! Website: theprose.com/LyndseyEH*

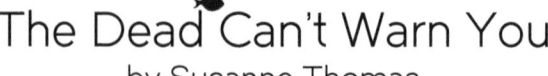

The Dead Can't Warn You
by Susanne Thomas

Another body washed up on shore, pocked by circles like the others. Giant rings were gruesome reds and purples on the bloated, rotting, grey flesh. Access to the beaches had been revoked for the millions of tourists and residents of the city. Not that it seemed to matter.

Patrick had the misfortune of examining each cadaver. He watched the water's surface with fear. He was just a coroner, and bravery wasn't his strong suit. A glint in the water caught his eye, and he approached the water's edge, staring into the distance. He never saw the tentacle that grabbed him.

Susanne Thomas reads, writes, parents, and teaches from the windy west in Wyoming. She's an MFA graduate of the University of Arkansas at Monticello Creative Writing Program and she loves fantasy, science fiction, speculative fiction, poetry, children's books, science, coffee, and puns.
Website: www.themightierpenn.com

Even sharks can be prey
by Stephen Herczeg

The shark swam through the deep cold water. Summer was coming and with it the rise in fish stocks and the chance for something larger. The dark seals were a delicacy, but not the larger pale seals. Too many bones.

Deep below, a large shape surfaced from the murky depths. Its powerful tail thrust towards the shark.

Awakened from its frozen slumber, the giant Kronosaurus rose. Massive jaws snapped the shark in half and gulped it down.

After so long, the hunger gnawed away inside.

It sensed prey splashing in the shallows nearby. They were small, but they were many.

Stephen Herczeg is an IT Geek based in Canberra Australia. He has been writing for over twenty years and has completed a couple of dodgy novels, sixteen feature length screenplays and numerous short stories and scripts. His horror work has featured in Sproutlings, Hells Bells, Below the Stairs, Trickster's Treats #1 and #2, Shades of Santa, Behind the Mask, Beyond the Infinite; The Body Horror Book, Anemone Enemy, Petrified Punks and Beginnings. He has also had numerous Sherlock Holmes stories published through the Belanger Books - Sherlock Holmes anthologies.
Amazon: amazon.com/-/e/B07916SQQS
Facebook: stephenherczegauthor

Bad Luck
by Jade Wilburn

Bad luck to have a woman onboard.

That's what the sailors said when they tossed Veronica overboard, a sacrifice to appease the raging sea.

What was a woman's life in comparison to the fear of fifty men?

Luckily, the sea gifted its new daughters with water-breathing and tails.

"It's time," Veronica called, sharing a fanged smile with her sisters as they bobbed in the water beside a ship. A haunting melody spilled out their lips, and bodies began to fall from overhead.

She and her sisters had drowned for something that wasn't their fault; every sailor deserved that same courtesy.

*A native of Rochester, New York, **Jade Wilburn** is currently earning an M.S. in User Experience and Interaction Design at Thomas Jefferson University. In between studying like a good student, she devours fairytales and composes fantasy stories. Her work has appeared in Enchanted Conversation Magazine. Twitter: @_Jade_Green_*

Sink or Float
by Radar DeBoard

Tommy's favourite game was walking to the end of the dock by his oceanside home and tossing things into the water. He loved to discover if each item would sink or float.

His favourite moment was that brief second where he couldn't tell what was going to happen.

Secretly, Tommy liked watching items sink way more than seeing them float.

He was having trouble getting his latest object pushed off the dock since it was so heavy.

With a final push he managed to shove his father's body off the edge. Tommy smiled as his dad sank into the ocean.

Radar DeBoard is a horror movie and novel enthusiast who resides in the small town of Goddard, Kansas. He occasionally dabbles in writing, and enjoys to make dark tales for people to enjoy. He has had drabbles and short stories published in various electronic magazines and anthologies.
Facebook: WriterRadarDeBoard

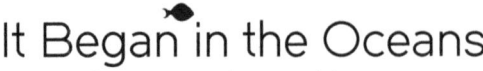

It Began in the Oceans
by Crystal L. Kirkham

It began in the oceans.

A war unlike others.

Dolphins organised the sea creatures. Whales crashed down and destroyed ships. Jellyfish sought out the swimmers.

Soon, the seas were untouchable, the beaches abandoned.

It was war, and we weren't going to give up. They fought dirty, we fought dirtier.

Poison. Disease. Bombing.

We defeated them, but we did not win.

Our oceans were destroyed. Unusable. Fresh water was at a premium.

Parched and choking, all living things perished.

The empty Earth had time to heal and life could once again find a way.

As always, it began in the oceans.

Crystal L. Kirkham *is a multi-genre speculative fiction author. She has published novels across several genres including her fantasy adventure Feathers and Fae (October 2019 from Kyanite Publishing) and her self-published urban fantasy series, Saints & Sinners. She is also a contributing author to multiple best-selling anthologies. Hailing from the wilds of Canada, she is an avid outdoors person, unrepentant coffee addict, part-time foodie, servant to a wonderful feline, and companion to three delightfully hilarious canines - Treble and Freddie the Standard Poodles, and Nahni the Australian Shepherd.*
Website: www.crystallkirkham.com

Man O' War
by Antonia Rachel Ward

I swam as far from the beach as I dared. The ocean was drenched in sunlight. I floated adrift, feeling free, until electric prickles seared up my limbs.

Turning my head, I saw the water swarming with cellophane forms. They looked so delicate. So harmless. I reached out to them. Feathery tendrils wrapped around my arms and legs. The pain turned me translucent. I became atoms on the surface of the water.

My rescuers told me I was lucky. The amount of venom in my blood should have killed me. But they don't understand.

I brought death back with me.

Antonia Rachel Ward is a writer of Gothic, horror, and futuristic fiction based in Cambridgeshire, UK. She holds an MA in English Literature with a specialism in Eighteenth-Century Gothic, and is currently working on her first novel.

To Die or Not to (Not) Die

by K.B. Elijah

There was only one choice for the crew of the *Bountiful*: death by dehydration or death by drowning.

On a steadily sinking ship whose mast had been lost in the storm three days prior, and now lay adrift in a desolate part of the ocean far from shipping lanes, that choice was all they had.

Would they give themselves to the sea, that unforgiving and temperamental mistress? Or would they clutch at the vestiges of a forlorn hope; attempt to hold on to life until their thirst stole it from their bones?

Then the Kraken arrived and stole their choice.

K.B. Elijah is a fantasy author living in Brisbane, Australia with her husband and three cockatiels. A lawyer by day, and a writer by...also day, because she needs her solid nine hours of sleep per night (not that the cockatiels let her sleep past 6am). K.B. writes for various international anthologies, and her work features in dozens of collections about the mysterious, the magical and the macabre. Her own books of short fantasy novellas with twists, The Empty Sky and Out of the Nowhere, are available on paperback and Kindle now.
Website: www.kbelijah.com
Instagram: k.b.elijah

The Longest Voyage
by Kimberly Rei

The discovery of an ancient sea-faring vessel in the middle of a prairie had brought Sam to the abandoned farmhouse on a survey mission.

He stared in wonder and pressed his palm to the oddly preserved wooden hull.

The sound of crashing waves snapped his gaze to the horizon. He had to be hearing things. The air felt heavy, as if a storm was approaching. Icy water, unseen to the mortal eye, slammed into him and spun him off his feet. He struggled for air, blacking out as the ship slid past.

The ocean had come to reclaim its own.

Kimberly Rei has been writing for as long as she can remember. At five years old, her parents gifted her with a set of Children's Classics that she had no hope of reading. Yet. The potential alone sparked a love of words that has never wavered. Kim has taught writing workshops and edited novels for Authors You May Recognize. She has published several short stories and now can't stop chasing paper dragons. She currently lives in Tampa Bay, Florida with her wife and an abundance of gorgeous beaches to explore.

Qalupalik Part 2
by V.A. Vazquez

She waited.

Shotgun clutched tight in her hands, puffs of breath steaming and dissipating in the arctic winds. Finally, the *qalupalik* climbed out of the breathing hole; its lurching, consumptive frame silhouetted against the lights of the town.

Her town.

"Do you remember me?"

Its voice was cracked and seeping.

She looked closer at its pale face, its damp-blue eyes.

The outsider boy.

The one who'd chased her onto the ice years ago.

"I've been living all this time—" It pointed its stuttering finger towards the breathing hole. "—down there."

The night breathed.

"I suppose it's your town too then."

V.A. Vazquez writes urban fantasy and paranormal romance. She currently lives in Glasgow, Scotland with her husband and small doggo.
Website: www.vavazquez.com

The Artist
by Bec Lewis

The luxury yacht—her floating studio—lurched. Water spewed in.

Bella grabbed her precious paintings.

"Where d'you get such amazingly iridescent colours?" buyers always asked.

She never told. Tattoos snaking down her arms gave a clue: seaweed, coral…and mermaids. Papa's fishing trips were not for food. The ground-up scales were like liquid mother-of-pearl.

The water rose rapidly.

A woman appeared alongside the floundering Bella and pointed at bobbing seascapes.

"You like my art?" Bella gasped, spotting the fishy tail. The mermaid stroked Bella's tattoos, nodded, smiling, before whipping out a sharp razor shell and starting her own art collection.

Bec Lewis lives in Kent, England. She's had stories published in a number of e-zines and print magazines.
Website: www.beclewisfiction.com

The Lady and the Whale
by Nicola Currie

Something draws the creature, I think as I observe from the helm, as I am drawn to his melancholy song. Days he has followed our ship, ever singing.

Could it be? I think as I fuss the odious whalebone pendant my husband bids me wear, ever reminded of his cruelty.

How many seas would I cross if I loved someone to their bones?

My husband approaches, harpoon ready. He ignores my implorations, leans overboard, aims at the mellifluous angel.

For my melancholy or the creature's, I know not, but I push.

Silently, the beauty enjoys his vengeance.

Bone by bone.

Nicola Currie is from Cambridge, UK where she works in educational publishing. She has published poetry in literary magazines, including Mslexia and Sarasvati, and short stories in various anthologies. She has also completed her first novel, which was longlisted for the Bath Children's Novel Award. Website: writeitandweep.home.blog

Caged

by Jodi Jensen

Down, down, down she went, safe inside the shark cage, camera in hand. The deeper she went, the darker it got.

A bump against the cage sent her heart racing.

Lifting her camera, she wondered what species of shark she was about to capture. A hammerhead, she hoped.

She waited…

And waited…

Something tugged at her foot.

She glanced down…

Tentacles?

One around her ankle, another around a bar. A head squeezed through the cage, then a body.

She dropped the camera and fumbled with the cage door.

The giant squid wrapped her in its tentacles and swallowed her screams.

Jodi Jensen, *author of time travel romances and speculative fiction short stories, grew up moving from California, to Massachusetts, and a few other places in between, before finally settling in Utah at the ripe old age of nine. The nomadic life fed her sense of adventure as a child and the wanderlust continues to this day. With a passion for old cemeteries, historical buildings and sweeping sagas of days gone by, it was only natural she'd dream of time traveling to all the places that sparked her imagination.*
Twitter: @WritesJodi
Facebook: jodijensenwrites

Easy Kill
by Wendy Roberts

The scent of blood is strong, leading him straight toward an easy kill that will allow him to find a dark space to hunker down and rest for a while. As the smell grows stronger, the huge beasts that lurk above the ocean move, along with something else. The new scent makes him swim a bit faster. Determined to get his prize and as far from the strange hunters as possible when something rips into his side. He snaps at this new enemy, turning to escape the pain, when something wraps around him to pull him toward the beasts above.

Writing short stories and novels started as a past time for **Wendy Roberts** *and has now become a fully fledged passion. She posts short stories on her website and can be found most days on Twitter.*
Website: flippinscribbler.com
Twitter: @_WARoberts

Fish Judgement
by Will Christian

Bright flashing lures, fat juicy worms, feathers or plastic eels: you spend futile hours on shore and craft.

But we see you and we pity you.

There's no art to your fishing, dangling a line with the hope that you will take back a prize catch to show off to others on a big dish. Waiting for us to jump on the hook—do you think we are foolish?

Inconsequential humans, we only give up the dregs and wastrels of the deep.

Our own piscatorial courts pass sentence to those who stray: onto the hook with their lives, they pay.

***Will Christian** is a father of two writers and a husband to his beautiful wife (who paid him to write that). With a sense of humour that his eldest daughter calls "adorable and groan-worthy dad jokes with surprising creativity", Will can usually be found wandering the local beaches, writing poetry and drabbles, and wistfully daydreaming about the boat that his girls haven't yet agreed to buy him.*

Into the Depths
by Megan Willette

It was bad luck to allow a woman to stay aboard, so they tied a weight around her legs and pushed her from the ship. The sky was full of stars as she sank into the depths of the ocean.

On the verge of death, there was a pain beyond anything she had ever experienced. When it subsided, she was transformed: a tail where she once had legs, and the ability to breathe beneath the waves.

Her beauty and song would lead hundreds to their deaths, for mermaids are the unfortunate victims of superstitious sailors, gifted a chance for revenge.

Megan Willette is a registered cardiology technologist living in St. John's, Newfoundland. While most of the time she can be found reading various types of stories, she sometimes tries to write them. Fantasy themes come easiest to her but she has attempted fiction, sci-fi, and mystery as well. There are currently two unfinished fantasy novels sitting on her computer which may or may not eventually be shared with other people if she can ever manage to finish them.

The Sea Witch
by Zoey Xolton

Standing upon the rocky shore the ancient, but deceptively youthful looking sea witch raised her arms, her fingers and hands performing intricate motions through the air—swirls of magic whorled around them as she worked.

In return for her long years, her beauty and her power, she owed Poseidon tribute, once a year; a tithe of blood to be paid to the old god beneath the waves.

In the distance a ship could be seen battling the choppy waters. Answering her summons, the ocean swelled and raged. The mast snapped, the vessel sank, and all the souls aboard were lost.

Zoey Xolton is an Australian Speculative Fiction writer, primarily of Dark Fantasy, Paranormal Romance and Horror. She is also a proud mother of two and is married to her soul mate. Outside of her family, writing is her greatest passion. She is especially fond of short fiction and is working on releasing her own themed collections in future.
Website: www.zoeyxolton.com

Funnel of Death
by Nerisha Kemraj

Captain Erickson stood before the ship's wheel, steering against the current, trying to shield the lifeboats that struggled to get away from the magnetic pull of a massive whirlpool. As passengers climbed onto the remaining lifeboats, the anchor gave way, snapping onto the ship.

Within seconds, the giant vessel swirled into the midst of the rotating mass of water. Screaming passengers were flung overboard and sucked into the funnel when the ship began to spin.

The captain could do nothing but painfully watch as the raging ocean swallowed his beloved *Betty* into its depths while he held onto her wheel.

Nerisha Kemraj resides in Durban, South Africa with her husband and two mischievous daughters. Writing since 2017, she has had over 100 short stories and poems published in various publications, both print and online. She has also received an Honourable Mention Award for her tanka in the Fujisan Taisho 2019 Tanka Contest. She holds a Bachelor's degree in Communication Science, and a Post Graduate Certificate in Education from University of South Africa.
Amazon: amazon.com/author/nerisha_kemraj
Facebook: Nerishakemrajwriter

The Coral Garden
by Paula R.C. Readman

Such a perfect ending to a crappy holiday, Wendy thought while floating on her back. As a light breeze brushed her cheek, she rolled over to gaze down.

Through the crystal clear water, she saw her husband, Tom, waving at her. He swam seal-like among the brightly coloured corals and darting fish.

Wendy calmly pulled the harpoon trigger. She enjoyed Tom's shocked expression as the spear passed straight through him.

No more than the bastard deserved, she deemed, since finding out about his betrayal.

Soon the circling sharks would follow the bloody trail. With determined strokes, Wendy headed to shore.

Paula R.C. Readman learnt 'How to Write' from books which her husband purchased from eBay. After 250 purchases, he finally told her 'just to get on with the writing'. Since 2010, she's had 34 stories published.
Blog: paulareadman1.wordpress.com

Tsunami
by Paul Eric Carberry

The ocean retreats from the shore without reason. Fishermen rush to the exposed, craggy ocean floor to assess the damage to their boats. They stand there puzzled. Amongst the chatter, theories and rumours spread like wildfire. An ominous silence washes over them as the powerful raging ocean rushes back to reclaim its rightful place. Cries are drowned out by the overpowering roar as the one hundred foot tidal wave asserts its dominance. Water pounds the shore with unfathomable power. Nothing is left intact; houses, boats, vehicles, animals and people are washed out to their watery grave in an instant. Tsunami.

Paul Eric Carberry is the author of the Zombies on the Rock series. His tales of the zombie apocalypse in Newfoundland are inspired by George A. Romero's Living Dead series. He has also published several short stories over three "from the Rock" anthologies including "Halloween Mummers", "The Light of Cabot Tower", "Into the Forrest" and "Harmon Field". His Zombies on the Rock series currently has three novels, "Outbreak", "The Viking Trail" and "The Republic of Newfound" and is currently working on the fourth novel "Extinction". Paul is from Newfoundland and is currently living in Shearwater, Nova Scotia.
Website: engenbooks.com/zombies-on-the-rock

Frozen
by Terri A. Arnold

I run, flat out, my breath coming in agonised puffs. I've never been thankful for living so far north as I am right now. It burns as my bare feet hit the snow. I know I'm leaving a trail of blood behind me, blood drips from every orifice.

Survival isn't likely, but after hours of torture, when I saw a chance, I ran. All I wear is a parka and my panties, I push myself to run faster. The frozen ocean could be my saviour as I run over it towards town. My body slows, and I pray for rescue.

Terri A. Arnold is an avid reader turned writer from a small town in Nova Scotia, who has spent her life reading and wishing she was writing. Although she has written a lot in those years, she has only recently begun to submit pieces for publication. With ongoing encouragement from family and writing challenges with friends, Arnold felt the urge to try her hand at publishing.

Fateful Expansion
by C.L. Williams

Today could be the final day of life on Earth. After millennia of treating the ocean as our dumping grounds, life in the ocean retaliated. It turns out, many of the animals living in the ocean live in water by choice. Jellyfish, sharks, and creatures I've never seen before attacked all living organisms on land.

The worst of it happened when the ocean waters themselves expanded onto land throughout the globe. Taking down cities, expanding the reaches of the ocean. All that remains is an island once known as Oklahoma.

Today could be the final day of land on Earth.

C.L. Williams is an international best-selling author currently living in central Virginia. He has written eight poetry books, four novellas, one novel, and a contributor to a multitude of anthologies and magazines. His most recent anthology appearance ANGELS: Dark Drabbles #2 from Black Hare Press became a number one in hot new releases. C.L. Williams is currently working on his second novel and a new poetry book.
Facebook: writer434
Twitter: @writer_434

The Mermaid
by Timothy Friesenhahn

Her beauty brought upon a feeling of pure euphoria. The arms of the enchantress were crossed as she sat perched on his small raft. The young seaman was fishing; a morning ritual he made routine since his crash on the island days ago. The sunlight sparkled in her blazing red hair. Her voice was soft when she spoke. She asked, "Come a little closer, feel my touch."

Resisting would bring on years of regret. His life was already lost to the sea. Face to face with the sea-goddess, he saw her teeth were razor sharp. Pulling him overboard, she fed.

Timothy Friesenhahn is thirty years old from Texas, where he lives with his fiance and two dogs. He has been writing since eight years old rather it be stories, poems, or lyrics. He played in a band off and on for several years until he was electrocuted. His lifestyle had to change from there and he went to a WFPB diet and settled down and decided to pursue his dream of writing novels.

Meal for a Mermaid
by Elizabeth Tackett

Still as the night, watching the herd unwittingly swim above the reef where she lies. Grey skin mimicking the rocky surface, going undetected by her meal. A human strays from the pack; her mark is clear. Her heart pounds, the scent of her feast strengthens as it draws near. Advancing upon its predator with little suspicion that something is amiss; curiosity damning it to the fate of the feline. Her victim within inches, it's back is turned. It's feeding time. Her claws sink deep into flesh, releasing the intoxicating aroma of blood, dragging her bounty to its final resting place.

Elizabeth Tackett is an emerging fiction writer based in LaGrange, GA, where she lives with her husband and three young sons. As a homemaker, she uses her creative talents daily and has a yearning to share those talents beyond the confines of her home.

Human Leg Soup, Anyone?
by Wondra Vanian

How long can you dump pollutants into the oceans before you change the genetic makeup of the creatures living there? Scientists never got around to asking. They didn't have to.

The effect of manmade contaminants on marine life became obvious when the first shark walked onto land. That level of evolution should have taken hundreds of thousands of years but had been helped along considerably.

How long can you hunt a species for their fins before they seek revenge? Reporters never got around to asking. They didn't have to.

Their desire for revenge became obvious when the first shark attacked.

Wondra Vanian is an American living in the United Kingdom with her Welsh husband and their army of fur babies. A writer first, Wondra is also an avid gamer, photographer, cinephile, and blogger. She has music in her blood, sleeps with the lights on, and has been known to dance naked in the moonlight. Wondra was a multiple Top-Ten finisher in the 2017 and 2018 Preditors and Editors Reader's Poll, including the Best Author category. Her story, "Halloween Night," was named a Notable Contender for the Bristol Short Story Prize in 2015.
Website: www.wondravanian.com

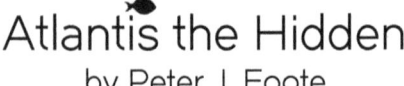

Atlantis the Hidden
by Peter J. Foote

"There's nothing here, Professor, and between the reef and the mist, your life is in jeopardy."

"You accepted my money, Caspian, to sail me here, I say we continue on!" The professor leans against the ship's railing, willing the fog to part, and shouts in delight as the crystal city of Atlantis pokes out of the ocean.

"I knew it! Everybody at the university laughed at my theories, but when I return..." The harpoon pierces his back, rupturing organs, killing him.

"I'm sorry, Professor, but I must defend my home," Caspian says and pitches the body to the circling sharks.

Peter J. Foote is a bestselling speculative fiction writer from Nova Scotia. Outside of writing, he runs a used bookstore specialising in fantasy & sci-fi, cosplays, and alternates between red wine and coffee as the mood demands. His short stories can be found in both print and in ebook form, with his story "Sea Monkeys" winning the inaugural "Engen Books/Kit Sora, Flash Fiction/Flash Photography" contest in March of 2018. As the founder of the group "Genre Writers of Atlantic Canada", Peter believes that the writing community is stronger when it works together.
Twitter: @PeterJFoote1
Website: peterjfooteauthor.wordpress.com

To Find Peace
by T.A. Ulven

My father loved the endless horizon and the vast depths. There's a peace here, he told me, that you can't get anywhere else. I guess that's why I keep coming back. To feel close to him.

And he was right; there's this special feeling when you look around and there's nothing but the ocean. Nothing but the fathomless blue. It makes you feel insignificant and small. Just like he made me feel.

So I visit him. Dive down to his final resting place, his body anchored for eternity. They'll never find him. He's all alone.

I find peace in that.

T.A.Ulven is a father, husband, and horror fiction writer hailing from the cold mountains of Norway. He became known through his horror persona hyperobscure, primarily posting short stories on the vast writing subreddit of NoSleep. He has since had work published in several anthologies, and will continue to expand his dark universe for as long as people will visit it.
Facebook: hyperobscure
Reddit: hyperobscura

Safe in the Dark
by Lynne Phillips

The malevolence that emanated from the vial was overpowering. Manweolf tried to counter the spell but failed.

In exasperation he muttered, "I cast you into the deepest ocean where no light penetrates, and you can't do evil."

His words held for a thousand years until a two-man bathysphere sank to the bottom of the ocean. The light from the undersea vehicle woke the monstrosity in the vial. Its spores clung to the vehicle and were carried to the surface. When exposed to sunlight, the flesh-eating bug multiplied and spread. The two divers were the first to succumb, others swiftly followed.

Lynne Phillips, a retired teacher, lives in the beautiful Northern Rivers Region of New South Wales Australia. Her stories, across all genres, have been published in anthologies and various online magazines. Her priority is spending time with her family. Her passions are reading, writing and keeping fit.

H.M.S. Tempest
by E.L. Giles

Captain Scott was pulled from slumber as the annoying hum of the speakers died and the eerie, distorted transmission filled the control room.

"Mayday! Mayday!" the voice repeated. A long silence followed, and then the voice haunted the control room again. "This is the HMS *Tempest*…are sinking…"

Captain Scott's stomach dropped. His blood ran cold. He picked up the microphone, feverishly adjusted the frequency, and spoke, "This is Captain William Scott. Do you copy? Did you say the HMS *Terror?* Please confirm."

Scott's forehead gleamed with sweat.

"What's the matter?" asked an officer.

"The HMS *Tempest* disappeared fifty years ago."

E.L. Giles is a dreamer, passionate about art, a restless worker and a bit of a weird human. He started his artistic journey as a music composer until the need to put his thoughts and stories down on paper grew too strong for him to resist it any longer. He lives in the French Province of Quebec, Canada, with his girlfriend and two boys.
Facebook: elgilesauthor
Website: www.elgilesauthor.com

You darkened my Soul
by Chris de Monclin

Foolishness and ignorance are killing me.

Humans always took me for granted, believing I would right their wrongs. Oil spills spreading darkness, a continent of plastic dispersing into the food chain, radioactive wastes leaking into my depths…all poisons asphyxiating me slowly.

Once, I hosted millions of species living in symbiosis; they're now all joining me in this journey towards the inevitable.

So, I take my revenge, blindly taking lives. An imprudent sailor, a presumptuous surfer, maybe an appetising swimmer or a diver. Who will be next?

What did you expect? That I'd die without fighting? You perverted me, fools!

Chris de Monclin has lived in Germany, France, Australia, and the USA, visited 35+ countries and enjoyed every encounter. Passionate about Franco-Belgian graphic novels, he writes to challenge himself in storytelling, put into words his nightmares, or when his talented author wife doesn't adapt his ideas the way he likes.

Shark Fin Soup
by McKenzie Richardson

Tossing the last of the de-finned sharks into the now blood-sullied water, Marcus stretched with a groan. His back had been bothering him lately. Hunching over thrashing sharks didn't help matters.

He cast his eyes out over the open water. In the distance, a boat approached, its tall sail cutting the sky.

His forehead rumpled. It was going awfully fast; must have a motor of some sort.

Suddenly, an enormous creature erupted from the water beneath what he now saw was a fin. Massive mouth agape, serrated teeth looming.

Marcus cried out before the entire boat was plunged into darkness.

McKenzie Richardson lives in Milwaukee, WI. Her horror stories have been featured in various anthologies including Evil Lurks, Pandemic, and After: Undead Wars. She has also published a variety of poems and flash fiction pieces.
Facebook: mckenzielrichardson
Blog: www.craft-cycle.com

Song of the Sirens
by Rowanne S. Carberry

Wind howls through the sails.

Thick, black clouds cover the only light.

Each drop of rain like bullets.

"Drop the anchor, we aren't going further tonight."

They scramble to do as they're told.

The captain heads to his quarters for the night.

Sometime later he hears singing.

I'm not the only one on the whiskey tonight.

The ship moves.

Running onto deck, he stares as his crew steer the ship in a trance.

He hears a soft, sweet voice, calling out to all who pass for help.

Taking his place, he steers the ship towards the voice, and into oblivion.

Rowanne S. Carberry *was born in England in 1990, where she stills lives now with her cat Wolverine. Rowanne has always loved writing, and her first poem was published at the age of 15, but her ambition has always been to help people. Rowanne studied at the University of Sunderland where she completed combined honours of Psychology with Drama. Rowanne writes to offer others an escape. Although Rowanne writes in varied genres each story or poem she writes will often have a darkness to it, which helped coin her brand, Poisoned Quill Writing – Wicked words from a poisoned quill.*
Facebook: PoisonedQuillWriting
Instagram: @poisoned_quill_writing

The Stowaway
by Crmetheus Christopher

"Good lord!" Mason croaked in disbelief, frantically pacing back and forth.

"All I did was my job, same as every day."

He glanced nervously back down into the ship's bilge where a small hand could be seen just breaking the surface of the water in the boats recess.

Looking up towards the engine room door, he saw the ship's captain was fast approaching accompanied by a distressed looking couple, and immediately he began to feel a terrible sadness well up inside of him.

"All I did was my job," Mason said, gazing out at the ocean, same as every day."

Crmetheus Christopher is an author from Boston Massachusetts. He is an eclectic artist who writes with a unique passion and flair for storytelling, he is the author of two books. When The Lions Came(Fantasy) and Mayhaps Tomorrow(Psychological Thriller). He is also the creator of The Authors Embers Podcast.

Hunting in the Shallows
by G. Allen Wilbanks

She watched the child playing in the shallow waves on the beach. His parents lay contentedly sunning themselves on a blanket a few yards further away.

"Hello, Sweetie. Are you enjoying the water?" she called to him.

The boy glanced to where she waited, seeing only her head above the surface.

"The ocean is nice and warm over here. Can you swim out to me?"

The boy laughed and waded toward her.

"Such a sweet boy," she said, urging him on. She smiled at his progress, careful not to reveal her long pointed teeth until it was far too late.

G. Allen Wilbanks is a member of the Horror Writers Association (HWA) and has published over 100 short stories in various magazines and on-line venues. He is the author of two short story collections, and the novel, When Darkness Comes.
Website: www.gallenwilbanks.com
Blog: DeepDarkThoughts.com

Surf & Turf
by Jacob Baugher

I remember when we found them. We dived into the black. Blinking cyan and sea-green indicators illuminate the submersible's cockpit. Megan sits beside me, manning the hydro-propulsion thrusters. Outside, it's like inky outer space. Constellation Marianas.

The exterior lights flicker on, illuminating squidy faces. Over the comm, a mucous-filled voice burbles, "Greetings."

They take us to their city. Glowing bubbles cling to the trench like barnacles. Slimy, tentacled handshakes are exchanged. We'll return. Diplomacy is important.

When we dive again, a fat man in a chef's hat sits in Megan's chair. He says, "Yes, they'll do nicely. Ready the steamers."

Jacob Baugher teaches Creative Writing at a small university near Pittsburgh, PA. When he's not teaching or coaching the track team, he can be found in the Cuyahoga Valley hiking with his wife and son or brewing beer on his front porch. He's received honourable mentions for his work in the Writers of the Future contest and he co-edits a series of Fantasy and Science Fiction anthologies titled Continuum. His work also appears in Black Hare's Deep Space and Area-51 anthologies, as well as in the Dark Drabble Anthologies Worlds, Angels, Monsters, Beyond, and Unravel. He also hates pineapple on pizza.

Evolution
by Catherine Kenwell

When research divers discovered a new, brilliantly fuchsia brain coral along the Great Barrier Reef, they marvelled at its unique beauty. The ocean life had been dwindling; climate change and human interference had killed many of the sea creatures.

Collectors weren't far behind its discoverers; thieving divers chipped away at the bright-pink brain, killing off large areas of the magnificent specimen of sea life.

Now, I've heard from a friend of a friend, that only when the coral is exposed to the air does it explode, emitting chemicals that kill everyone within several meters. True? Could be. Evolution, you know.

Catherine Kenwell is a Barrie, Ontario, mediator and author. After 30 successful years in corporate communications, she sustained a brain injury, lost her job, and joined the circus. She writes both horror/dark fiction and inspirational non-fiction. Her works have been published in Chicken Soup for the Soul, Trembling with Fear, Siren's Call, and HellBound Books. Website: www.catherinekenwell.com

Hammer - God - Serpent
by Umair Mirxa

Hvitserk wiped the ocean's spray off his face and attempted, once again, to understand the sight before him. The storm, rapidly gathering to the north, did not help visibility.

Thunder struck; it split the clouds asunder. The sea roared; its wrath awakened.

From the waves emerged a form as monstrous as it was majestic. From the skies dropped a hammer onto its head.

Thor followed in mighty Mjölnir's wake and wrestled Jörmungandr back underwater.

It was the last sight Hvitserk beheld before the ocean swallowed his ship.

The end of the world had begun. It was the time of Ragnarok.

Umair Mirxa *lives and writes in Karachi, Pakistan. His first published story, 'Awareness', appeared on Spillwords Press. He has since had stories accepted for publication in anthologies from Zombie Pirate Publishing, Blood Song Books, Black Hare Press, Iron Faerie Publishing, Clarendon House Publications, Fantasia Divinity Magazine & Publishing, and The ReAnimated Writers Press. He is a massive J.R.R. Tolkien fan, loves everything to do with mythology, fantasy, and history, and wishes with all his heart that dragons were real. When he's not writing, he enjoys reading novels and comic books, playing video games, listening to music, and watching movies, TV shows, and football as an Arsenal FC fan.*
Website: umairmirxa.com

Fun Cruise
by Nicole Henning

The rowboat rocked as the water churned around it. She looked around wildly, seeking out other survivors. The only thing that greeted her was more rioting water as it swallowed what was left of the splintered cruise ship.

Groaning, she grabbed her aching head with both hands and tried to stay focused. She was alive and needed to start rowing if she wanted to stay that way. Before she could grab the oars, a pale grey hand reached out of the water and gripped her wrist. Squeezing, the hand pulled her into the water, where she floated with the rest.

Nicole Henning is a book-a-holic who lives in a big-little town in Wisconsin. She surrounds herself with all things scary and bizarre and enjoys creating unique art. When she isn't writing she enjoys playing video games and spends a lot of time snuggling with her dog Allie aka Princess Prissy Pants. Reading, writing and horror are her biggest passions in life.

Fashionably Late
by John H. Dromey

After briefly researching her family origins for a school project, Maureen became obsessed with genealogy. She worked diligently to identify not only all of her immigrant ancestors—those who'd made at least one transoceanic voyage to reach their new home—but also those they'd left behind.

One day, wearing only a bikini and flip-flops, Maureen picked up her car keys and headed for the door.

"I thought you were going to visit your great-great-grand-pappy Stewart's grave, today," her roommate said.

"I am."

"Dressed like that? Are you being properly respectful?"

"I don't have much choice. He was buried at sea."

John H. Dromey was born in northeast Missouri, USA. He enjoys reading—mysteries in particular—and writing in a variety of genres. In addition to contributing to the Black Hare Press series of Dark Drabbles anthologies, he's had short fiction published in Alfred Hitchcock's Mystery Magazine, Martian Magazine, Mystery Weekly, Stupefying Stories Showcase, Thriller Magazine, Unfit Magazine, and elsewhere, as well as in numerous anthologies, including Chilling Horror Short Stories (Flame Tree Publishing, 2015).

Twilight on the Sea
by Timothy Friesenhahn

The stars reflect from the still sea waters. Slipping in out of consciousness, I cling to the hope of rescue. The small raft I salvaged from the wreckage was I all could find, and I was lucky I found it. From the depths it came in the night. A beast of the waters, a monstrosity of catastrophic desires. In one swift swipe of its enormous tentacle it took our ship. Like a vacuum, it inhaled most of the wreckage and my shipmen. Slipping in and out of consciousness, I pray to the stars that the Kraken doesn't come for me.

Timothy Friesenhahn is thirty years old from Texas, where he lives with his fiance and two dogs. He has been writing since eight years old rather it be stories, poems, or lyrics. He played in a band off and on for several years until he was electrocuted. His lifestyle had to change from there and he went to a WFPB diet and settled down and decided to pursue his dream of writing novels.

The Shark and The Sea Cloud
by Lyndsey Ellis-Holloway

Duuunnn dun.

Spindly legs paddled at a desperate pace.

Duuunnn dun.

The sheep bobbed up and down on the ocean surface as it swam, its beady black eyes fixed upon the horizon; on the ship it had fallen from. Never looking back at the exposed fin.

Duuunnn dun dun dun.

What a delicacy the shark had come across. It had never seen a sea cloud before, only lots and lots of land ones, and the unreachable sky ones.

Dun dun dun dun.

So close, its rare treat in reach, the shark could already *taste* it…

DUN DUN DUN DUN DUNNNN.

Lyndsey Ellis-Holloway is a writer from Knaresborough, UK. She writes fantasy, sci-fi, horror and dystopian stories, focussing on compelling characters and layering in myth and legend at every opportunity. Her mind is somewhat dark and twisted, and she lives in perpetual hope of owning her own Dragon someday, but for now she writes about them to fill the void… and to stop her from murdering people who annoy her. When she's not writing she spends time with her husband, her dogs and her friends enjoying activities such as walking, movies, conventions and of course writing for fun as well! Website: theprose.com/LyndseyEH

Addicted

by Theresa Halvorsen

I wait for the fog to roll in and surface, water beading on my skin. I'm empty. Hungry. Humans play in the waves, standing on wood. I submerge and swim closer. They'll see me as a piece of seaweed, a hunk of wood. I nudge a board and one falls. I take a quick sip. She's mine. Addicted. Her heart will pound, hands will shake without me, without the ocean. She'll visit in the morning, at night. Float on the waves. And each time I'll take more. She'll think she loves the ocean. But she's wrong. It's only me. Forever.

Theresa Halvorsen is a speculative fiction writer, and the author of the Dad's Playbook to Labor and Birth. Website: www.theresahauthor.com

Fluorescent Hell
by Paul Eric Carberry

In the chill of night, adrift at sea, a sailor enveloped by complete darkness glances over the edge. A brilliant orchestra of rich colours cries out to him from below, inviting him to join them. Eerily beautiful, hauntingly peaceful, hypnotised by display, he answers their call. Jolted awake by frigid, cold waters, the sailor kicks his limbs. A swarm of hellish fish race towards him. From the depths where no man should go, devils of the deep with luminous, hideous bodies devour the sailor. Snarled teeth ravage the flesh, tearing and shredding jaws drag him down into a fluorescent hell.

Paul Eric Carberry *is the author of the Zombies on the Rock series. His tales of the zombie apocalypse in Newfoundland are inspired by George A. Romero's Living Dead series. He has also published several short stories over three "from the Rock" anthologies including "Halloween Mummers", "The Light of Cabot Tower", "Into the Forrest" and "Harmon Field". His Zombies on the Rock series currently has three novels, "Outbreak", "The Viking Trail" and "The Republic of Newfound" and is currently working on the fourth novel "Extinction". Paul is from Newfoundland and is currently living in Shearwater, Nova Scotia.*
Website: engenbooks.com/zombies-on-the-rock

Surf's Up, Surfer's Down
by Brandi Hicks

"Bruh, I'm telling you, don't go out there today. The guys said they saw, well, they don't know what they saw, but it wasn't good," Sam begged his friend.

"Listen, man, they were probably smoking and saw some seaweed floating. The swell is massive." Drew grabbed his surfboard and headed toward the beach.

Drew paddled out. He turned around to get in position for a ride and waved at Sam. Sam was frantically waving back, but Drew didn't notice, he was focused on the shadow that swam by him. The shadow breached, opening its massive mouth, and swallowed Drew whole.

*Growing up in West Virginia, **Brandi Hicks** loved to have her nose in a book, her eyes toward the night sky and putting a pen to paper. Her imagination was always sparked by her grandfather and her mom taking her to new places and teaching her about the unusual. She loves fantasy, sci-fi, and learning about science and history. She has two beautiful children, and hopes to instill creativity and a love of reading in them. Finding new crafts to try keeps her busy when not playing with her kids or working.*

Siren Song
by Musaab Sultan

"Just three more miles till we reach Varus port, Cap'n," the first mate called,

The ship gently rocked as they moved towards their destination. There was not a star nor moon in the sky. Captain Haggard was at least thankful that the sea was calm.

"Cap'n, look! A fogs rollin' in," a sailor called suddenly from the crow's nest.

At the same time, a mesmerising sound began to flow through the wind.

One by one, the sailors fell unconscious until only the captain remained.

"One more to the siren's song," Haggard said, entranced, as the ship disappeared into the fog.

Musaab Sultan is a 22 year old university student and aspiring writer from Karachi Pakistan who spends his time buried in fictional universes, books and animes when not battling to keep his grades afloat.

The Ghost of Bosun Gregory
by Cecelia Hopkins-Drewer

It was wild and windy the noxious night
Boson Gregory was washed overboard.
A wave rose from the deep and rose to height,
Drenching dank deck wet from aft to forward.

The sailor cried and clutched at the mast,
Horror frozen face, flushed like a turd,
Battered and bashed, forward fell fast;
Gregory gasped to breathe his last word.

The wind howls, wet footprints patter the deck,
I shudder with fear, think a thought absurd;
Cabin doors rattle, I pray and genuflect.
But the specter crosses the floor undeterred.

"I couldn't save you…" I averred.
"Too late!" My vision blurred.

Cecelia Hopkins-Drewer lives in Adelaide, South Australia. She has written a Masters paper on H.P. Lovecraft, and her weird poetry has been published in THE MENTOR (edited by Ron Clarke), and SPECTRAL REALMS (edited by S.T. Joshi). Her novels include a teenage vampire series commencing with MYSTIC EVERMORE. Short stories have been published in WORLDS, ANGELS & MONSTERS, BEYOND, STORMING AREA 51, and UNRAVEL. (Dark Drabbles anthologies edited by Dean Kershaw).

Amazon: amazon.com/Cecelia-Hopkins-Drewer/e/B071G968NM
Website: chopkin39.wixsite.com/website

Siren Song
by Sara Burke

A surface cracked by foam, rolling like thunder, crashes into a deep green cliff face.

Splintering waves grope the rocks. Reaching, tumbling forward. She stood on the precipice, scanning the horizon for a sign of a ship.

A tiny dot flickered on the line between the sky and sea. This metal bobber set lanterns ablaze as the sun sunk behind it.

"Almost home," she whispered, clasping her bony fingers to her wispy shawl.

Icy spray from the churning waters rose to greet her. From her lips fell haunting notes, summoning an impenetrable mist, and beckoning the ship to come closer.

Sara Burke is a writer living in Newfoundland, Canada. New to the writing scene, she has had three short stories published since the winter of 2018. The first two are flash fictions published via the "Kit Sora the Artobiography" contest. Sara was the first to win this monthly competition twice. The third short story is found in "Flights from the Rock" published by Engen Books. In her spare time she helps coordinate a local sci-fi convention, and enjoys painting and other crafts.

Storm Sent
by Katie Conrad

The storm arrived quickly but lasted three days. The little ship pitched and rolled until the captain lost all notion of navigation, focusing on remaining upright.

When the clouds finally cleared, the call came from the crow's nest. "Land ho!"

The harbour didn't resemble any the captain had seen, but she hadn't visited every port on earth. Still, those towers didn't look like any architecture she knew, and the stars didn't match any of their charts. When the second moon rose in the sky, she had to face facts: the storm had blown them more than a little off course.

Katie Conrad is a writer and lawyer from Halifax, NS. When not writing, she enjoys tea, camping, and fiction podcasts. She has been published in several anthologies from TL;DR Press and won the 2019 Songs From Luna 48-hour flash fiction contest.
Twitter @KatieAConrad

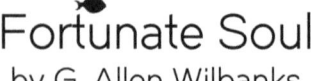

Fortunate Soul
by G. Allen Wilbanks

The young sailor guided his small craft through the jagged rocks. Deaf from birth, he had only his keen eyes to keep his boat intact in these hazardous waters, so he did not let his attention lag for an instant.

He had navigated this journey before. He could make it through. In fact, he was the only one in his village who could.

He spied two of the sirens huddled among the rocks, their hungry, malevolent gazes locked on him. There were days he wished he could hear like everyone else, but today certainly was not one of those days.

G. Allen Wilbanks is a member of the Horror Writers Association (HWA) and has published over 100 short stories in various magazines and on-line venues. He is the author of two short story collections, and the novel, When Darkness Comes.
Website: www.gallenwilbanks.com
Blog: DeepDarkThoughts.com

Tale of the Hydrodragon
by C.L. Williams

The legends are that the worst animals of the ocean have yet to be discovered. I can say I have seen the worst. The worst entity in the ocean is none other than the Hydrodragon. It doesn't blast fire towards its enemies; it sends blasts of water hurdling at speeds that cause certain death.

Everything is its prey, even the microorganisms that are crumbs to the Hydrodragon. My friends and I stumbled upon it by accident and nothing remain of my friends, not even their bones. I was only left alive for one reason; warn everyone about the dangerous Hydrodragon.

C.L. Williams is an international best-selling author currently living in central Virginia. He has written eight poetry books, four novellas, one novel, and a contributor to a multitude of anthologies and magazines. His most recent anthology appearance ANGELS: Dark Drabbles #2 from Black Hare Press became a number one in hot new releases. C.L. Williams is currently working on his second novel and a new poetry book.
Facebook: writer434
Twitter: @writer_434

Don't Scream
by C.L. Steele

"Student-Mini-sub-1 to base, over."

"Images sent, but no response from base."

The aquanauts pressed against their seats as the bubble-gum looking glob turned inside-out again, doubling in size.

"It can't be harmful, no teeth, right?"

"0ctopus; no teeth, still deadly. Plus, this thing morphs."

The sub screeched with the changing pressure.

"I never get used to that."

"Looks like gummy here doesn't like it either. It's morphing, again."

"Getting bigger, maybe we should leave."

"Gotta stay for Base to answer."

"Student-mini-sub-1 this is base. That's a prehistoric... *crackling...* it responds to noise. Go silent. Repeat go si....*squelch.*"

"Base, base! It's enveloping us....*scree...*"

C.L. Steele *creates new worlds and mystical places filled with complex characters on exciting journeys. Her typical genre is Sci-Fi/Fantasy, where she concentrates on writing in the sub-genres of Magical Realism, Near Future, and Futuristic worlds. Published in numerous anthologies, she looks forward to the release of her debut novel. In the interim, she works on other novels and continues to write short stories, novellas, and poetry. She is featured as one of five international authors in ICWG Magazine through Clarendon Publishing House and is a contributing author to Blood Puddles Literary Journal.*
Facebook: *author.CLSteele*
Instagram: *@clsteele.author*

A Final Wave Goodbye
by Shawn M. Klimek

After her swim, Patty scampered across the hot sand to fling herself face down upon her beach towel. Exhausted and lulled by the sun's warmth, she soon drifted off, listening to the sounds of distant seagulls and chattering beach goers, against the background of rhythmically sussurant surf. In her dream, she found herself sleeping instead on a sailboat. The sensation of a rocking deck was so vivid that her subconsciousness argued that the boat must be reality, and her beach experience mere memory. Because other sensations were consequently subverted to this rationale, the shouts of "Tsunami" failed to wake her.

Shawn M. Klimek is an internationally best-selling short-story writer and poet, and author of Hungry Thing. More than 150 of his works have been published online or in such anthologies as BHP's Deep Space, Eerie Christmas, Bad Romance, Jibbernocky, and every book in the Dark Drabbles series.
Website: jotinthedark.blogspot.com
Facebook: shawnmklimekauthor

Cosa Negra
by Andrew Anderson

"Let's go to Cosa Negra," I'll say.

They'll laugh and correct it to "Costa." I let them think that.

I bring all my men here, to sit with me on the sand and watch the sunset. Distracted as they lean in for a kiss, they always fail to spot the black tentacle emerge from the water, which coils around their throat and drags them in.

I've nothing to fear.

My men are not nice men; they deserve to be punished for what they've done.

Cosa Negra—*Black Thing*—feeds on dark hearts. I already know who's next on the menu.

Andrew Anderson is a spare-time writer of microfiction, flash fiction and short stories, from Bathgate, Scotland. His work has been published on FlashFlood and Re:Written, and published in Black Hare Press anthologies.
Twitter: _soorploom_

The Sea of Grief
by Nerisha Kemraj

"Mommy!"

Myrtle frantically searched for the source. She swore it was Anna calling her.

"Mommy! Help me."

She ran towards the sea, kicking sand as her steps became desperate.

"Honey?" Tears welled as she spotted Anna, a long way off from where the waves receded.

"Mommy!" Anna's hand reached out to her mother.

Even though she couldn't swim, Myrtle ran into the choppy waters to save her daughter.

But Anna was nowhere to be found.

The beach was quieter since Anna drowned exactly one month before.

And now, gasping for air, Myrtle's feet could no longer feel the ocean floor.

Nerisha Kemraj resides in Durban, South Africa with her husband and two mischievous daughters. Writing since 2017, she has had over 100 short stories and poems published in various publications, both print and online. She has also received an Honourable Mention Award for her tanka in the Fujisan Taisho 2019 Tanka Contest. She holds a Bachelor's degree in Communication Science, and a Post Graduate Certificate in Education from University of South Africa.
Amazon: amazon.com/author/nerisha_kemraj
Facebook: Nerishakemrajwriter

The Flood
by Charles Welch

God wasn't supposed to flood the world again. God is a fucking liar. We had very little warning.

Because of global warming, the storms were fierce, and precious few of us made it to a boat.

Didn't matter, they were soon capsized anyway. Sharks and barracudas got most of the people I saw. It was gruesome. Even with the volume of water, it was still tinged red. So far, I have been spared, although I'm covered in jellyfish, begging for death. Anything to be free. It'll be hard, but I think I'll drown myself. One, two, three, here I go...

__Charles Welch__ is an aspiring writer and a prolific reader—the weirder and odder the better. He is strange and unusual, like Wednesday Addams is quoted as saying.

Tall Tales
by David Bowmore

I'm only a simple fisherman, making a modest living alone in a small boat hauling cold, wet nets by hand.

I've had some rare old catches in my time. Pulled a mermaid in once, I did. Truth. Don't look at me like that.

She weren't no looker, anyway.

'Nother night, a dead body ends up in the nets. 'Eadless it were, naked and bloated too. Nearly shit myself, I did.

I threw it back. Nothing I could do for the poor sod, was there?

The look on your fizog tells me ya don't believe me.

No one ever believes fishermen.

David Bowmore has lived here, there and everywhere, but now lives in Yorkshire with his wonderful wife and a small white poodle. He has worn many hats in his time; head chef, teacher and landscape gardener. His first collection of short stories 'The Magic of Deben Market' is available from Clarendon House.
Website: davidbowmore.co.uk
Facebook: davidbowmoreauthor

The Cave

by Brian Rosenberger

I had heard of sea caves but never seen one. Neither had Clarissa, my beautiful new bride. We were honeymooning off the coast of Thailand, snorkelling near Phag Nga Bay, when we discovered the cavern by chance.

I knew the battering of waves created sea caves. We wondered how many centuries of contestant pounding created this one. The cavern was roughly the size of an SUV.

Salt water lapped our waists. The cave walls felt like limestone and resembled the patterns of coral.

Clarissa posed against one of the stalagmites as I focused the camera.

No cave. Not stalagmites.

Teeth.

Brian Rosenberger lives in a cellar in Marietta, GA (USA) and writes by the light of captured fireflies. He is the author of As the Worms Turns and three poetry collections. He is also a featured contributor to the Pro-Wrestling literary collection, Three-Way Dance, available from Gimmick Press.
Facebook: HeWhoSuffers

Splash Down
by Peter J. Foote

"3...2...1... Splash down!" Hafsa says as the command module strikes the alien ocean, violet water cascading over the spacecraft as it bobs to the surface.

The lone pilot powers down her craft and continues speaking. "Log of Commander Hafsa Khalid continues. Survey probes of Vega Atheni show a perfect world for colonisation. The air, water, and land all fit for humans, it's paradise compared to the mess we've made of Earth. I've landed near the largest landmass and hope—"

Rising out of the alien ocean, the colossal sea creature swallows the spacecraft whole before returning to the depths.

Peter J. Foote *is a bestselling speculative fiction writer from Nova Scotia. Outside of writing, he runs a used bookstore specialising in fantasy & sci-fi, cosplays, and alternates between red wine and coffee as the mood demands. His short stories can be found in both print and in ebook form, with his story "Sea Monkeys" winning the inaugural "Engen Books/Kit Sora, Flash Fiction/Flash Photography" contest in March of 2018. As the founder of the group "Genre Writers of Atlantic Canada", Peter believes that the writing community is stronger when it works together.*
Twitter: @PeterJFoote1
Website: peterjfooteauthor.wordpress.com

A Deadly Dive
by Nerisha Kemraj

Dylan dived into the waters with James right behind him, eager to explore the ocean to see what treasures she held today.

Moments after reaching the ocean bed, James turned to see Dylan thrashing about in the water.

Just great, pycnogonids! Remembering Dylan's phobia, he rushed over to his friend as the swarm of sea-spiders closed in.

Fending them off, James realised Dylan had released his oxygen tube, which now filled with the creatures. Placing his oxygen into Dylan's mouth proved futile; three tiny spiders floated out of his open mouth. Dylan's face, frozen with fear, stared at him, unresponsive.

Nerisha Kemraj resides in Durban, South Africa with her husband and two mischievous daughters. Writing since 2017, she has had over 100 short stories and poems published in various publications, both print and online. She has also received an Honourable Mention Award for her tanka in the Fujisan Taisho 2019 Tanka Contest. She holds a Bachelor's degree in Communication Science, and a Post Graduate Certificate in Education from University of South Africa.
Amazon: amazon.com/author/nerisha_kemraj
Facebook: Nerishakemrajwriter

Skull Island
by Zoey Xolton

Jason clung to the old red buoy desperately as it bobbed wildly upon the sea. Would his friends come back for him? It'd been hours...surely they'd noticed his absence?

Night fell—and his strength failed him.

Blinking, Jason's vision took a moment to adjust. It was daylight, and he felt wet sand beneath his fingers. Pulling himself up, he tried to gain his bearings. Palms swayed in the salty breeze, and the sea lapped gently behind him.

Beyond the lush tropical forest, he spied a derelict fort perched high above the island. Steeling his nerve, he ventured into the unknown.

Zoey Xolton is an Australian Speculative Fiction writer, primarily of Dark Fantasy, Paranormal Romance and Horror. She is also a proud mother of two and is married to her soul mate. Outside of her family, writing is her greatest passion. She is especially fond of short fiction and is working on releasing her own themed collections in future.
Website: www.zoeyxolton.com

I Know
by Gabriella Balcom

"I need to talk," Walsh said. "Please come."

Rod sighed. "Okay."

Soon, Walsh sped across the Atlantic, not stopping his motorboat until they were hundreds of miles out at sea.

"Edie's cheating," he announced, watching the other man's eyes widen. "Don't play dumb. I know."

Stiffening, Rod glanced away.

Walsh grabbed him, tossing him overboard.

Rod's head went under. He surfaced, coughing up liquid. "*Please!* I can't swim."

"You shouldn't've screwed Edie."

"*Help*!" Rod flailed around wildly for a while, water flying everywhere, before he sank. Bubbles appeared in the water.

Starting his boat, Walsh raced away, not looking back.

Gabriella Balcom lives in Texas with her family, loves reading and writing, and thinks she was born with a book in her hands. She works in a mental health field, and writes fantasy, horror/thriller, romance, children's stories, and sci-fi. She likes travelling, music, good shows, photography, history, interesting tales, and animals. Gabriella says she's a sucker for a great story and loves forests, mountains, and back roads which might lead who knows where. She has a weakness for lasagne, garlic bread, tacos, cheese, and chocolate, but not necessarily in that order.
Facebook: GabriellaBalcom.lonestarauthor*

Her Return
by Deanna Bollinger-Hill

From sunrise to sunset, the woman was found kneeling, facing the wide blue ocean.

The beachgoers noticed the pained expression on her face, the tears that stained her cheek. Children avoided her while they played. The adults looked on, not wanting to bother the strange woman.

After a few days, the beachgoers noticed that the woman never moved from her spot. She wore the same clothes, the same pained expression.

Concerned, a man approached her and asked if she was alright.

The woman turned to him, "My daughter, Abby, was swept away. I'm waiting for the ocean to return her."

Deanna Bollinger-Hill lives in Missouri with her husband and their adorable fur babies. She is a writer that loves to introduce readers to her dark side with her own brand of horror, mysteries and the paranormal. When she's not writing, she loves to read, create roleplaying games and spend time with friends.

Unmoored, Evermore
by Catherine Kenwell

"What *is* that up ahead?" the captain asked.

The behemoth silently slipped through the dense fog.

"It's gone, Captain. No sign of it now."

An unearthly groan from behind; the crew turned in unison.

"It's a ship, Captain. A massive vessel."

"Ahoy, up ahead!" shouted the captain. "You there! Identify yourself!"

Again, the monster ship faded into the impenetrable mist.

"Captain, what is it? It seems to be everywhere, yet… nowhere!"

"Hogwash," muttered the Captain. "It can't be…"

Sky and sea turned dark. They drifted into the peculiarly stifled stillness.

A bloodcurdling snap. The ship shuddered.

"We're *inside* something, Captain!"

Catherine Kenwell is a Barrie, Ontario, mediator and author. After 30 successful years in corporate communications, she sustained a brain injury, lost her job, and joined the circus. She writes both horror/dark fiction and inspirational non-fiction. Her works have been published in Chicken Soup for the Soul, Trembling with Fear, Siren's Call, and HellBound Books. Website: www.catherinekenwell.com

Shipwrecked
by D.J. Elton

Floating through a pale green sea. My energy has finally left. For long hours trying to stay afloat, yet cold and fear are both biting. Such a burden, so I just let go completely.

Down, down…so graciously, sliding into this gentle fluid tomb.

Eventually, it seems I took my leave, and left. Silently giving up the pull of gravity. Just slipped out, and my body was free, light like a rubber ball. It bent and bounced through coral, rock, sea weeds.

They'll say I drowned, but I know better—that it was just my body left to decompose.

D.J. Elton is a writer living in Melbourne's west. As a child she came from England to Australia, on the last boat down the Suez Canal, where she underwent a sacrificial dunking ritual in the court of King Neptune, and has never looked back. She likes creating speculative micro fiction and short stories, as well as random essays. Her work has been published in several anthologies, and she has written a historical fantasy novella, 'The Merlin Girl.' When not playing with a pen, she likes most of all to go to the green country.

Killer Waves, Wretched Hearts
by Russell Hemmell

Sun-scorched, seasick, Alina stumbles towards her lover's body, once riding the oceans and now lifeless on the shore.

"I'll conquer that wave for you," Kara had said.

But night had fallen, and shoals of intruders had come. The tapestry of Alina's skin had turned into a constellation of pain when she had fought them off, back into the sea.

Marine creatures were famished, but not as much as Kara.

Hungry for life, chasing the waves.

Then she was gone, leaving nothing behind but salt-soaked memories, a surfboard of the colour of blood, the caress of Kona wind over empty seashells.

Russell Hemmell is a French-Italian transplant in Scotland, passionate about astrophysics, history, and speculative fiction. Winner of the Canopus Awards for Excellence in Interstellar Writing. Recent stories in Aurealis, Flame Tree Press, The Grievous Angel, and others. SFWA, HWA, and Codexian. Twitter: @SPBianchini

The Return
by Chris Bannor

The fog rolled in from the ocean, and no one noticed the silence creeping in with it. The grey of isolation surrounded them and they stumbled, unaware of the dangers it contained.

Humans were on guard in their vulnerable places; the streets and alleyways, the closed offices and secluded corners. Here, in nature, they forgot that, though they might be top of the food chain, they were not the only predators.

Screams pierced the air, though the fog ate their source even as they left terrified mouths.

They said from the ocean, all life began. It was time to return.

Chris Bannor is a science fiction and fantasy writer who lives in Southern California. Chris learned her love of genre stories from her mother at an early age and has never veered far from that path. She also enjoys musical theater and road trips with her family but is a general homebody otherwise.
Facebook: chrisbannorauthor
Website: ChrisBannor.com

Swallowed
by C.L. Williams

Steve takes his girlfriend Kasey to the beach for a day of fun. Steve finishes his bottle of water and throws the bottle into the ocean. A stunned Kasey looks at her boyfriend in disgust.

"Babe, you know the ocean doesn't like when you throw pollution into it."

"What's the ocean going to do?" Steve laughs.

A wave comes to shore and grabs Steve. He can't move, as the ocean has him by the foot.

"STEVE!" Kasey screams.

The ocean forms a mouth and swallows Steve before going back to gentle waves.

"I tried warning him," Kasey says before leaving.

C.L. Williams is an international best-selling author currently living in central Virginia. He has written eight poetry books, four novellas, one novel, and a contributor to a multitude of anthologies and magazines. His most recent anthology appearance ANGELS: Dark Drabbles #2 from Black Hare Press became a number one in hot new releases. C.L. Williams is currently working on his second novel and a new poetry book. Facebook: writer434 Twitter: @writer_434

Behemoth

by Maxine Churchman

I come, not with gaping maw and gnashing teeth, but with stealth and subversion; an indiscriminate killer; adept at generating great suffering and slow lingering deaths.

For eons you have known me; you created me, and didn't fear me.

Ignored for so long, I drifted on tides and currents. From the deepest depths to the nearest shores, I spread. The world is mine and your puny efforts to contain me scare me not—I have no feelings, no chink in my armour, no weakness you can exploit.

See me and weep; for I am the thing of nightmares— your pollution.

Maxine Churchman lives in Essex UK and has recently started writing poetry and short stories to share. Her interests include learning to improve her writing, reading, knitting, walking and teaching yoga. She is also planning a novel.

Dr. Ventham's Log
by Sara L. Uckelman

Once, no one believed there was water on Mars. Then Phoenix came along and proved all of us wrong, and soon everyone believed there was water on Mars. Cold water. Ice water. Which is just ice, I guess.

I'm writing this for Gryphon to send back to Earth. Everyone believes that there's ice on Mars, but even my team doesn't believe there's an ocean, hidden deep beneath the cryosphere, full of real, liquid, pure water.

But I've seen it. And I've seen the lizards that live in the depths, the Martians no one believes in. Check my logs. You'll see.

Sara L. Uckelman is an assistant professor of logic and philosophy of language at Durham University by day and a writer of speculative fiction by night. Her short stories are published or forthcoming in Manawaker Studio Flash Fiction Podcast, Pilcrow & Dagger, Story Seed Vault, and The Martian Wave, and anthologies published by Exterus, Flame Tree Publishing, Hic Dragones, Jayhenge Publications, QueerSciFi, and WolfSinger Publications. She is also the co-founder of the reviews site SFFReviews.com.

Soldier of Fortune
by David A.F. Brown

A rainbow of corals and anemones illuminate the azure grotto. The raider swims to the wooden chest at the cave's end, exactly where the villagers said it would be. Lifting the lid, he sees a small emerald engraved with a crying face—the Medusa's Tear. He grabs the stone and dives back into the water.

In his haste, he fails to notice the swarm of pulsating, purple jellyfish propelling towards him. Their tentacles strike, barbs stinging and ripping his flesh, until his lifeless body sinks to the ocean floor. Trailing behind him, the Medusa's Tear, its etched face now smiling.

David A.F. Brown is a Canadian author whose fiction has appeared in various anthologies, magazines and podcasts, including Tales to Terrify, Tell-Tale Press, Deep Fried Horror, Forgotten Ones, Forest of Fear – Volume 1 and Love: Dark Drabbles #7, and is forthcoming in Ancients: Dark Drabbles #10. He was a finalist in the NYC Midnight Short Story Challenge 2019, an international competition of over 4,500 writers. He holds a BA (Hons) from Western University and resides in Caledon, Ontario, with his wife and son.
Facebook: browndavidaf

Monster from the Deep
by Cecelia Hopkins-Drewer

The leviathan scratched its scaly back with lazy claws as it watched the shadow cast by the hull. Should it attack?

The monster weighed the satisfaction of a full stomach against the annoyance of torpedoes; before concluding that this ship was not grey and might be a cruise liner.

Juicy passengers! Its salivary juices began to water.

The leviathan crawled up over the structure and crashed through the flimsy sundeck onto the open entertainment area. Bored vacationers eating ice-cream began to scream. The frenzied crew ran around looking for a harpoon launcher.

Meanwhile, the cold-blooded behemoth gulped down its fill.

OCEANS

Cecelia Hopkins-Drewer *lives in Adelaide, South Australia. She has written a Masters paper on H.P. Lovecraft, and her weird poetry has been published in THE MENTOR (edited by Ron Clarke), and SPECTRAL REALMS (edited by S.T. Joshi). Her novels include a teenage vampire series commencing with MYSTIC EVERMORE. Short stories have been published in WORLDS, ANGELS & MONSTERS, BEYOND, STORMING AREA 51, and UNRAVEL. (Dark Drabbles anthologies edited by Dean Kershaw).*
Amazon: amazon.com/Cecelia-Hopkins-Drewer/e/B071G968NM
Website: chopkin39.wixsite.com/website

Awakened
by Gabriella Balcom

The hafgufa twitched in his sleep, sensing something wrong, then woke completely. Emerging from his deep ocean crevice, he narrowed his eyes and propelled himself upward, shooting through the strong undercurrents as if they didn't exist.

Ripples soon spread on the water's surface, but the men constructing the oil platform didn't notice.

"Monster!" someone screamed when the huge creature exploded from the ocean.

Grabbing men in his tentacles, he ate one whole and bit a second in half. Another tried to escape by boat, but the hafgufa shattered it with one blow.

He killed everyone, then eyed the distant shoreline.

Gabriella Balcom lives in Texas with her family, loves reading and writing, and thinks she was born with a book in her hands. She works in a mental health field, and writes fantasy, horror/thriller, romance, children's stories, and sci-fi. She likes travelling, music, good shows, photography, history, interesting tales, and animals. Gabriella says she's a sucker for a great story and loves forests, mountains, and back roads which might lead who knows where. She has a weakness for lasagne, garlic bread, tacos, cheese, and chocolate, but not necessarily in that order.
Facebook: GabriellaBalcom.lonestarauthor

Someone's Daughter
by Hari Navarro

Someone's daughter loves to dance. The tips of her bare toes scrawl her name as their broken calligraphy pirouettes and carves across the sunken dunes and into the inky Indian pitch.

Tiny arms conduct the pull and push of the swell and waxy bloating flesh unfurls, shedding away from her bones.

Someone's mother gazes through the tempest's tears as they rake the cold cockpit glass beneath the splay of her fingers.

Her gaze hangs upon a vast plain of foam whipped peaks and the majestic closing yawn of innumerable troughs, and she knows.

She knows her little dancer is lost.

Hari Navarro has, for many years now, been locked in his neighbours cellar. He survives due to an intravenous feed of puréed extreme horror and Absinthe infused sticky-spiced unicorn wings. His anguished cries for help can be found via 365 Tomorrows, Breachzine, AntipodeanSF, Horror Without Borders, Black Hare Press and HellBound books. Hari was the Winner of the Australasian Horror Writers' Association [AHWA] Flash Fiction Award 2018 and has, also, succeeded in being a New Zealander who now lives in Northern Italy with no cats.
Amazon: amazon.com/Hari-Navarro
Tumblr: harinavarro.tumblr.com/

Suicidal Sea
by Nerisha Kemraj

Raging waters, rapid swells,
the sea cries out in pain.
Stormy ocean—rising hell.
Unrelenting rain.

Remorseless wrath, undying anger.
A fierce rise in tide.
Heaving sighs, absent languor.
Watching waves collide.

The growing moon invites her fury
as worlds begin to fall.
And soon it starts to spell the end
for creatures great and small.

It's far too late for mercy,
we abused her all the time,
and now she's paying back slowly.
We were ignorant to the signs.

Destruction flows, pitiless.
She can't control her anguish.
Body of blue—so perilous.
Wild, she's left to languish.

Nerisha Kemraj resides in Durban, South Africa with her husband and two mischievous daughters. Writing since 2017, she has had over 100 short stories and poems published in various publications, both print and online. She has also received an Honourable Mention Award for her tanka in the Fujisan Taisho 2019 Tanka Contest. She holds a Bachelor's degree in Communication Science, and a Post Graduate Certificate in Education from University of South Africa.
Amazon: amazon.com/author/nerisha_kemraj
Facebook: Nerishakemrajwriter

Blue Escape
by Carole de Monclin

The men are kept below deck in leg irons. At least I can see the sky, but the vast expanse of water terrifies as much as it fascinates. Some say it's like a giant lake.

I'm scared of what awaits on the other side.

The rolling and cracking have become familiar, but I don't recognise this world where pale-skinned intruders wave strange weapons, bellowing unintelligible orders. Where my people are beaten, imprisoned, and starved.

Patiently, I've frayed the ropes binding me.

I stand and lean over the rail. The water calls, promising an end to the nightmare.

I jump.

Free.

Carole de Monclin travels both the real world and imaginary ones. She's lived in France, Australia, and the USA; visited 25+ countries; and explored Mars, Ceres, and many distant planets. She writes to invite people on a journey. Her stories can be found in The Arcanist, The Deep Space Anthology, and every volume of the Dark Drabbles series.
Website: *CaroledeMonclin.com*
Twitter: *@CaroledeMonclin*

Selkie Soft Skin
by N.M. Brown

A beautiful woman climbed the largest rock near the shoreline; laying on her back to bask in sunlight. The waves didn't affect her; she had lived in them for decades. Her kind doesn't age like the rest of us do.

One sailor rushed the selkie, attempting to steal her sealskin and freedom. If he stole her outer shell, she'd have to marry him, leaving her ocean home forever.

She couldn't let that happen. The woman clutched his throat the moment his finger touched her outer layer, making a mural on the rock of his intestines, brain matter and bone fragments.

*Since **N.M. Brown** made her first post to a popular Internet forum, she's taken the horror community by storm. Her ability to create, terrify, and drive home her stories is insurmountable. N.M. Brown's published works can be found in multiple anthologies for all to read, but be forewarned, if you do... you may want to call your therapist after, her stories are terrifying, disturbing and devilishly unsettling. She is not only a fright visually, but also has a creepy tentacle in horror podcasting as well. Sinister Sweetheart writes, voice acts and is the media director of the Scarecrow Tales podcast.*
Website: Sinistersweetheart.wixsite.com/sinistersweetheart
Facebook: NMBrownStories

When the Balen Strikes
by D.J. Elton

Weary sun sinks low, and shadows filter. In dark, cold, blue poisonous blood, the Balen slides forth. A giant salamander creeping on six legs, looking for solace in the open seas.

An old and ugly creature of the deep, unlike others in packs, its one cruel gift from Nature the Mother is to be alone. For several hundred years, the Balen has slowly grown to immense proportions, devouring all in its path, especially the still and pretty.

Yet it is significant, the need to breed. Then die, fully satisfied. Oceans spit, whirl, yielding tsunamis as the Balen seeks its mate.

D.J. Elton is a writer living in Melbourne's west. As a child she came from England to Australia, on the last boat down the Suez Canal, where she underwent a sacrificial dunking ritual in the court of King Neptune, and has never looked back. She likes creating speculative micro fiction and short stories, as well as random essays. Her work has been published in several anthologies, and she has written a historical fantasy novella, 'The Merlin Girl.' When not playing with a pen, she likes most of all to go to the green country.

The Last Resort
by Sara A. Mosier

Every full moon, he dived into the water until he could thread the gritty sand between his fingertips, feel the grains against his palm. He would turn, rest, cast his eyes upwards where he could catch the glinting light of starlight. Plunging into the dark water night after night, the smell of seawater taking on a heavy smell of blood each time. The world began to grow darker around him, heavier, until he could no longer swim to the surface. It was only then that, instead of the diamond-like sand, he cradled his own skull, hollow eye-sockets swallowing up light.

Sara A. Mosier is a Nebraska author, poet, and recent graduate from the University of Nebraska-Lincoln where she received a BA in English. Her writing focus is fiction and poetry of which she enjoys typing on an old 1950's typewriter. She has poetry published in several issues of Laurus Magazine, Cocky-Tales anthology, and University of Nebraska Press's 75th Anniversary edition of "Voices of Nebraska". Her romantic short stories "Sparkling Human Conundrum" and "Summer Dilemma" can be found in the anthologies Love Dust and Salty Tales on Amazon.

Qalupalik
by V.A. Vazquez

"Chase me!"

The tourist boy came tumbling after her, unable to get any traction on the ice. *Qallunaat.* Outsider. She'd watched him disembark from the cruise ship that afternoon, trailing behind his mother, sugar-sticky thumb stuffed into his greedy mouth.

Her grandmother told her stories about the *qalupalik*, monsters that snatched children and dragged them under the ice. "Take him," she thought as the outsider boy's sneakers slipped out from under him again, his fall silhouetted by the glow of the floodlights. "Take him."

The ice cracked underfoot. Tree-branch fingers snatched the boy by his ankle, and he was gone.

V.A. Vazquez writes urban fantasy and paranormal romance. She currently lives in Glasgow, Scotland with her husband and small doggo.
Website: www.vavazquez.com

The Fins
by Alanna Robertson-Webb

I watched as a wrinkled, finned creature breached the surface, its finned head scanning the water around it.

I didn't dare move, or scream, in case it noticed me. The gilled face peered towards our ship, its blind eyes twitching away drops of salt water as it sniffed the air.

Needle-like fangs extended, and it let out a primal, blood-curdling scream. Within moments a dozen more fins sliced through the surface, and the creatures began ramming against the boat.

I felt my grip on the rail slipping, and a wordless cry escaped my lips as my fingers lost their hold.

Alanna Robertson-Webb is a New York author who enjoys long weekends of LARPing, is terrified of sharks and finds immense fun in being the chief editor at Eerie River Publishing. She lives with a fiancee and two cats, all of whom like to take over her favourite cozy blanket when they think they can get away with it. She is currently an MRO support member by day, and an editor and author by candlelight. While she has been published before, which is wonderful, she one day aspires to run her own nerd-themed restaurant.
Website: arwauthor.wixsite.com/arwauthor
Amazon: amazon.com/Alanna-Robertson-Webb/e/B07LFYJYS5

For Treasure
by Clint Foster

Many of us there are that would brave the tempestuous waves and whims of the water. Many of us there are that the landlocked might consider brave. Many more might consider us fools, and damned ones at that. Yet, when we come ashore with the plunder and booty of a hundred ships, and a hundred scars each to show for it, there is only one word upon our minds, and once our fortunes are spent on cheap drink, cheaper love, and a meal fit for kings, we hark upon the waves again to search for that which we love—treasure.

Clint Foster lives with his herd of four cats, beloved Basset, Zero, and wonderful wife, Nik. He loves to tell stories just as much as he loves to read them and is excited to share his work. A long-time consumer of media of all kinds, he enjoys giving back what he hopes everyone else thinks are good stories.
Facebook: ClintFosterAuthor

Photogenic
by Dawn DeBraal

Her fear of water was great. Convinced, she hesitantly went shallow diving.

"The saltwater won't let you sink," her boyfriend told her. Babette put on the mask and snorkel, plunging her face into the water. Her heart pounded out of her chest. Finally, she realised she was breathing underwater, and she was floating in the saltwater—it wasn't so bad.

Babette slowly propelled herself forwards, around the coral reef, snapping pictures of coloured fishes. It was mesmerising. The images on her underwater camera showed colourful tropical fish, jagged teeth, and the open mouth of the oncoming shark who ate her.

Dawn DeBraal lives in rural Wisconsin with her husband Red, two rat terriers, and a cat. She has discovered that her love of telling a good story can be written. Published stories with Palm-sized press, Spillwords, Mercurial Stories, Potato Soup Journal, Edify Fiction, Zimbell House Publishing, Clarendon House Publishing, Blood Song Books, Black Hare Press, Fantasia Divinity, Cafelit, Reanimated Writers, Guilty Pleasures, Unholy Trinity, The World of Myth, Dastaan World, Vamp Cat, Runcible Spoon, Dark Christmas, Siren's Call, Iron Horse Publishing, Falling Star Magazine 2019 Pushcart Nominee.
Amazon: amazon.com/Dawn-DeBraal/e/B07STL8DLX

Angels of the Deep
by Stephen Herczeg

"Can you hear them, Dmitri?"

"It's nothing, Nikolai. It's the boat moving against the rocks. It's the pressure on the hull."

"I can hear singing. Voices like angels."

Nikolai moved to the periscope and peered through. The rest of the crew simply watched. We knew we were dead. The submarine was holed and filling fast. The depth charges had seen to that.

"I can see them out there," he said, climbing into the conning tower before anyone could stop him. "I'm going to join them."

"No!"

He blew the emergency exit charges. Water flooded the cabin.

It wouldn't be long.

Stephen Herczeg is an IT Geek based in Canberra Australia. He has been writing for over twenty years and has completed a couple of dodgy novels, sixteen feature length screenplays and numerous short stories and scripts. His horror work has featured in Sproutlings, Hells Bells, Below the Stairs, Trickster's Treats #1 and #2, Shades of Santa, Behind the Mask, Beyond the Infinite; The Body Horror Book, Anemone Enemy, Petrified Punks and Beginnings. He has also had numerous Sherlock Holmes stories published through the Belanger Books - Sherlock Holmes anthologies.
Amazon: amazon.com/-/e/B07916SQQS
Facebook: stephenherczegauthor

Still Waters
by D.B. McKenzie

Sarah hated going to the beach. She hated the people, she hated the sand, and she hated the fish that kept touching her no matter where she went.

Kicking out at the latest offender, Sarah scowled at the dark water.

"Cut that out," she snarled when something slimy trailed across her ankle.

The touch had bile clogging her throat, and Sarah was about done with this stupid trip.

She turned, suddenly ready to be back on solid ground, when something tugged at her leg.

"Cut that out," someone whispered in Sarah's ear, in a perfect mimicry of her own voice.

D.B. McKenzie is a 29 year old university graduate of Jamaican descent who has been writing horror and fantasy for over twenty years and is heavily influenced by the works of Neil Gaiman, Frank Herbert and Dean Koontz.
Website: medium.com/@deltabmckenzie

The Lure

by E.L. Giles

"Land!" The voice from the crow's nest resonated, waking the slumbering crew. They jumped to their feet, eyes wide, staring at the horizon, toward the dark mound drawing closer.

The captain joined the gathering of exited seamen, doubtful. He gazed out over the water, staring for a moment. Dread grew as he realised what was going on.

A faint movement—barely perceptible yet unmistakable—triggered some primal fear. He turned to his second officer, who seemed to understand. The land was moving.

"That's not land!" the captain yelled. "Kraken! Turn us around!"

"It's too late," answered the second officer. "Fire!"

E.L. Giles is a dreamer, passionate about art, a restless worker and a bit of a weird human. He started his artistic journey as a music composer until the need to put his thoughts and stories down on paper grew too strong for him to resist it any longer. He lives in the French Province of Quebec, Canada, with his girlfriend and two boys.
Facebook: elgilesauthor
Website: www.elgilesauthor.com

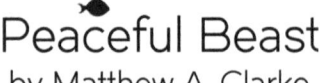

Peaceful Beast
by Matthew A. Clarke

I've heard that eighty percent of the ocean is still unexplored. That sounds accurate to me.

Once every ten years, I must surface for air. Perhaps once or twice I've seen a boat, and I'll give them a little show. I like to think I'm spoken about in tales of horrific sea beasts. It makes me chuckle.

They're good at navigating on top of the sea, I'll give them that, but they still haven't figured out how to reach me yet.

But they might, one day. My survival may depend upon my reputation.

Until then, I enjoy my peaceful sanctuary.

Matthew A. Clarke is a new face in the world of horror. He has been writing short fiction as a hobby for two years and has decided to share his passion with likeminded people. Matthew loves all things that go bump in the night, having been introduced to slasher movies at a young age. He lives on the South Coast of England with his fiancé, Isabelle, and a little dachshund called Frank.
Facebook: matthewaclarkeauthor

Mama Qucha Calls
by A.R. Dean

The village elder has come to our home. At moon rise it's our families turn to give. I gather the lama and my youngest brother, Dusi. We walk through the village to the cliff that overlooks the sea.

The elders wait for us. I hand them the rope to our lama. They gather, chanting. A blade sparkles in the moonlight. They stab it before sending it hurtling over the edge to the waves below.

I'm crying as they reach for Dusi. He will bring pleasure to Mama Qucha. I scream as they throw him struggling to the rocky coast below.

A.R. Dean is a dark and twisted soul. Dean has spent their whole life spreading fear with the tales from their head. Best known for stories that terrify and show the evilest side of human nature. So, look for Dean haunting your local cemetery or under your bed, because they're here to spread the fear. Turn off your lights and enjoy a scare. Dean is being published in Black Hare Press's Beyond and Unravel Anthologies. Keep a lookout for more stories.
Facebook: A.R. Dean Author & Ghoul

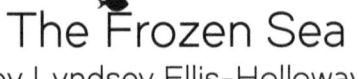

The Frozen Sea
by Lyndsey Ellis-Holloway

I thought I was free; thought I had escaped it.

And for a time, I think, I was.

I dragged myself from the frozen sea, the place I had always known. Fled the cold and saw the world beyond the ice-bound waves.

But when it's in your veins, when the frigid waves gave birth to you, there is no true freedom.

All the warmth was stolen from me, freezing once more.

I could feel it, pulling at me, calling me home, back to my grave.

I never wanted to go back to the ice, but it wouldn't let me go.

Lyndsey Ellis-Holloway is a writer from Knaresborough, UK. She writes fantasy, sci-fi, horror and dystopian stories, focussing on compelling characters and layering in myth and legend at every opportunity. Her mind is somewhat dark and twisted, and she lives in perpetual hope of owning her own Dragon someday, but for now she writes about them to fill the void... and to stop her from murdering people who annoy her. When she's not writing she spends time with her husband, her dogs and her friends enjoying activities such as walking, movies, conventions and of course writing for fun as well! Website: theprose.com/LyndseyEH

It's Your Turn
by Eddie D. Moore

Didrik grunted as he sat the treasure chest on the deck, and his eyes flicked nervously around the empty ship. He shouted into the night air, "You can have it all!"

Gold coins rained into the ocean as Didrik emptied the chest over the side of the ship. As the last of the treasure sank beneath the waves, apparitions appeared around him. Didrik let the empty chest fall over the side and asked with a trembling voice, "Happy now?"

A spectre resembling the captain pointed at a bottle of poisoned rum and softly said, "You did this. It's your turn."

Eddie D. Moore travels hundreds of hours a year, and he fills that time by listening to audiobooks. When he isn't playing with his grandchildren, he writes his own stories. You can find a list of his publications on his blog or by visiting his Amazon Author Page. While you're there, be sure to pick up a copy of his mini-anthology Misfits & Oddities.
Website: eddiedmoore.wordpress.com
Amazon: amazon.com/author/eddiedmoore

Survivors
by Tracy Davidson

The creatures gently guided the shipwreck's survivors towards shore. Bruised, battered and exhausted, the humans gave thanks to their unidentified protectors. They knew full well the dangers of sharks in these waters. But sharks stayed well away. There was safety in numbers. The beach was almost in reach...

The creatures gently guided the fresh meat towards their nursery, safe in the shallows.

Bruised, battered and tenderised, the humans would fatten up their young. Then they could spread, make new nurseries further along the coast, well away from the toxic spill that first created them. The oceans would soon be theirs.

Tracy Davidson lives in Warwickshire, England, and writes poetry and flash fiction. Her work has appeared in various publications and anthologies, including: Poet's Market, Mslexia, Atlas Poetica, Writing Magazine, Modern Haiku, The Binnacle, A Hundred Gourds, Shooter, Journey to Crone, The Great Gatsby Anthology, WAR and In Protest: 150 Poems for Human Rights.

The Gift
by Anika Claire

Nadine swims down, down to the deepest trenches—the only place the colonies can hide from the no-tails.

Once upon a time, they could go to the warm, bright waters, where the fish were plenty. "Once," the Eldest whispered, "I saw the sky."

"Nonsense," said the hunters. "The sky contains the no-tails and certain death, and the reefs are just a myth."

Now, Nadine has seen the bone-white rocks where the reefs were. She's met the no-tails—they're not so bad. She clutches the gift they gave her—a pretty necklace with a pulsing luminescence. The warriors will be jealous.

Anika Claire lives in Brisbane, Australia with her young family, where she alternates between making maps and escaping to other worlds, through either reading or creating them. You can find her reviewing and podcasting about books at;
Website: teainthetreetops.com
Instagram: @anni.treetops

Sinking Ship
by A.R. Dean

I escaped. Clinging to the lifeboat, I watched as the others went down. The sun beats on me, and I am parched. Days this wooden vessel has travelled with no end in sight of the blue. I give a glance to my companion. She is a girl no more than twelve. A fellow passenger that has lost as much as me.

When I can no longer fight the hunger, I try to strangle her. She stabs me with a small knife.

"Sorry." She shrugs with a small smile. "I'm very hungry."

I die as nourishment. Hope it makes her sick.

A.R. Dean is a dark and twisted soul. Dean has spent their whole life spreading fear with the tales from their head. Best known for stories that terrify and show the evilest side of human nature. So, look for Dean haunting your local cemetery or under your bed, because they're here to spread the fear. Turn off your lights and enjoy a scare. Dean is being published in Black Hare Press's Beyond and Unravel Anthologies. Keep a lookout for more stories.
Facebook: A.R. Dean Author & Ghoul

The Self-Sustaining Outpost
by Stuart Conover

Jameson had been alone on the outpost for nearly three years.

He'd long ago lost track of the days.

They all blended without being able to see the sun and moon.

The equipment that kept the environment running was working fine.

However, all the computers had gone out.

The idea had been to build a self-sustaining ecosystem for humanity to explore under water.

Now, he might very well be all that was left.

The systems had gone out on D-Day.

Nuclear winter.

The last reports said nearly everyone was gone.

So, who was in the ship that was currently docking?

Stuart Conover is a father, husband, rescue dog owner, published author, blogger, journalist, horror enthusiast, comic book geek, science fiction junkie, and IT professional. With all of that to cram in daily, we have no idea if or when he sleeps or how he gets writing done! (We suspect it has to do with having evil clones.) Stuart is a Chicago native and runs the author resource Horror Tree.

Sunken Treasure
by Jasmine Jarvis

The creature circles, taunting me by bumping against my raft. In desperation, I throw the cursed treasure overboard, thinking that that is what it wants.

Suddenly all goes quiet and still.

I collapse in relief, for the creature is gone.

The raft is struck so violently I am thrown overboard. The saltwater stings my blistered skin, burns my parched mouth and throat as it rushes into my lungs.

Only then do I realise the creature doesn't want the treasure; it wants me.

I go limp and let myself sink down into the dark depths of its great big open maw.

Jasmine Jarvis is a teller of tales and scribbler of scribbles. She lives in Brisbane, Australia with her husband Michael, their two children, Tilly and Mish; Ripley, their German Shepherd, and indoor fat cat, Dwight K. Shrute.

Blue Runner Bait
by Rich Rurshell

Jack planted his feet and reeled in his catch. The fish surfaced near the boat for a second, and to the fisherman's delight, it was a blue runner. Catching one would give him bragging rights down the *Pier Tavern* later.

Jack lifted it out of the water and onto the deck, then set the timer on his camera. He picked up the fish and felt a sharp pain in his hand. A thin, barbed tentacle was hooked through his palm. As the shutter clicked on his camera, Jack was hauled over the side of his boat into the ocean below.

Rich Rurshell is a short story writer from Suffolk, England. Rich writes Horror, Sci-Fi, and Fantasy, and his stories can be found in various short story anthologies and magazines. Most recently, his story "Subject: Galilee" was published in World War Four from Zombie Pirate Publishing, and "Life Choices" was published in Salty Tales from Stormy Island Publishing. When Rich is not writing stories, he likes to write and perform music.
Facebook: richrurshellauthor

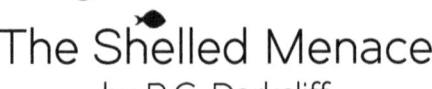

The Shelled Menace
by P.C. Darkcliff

Sheila picked the shell, pressed it against her ear—and screamed and collapsed into the sand as something inside the shell bit her.

Although she emerged from the coma, her limbs and lungs were useless, her skin scaly.

When I brought her back home, she kept staring through the window at the beach. Her eyes shone wildly above the oxygen mask as I wheeled her there.

The sea roared. A giant wave rushed at us and swept us away. When I scrambled back on shore, I found her wheelchair, but Sheila had disappeared.

Oh, God! Do you think she drowned?

P.C. Darkcliff is the author of two novels, Deception of the Damned and The Priest of Orpagus. In September 2020, he's going to launch Celts and the Mad Goddess, the first installment of The Deathless Chronicle.
Social Media: plu.us/p.c.darkcliff
Reader List: mailchi.mp/c5550d315607/pcdarkcliff

The Shark Fin
by Jim Bates

The middle aged couple skimmed their paddle boards across the idyllic Caribbean bay, but all he thought about was pushing her into the sea and watching her drown. She deserved it. Messing around with his best friend! He approached her fast and raised his paddle to strike when she turned and swung hers, hitting him hard in the face. Blood gushed as he fell. A school of sharks approached immediately in a feeding frenzy. She paddled away gleefully until a huge dorsal fin caught her board and she tumbled off. In seconds she joined what was left of her husband.

Jim Bates *lives in a small town twenty miles west of Minneapolis, Minnesota. His stories have appeared online in CafeLit, The Writers' Cafe Magazine, Cabinet of Heed, Paragraph Planet, Nailpolish Stories, Ariel Chart, Potato Soup Journal, Literary Yard, Spillwords (Dec, 2019, Author of the Month), The Drabble, The Academy of the Heart and Mind and World of Myth Magazine. In print publications: A Million Ways, Mused Literary Journal, Gleam Flash Fiction Anthology #2, the Portal Anthology and the Glamour Anthology by Clarendon House Publishing, The Best of CafeLit 8 by Chapeltown Publishing, the Nativity Anthology by Bridge House Publishing and Gold Dust Magazine.*
Website: www.theviewfromlonglake.wordpress.com

Suckers
by Rich Rurshell

Tony tried to reach his knife, but his arms were pinned to his sides. Through the murky ocean water, he saw more tentacles pulling the other members of his diving trip down to the seabed from the remnants of the yacht. He watched Patricia's head and torso disappear into the octopus' great maw. The beak snapped shut, severing her legs.

Already wearing his breathing apparatus had at first seemed like a blessing, but now as Tony watched the lifeless bodies of his companions being torn apart one by one as they were eaten, he realised what a curse it was.

Rich Rurshell is a short story writer from Suffolk, England. Rich writes Horror, Sci-Fi, and Fantasy, and his stories can be found in various short story anthologies and magazines. Most recently, his story "Subject: Galilee" was published in World War Four from Zombie Pirate Publishing, and "Life Choices" was published in Salty Tales from Stormy Island Publishing. When Rich is not writing stories, he likes to write and perform music.
Facebook: richrurshellauthor

Charybdis Smiles
by Kim Jackways

I've lived down here a long time, the restraints of their stories twining around me like seaweed. I hold my breath, though that's a game for the living, like mercy or hope.

Up above, the waffled waves. They came with their boats—floating unaware past jagged rocks and jade reflecting rips. Seducer, they styled me. Now crustaceans grow crunchy through my eye sockets.

I swallowed them whole in the dark of the storm. When the chill whirled them around, sucked them into obsolescence, they realised their mistake. Their legs paddled furiously.

And the world forgot.

A monster, I wait. Smiling.

Kim Jackways is a freelance writer and blogger from New Zealand. She has had fiction published in Flash Frontier and The Best Small Fictions and uses her background in Psychology and Linguistics to inspire her work.
Facebook: facebook.com/kimwriter
Website: www.writersideoflife.com

First Time at the Beach
by Derek Dunn

Joey splashed his feet in the cool ocean water. Sitting on the edge of the pier, he looked out at the gently rolling waves. It was his first time at the beach. The setting sun glowed more majestically than ever before. The song of the gulls rang through the air.

Something pricked at his feet. *It must be fish*, he thought. He couldn't see below the surface of the murky water. The little nibbles tickled his toes. But tickling turned to pain. He pulled his legs out and screamed for help—but where feet once were, only bloody stumps remained.

Derek Dunn is a film enthusiast and musician who writes primarily horror and mystery stories. After obtaining a degree in Media Arts Studies and dabbling in film production, he's turned his efforts to writing fiction. Several of his works have appeared in recent anthologies. He lives in the American northwest with his family, dog, and fish.
Twitter: DerekTDunn

Fin
by Paul Eric Carberry

Just out for a swim. Carefree, the cool waves soothe her sunburned skin. One arm over the other, each stroke accompanied by several swift kicks. Now out of sight from the shore, she is alone in a paradise. Out of the corner of her eye, a caudal fin is cutting its way through the waves with graceful ease. She is not alone, her paradise shattered. Panic floods her system, legs kicking wildly as she makes a desperate attempt towards shore. The fin changes direction, rushing towards her. Her heart beats so fast as the fin disappears below the calm surface.

Paul Eric Carberry is the author of the Zombies on the Rock series. His tales of the zombie apocalypse in Newfoundland are inspired by George A. Romero's Living Dead series. He has also published several short stories over three "from the Rock" anthologies including "Halloween Mummers", "The Light of Cabot Tower", "Into the Forrest" and "Harmon Field". His Zombies on the Rock series currently has three novels, "Outbreak", "The Viking Trail" and "The Republic of Newfound" and is currently working on the fourth novel "Extinction". Paul is from Newfoundland and is currently living in Shearwater, Nova Scotia.
Website: <u>engenbooks.com/zombies-on-the-rock</u>

Now We Know
by Eddie D. Moore

The research team applauded as the submersible reached record depths, but their celebrations faded as visibility approached zero.

A research assistant stated the obvious, "Well, this sucks. Two million dollars for a robotic submersible, and now we can't see more than six inches. Who knows what we're missing?"

Dr. Giordano sighed. "Give it a moment."

When the visibility cleared, a collective gasp filled the room.

"That's not humans living in that city," the assistant whispered.

The sonar display showed three small blips approaching the ship. Dr Giordano shook his head. "Now we know why so many ships have sunk here."

Eddie D. Moore travels hundreds of hours a year, and he fills that time by listening to audiobooks. When he isn't playing with his grandchildren, he writes his own stories. You can find a list of his publications on his blog or by visiting his Amazon Author Page. While you're there, be sure to pick up a copy of his mini-anthology Misfits & Oddities.
Website: eddiedmoore.wordpress.com
Amazon: amazon.com/author/eddiedmoore

Afloat
by L.P. Hernandez

I am a survivor. The ship, fires now extinguished, rests on the ocean floor fathoms below. My raft is beginning to fester, the knotted limbs of my shipmates pulling apart as their stretched sinews thin.

Drifting beneath a phosphorescent band of Milky Way, I hear predators emerge from the deep. A glimpse of dorsal fin. A quick bite and my raft quivers. Then silence once again. This is the longest night of my life.

At dawn my raft is depleted, just two torsos left, waterlogged and sinking. I am surrounded, and I fear they developed a taste for human flesh.

L.P. Hernandez is an author of horror and speculative fiction. His stories are featured in many collections, including Tavistock Galleria, Black Rainbow, and Monstronomicon. His work has also been adapted as audio productions on the NoSleep Podcast. He is an NYC Midnight Short Story Challenge Finalist and was awarded second place in the 2019 Writer's Digest Annual Writing Competition.
Website: www.lphernandez.com

Together-time
by Gabriella Balcom

"*Again?*" Delores complained. "All you do is scuba dive."

Tad shrugged.

After his scuba tank emptied, she carefully injected dust into it before it was filled.

He dived days later, admiring the coral and colourful fish and feeling energised by the ocean's fascinating underground world. A twinge of discomfort hit, but he ignored it.

Within moments, Tad's breathing was laboured, his chest strangely tight. He surfaced, passing out.

"Impaired respiratory function," the hospital doctor explained before discharging him. "Your body needs to heal."

"Too bad you can't dive," Delores murmured. "But we'll have plenty of together-time now."

Gabriella Balcom lives in Texas with her family, loves reading and writing, and thinks she was born with a book in her hands. She works in a mental health field, and writes fantasy, horror/thriller, romance, children's stories, and sci-fi. She likes travelling, music, good shows, photography, history, interesting tales, and animals. Gabriella says she's a sucker for a great story and loves forests, mountains, and back roads which might lead who knows where. She has a weakness for lasagne, garlic bread, tacos, cheese, and chocolate, but not necessarily in that order.

Facebook: _GabriellaBalcom.lonestarauthor_

261

Fiona Raven
by Luis Manuel Torres

The sea is full of many different creatures, from the tiny seahorse, to the largest whale. There're many wonderful animals at sea, but my favourites are the ones people don't actually know about. The ones called myths.

I've met an old kappa from the waters of Japan.

The colossal Jormungandr from the Atlantic ocean.

Let's not forget the Shen dragon from Asia.

My personal favourite would be the Kraken from the mysterious devil's triangle.

All these creatures are my friends and they do as I say.

My name is Fiona Raven, and you may call me Witch of the sea.

Luis Manuel Torres was born in Puerto Rico, lived in Boston Massachusetts for thirteen years and currently lives in Springfield Mass. He has a love for stories in all forms they come in, from books to television and video games. His work can be found in multiple anthologies with Zimbell House Publishing and Black Hare Press. He is always working on multiple writing projects. His debut short story collection Midnight Animals is now available on Amazon.
Website: luisitowrites.wordpress.com
Twitter: Luis1989Manuel

Monster Lunch
by Shelly Jarvis

"What's that?" I ask, pointing into the darkness.

"I don't see anything," Rick says, reaching for his glasses.

He wipes them off and moves to the ship's devices. I don't know what he's checking. I don't care. I'm only here to make sure everyone stays healthy.

A ping against the glass in front of me sends a jolt through my body. It's a diving helmet. With a face inside. Attached to *half* a body.

Rick curses behind me, but it's too late now. There's a massive mouth going around the sub, cracking *us* in half, as we become monster lunch.

Shelly Jarvis is a speculative fiction author from West Virginia, US. She found a life-long love of sci-fi and fantasy in the 3rd grade when she found Madeleine L'Engle's "A Wrinkle in Time." Shelly is an avid reader, a Whovian, the ideal viewer of dog rescue videos, and undoubtedly Ravenclaw. She currently has three YA sci-fi books available for purchase on Amazon. Website: www.ShellyJarvis.com

Lullaby
by Lydia F. Black

The water was calm at high noon.

"Land!" a mate yelled.

Ahead, rocky cliffs jet out into the water. The captain motioned for the sails to be released. The closer the ship got, the more confused the crew became. Wrecked ships, blood-stained water, and dead bodies floated everywhere.

"There!" someone shouted, pointing.

Three beautiful women sat waiting ashore. One blonde, the others, brunette. They had a tail, rather than legs. They opened their mouths; a sweet, alluring voice emerged. The men could not resist; they jumped and swam. The sirens sang once more, "How long can you hold your breath?"

*When she's not training for her third degree black belt, or slaving over the final days of school, **Lydia F. Black**, a ninja in Maryland, finds herself writing Drabbles, school papers, or the weird scenes in her head.*

Smile
by Paul Eric Carberry

It started with a smirk. Innocent enough from deep below. Then it began to grow out of control. From the depths, expanding quicker than he could have imagined. No time to react. A sinister snarl twisted on the creature's jaw, endless white tips bulging from the pink gums. A black hole opened up in the centre of the smile, swelling out of control. Razor-sharpened teeth outlined the ghastly void in space. His legs disappeared into the obscurity. Strips of flesh severed from legs, crimson rivers erupted around him. Enveloped in a sea of maroon blood. It concluded with a smile.

Paul Eric Carberry is the author of the Zombies on the Rock series. His tales of the zombie apocalypse in Newfoundland are inspired by George A. Romero's Living Dead series. He has also published several short stories over three "from the Rock" anthologies including "Halloween Mummers", "The Light of Cabot Tower", "Into the Forrest" and "Harmon Field". His Zombies on the Rock series currently has three novels, "Outbreak", "The Viking Trail" and "The Republic of Newfound" and is currently working on the fourth novel "Extinction". Paul is from Newfoundland and is currently living in Shearwater, Nova Scotia.
Website: engenbooks.com/zombies-on-the-rock

Quetzalcoatl's Revenge
by Joshua E. Borgmann

The great serpent slithered through the air. Finding the cruise ship, it came down upon it in a fury. Its many limbs grabbed screaming creatures from the pool deck. Then it slither-flew a few hundred feet up before unleashing a beam of fire that annihilated the ship's life boats. The beast coiled and uncoiled, hanging above the screaming passengers. Then it dived, cutting a path through the heart of the ship and nearly ripping it in half. These outsiders would no longer defile its temples, and the blood from the unbelievers it had claimed would again feed its pyramids.

Joshua E. Borgmann holds degrees from Drake University, Iowa State University, and the University of South Carolina. He grew up on horror and science-fiction and had long intended to become a great master of the art form before he was sucked into the bottomless pit of academia. He toils away his days as an English instructor at a small community college and dreams of being able to escape into a world of fantasy and terror where there are no student papers to grade. He and his wife reside in a nameless rural Iowa town surrounded by terrible cornfields where he is terrorized by several felines who have taken refuge in his home.

Neptune's Bounty
by Laurence Sullivan

It all started with a single shark washed up on the shore. Dead, bloated, a thick film of foam around its mouth. It was only a minor nuisance at first, quickly taken back out to sea by some local fishermen.

Then the rest arrived.

Whole schools of fish, dolphins, whales. Each new fish festering under the unforgiving sun. Within days the town was being choked out by the miasma; but the sea's bounty kept surging relentlessly.

Unable to afford to leave, most folks left it too late… Failing to stem the tide, the gangrenous grave would soon swallow every soul…

*Runner-up in the Wicked Young Writer Awards: Gregory Maguire Award, **Laurence Sullivan**'s creative writing has appeared in such places as: Londonist, The List, NHK-World, Literary Orphans and Crack the Spine. He became inspired to start writing during his studies at the universities of Kent, Utrecht and Birmingham – after being saturated in all forms of literature from across the globe and enjoying every moment of it. He is currently pursuing a PhD at Northumbria University in the Medical Humanities, exploring literary portrayals of women's domestic medicine during the eighteenth century.*
Website: www.laurencesullivan.co.uk
Twitter: @LozzySullivan

Uprising

by Emma K. Leadley

The divers rubbed their hands in glee at discovering the old, barnacle-encrusted chest. Hidden in the collapsed prow of a known pirate shipwreck, it had lain undisturbed for centuries. It was bound to be treasure-filled! They took turns at prising the lock, dreaming of riches whilst keeping watch on their air gauges. Plenty of time! Slowly, slowly, the old hasp broke through, and the lid opened to reveal a pile of rubies, doubloons and pieces of eight. Stuffing their bags full, they failed to notice the water shimmering around them—the ghosts of dead pirates rising to protect their hoard.

Emma K. Leadley is a UK-based writer, creative geek, and devourer of words, images and ideas. She began writing both fiction and creative non-fiction as an outlet for her busy brain, and quickly realised scrawling words on a page is wired into her DNA.
Website: emmaleadley.co.uk
Twitter: @autoerraticism

Eternal Lover
by K.B. Elijah

I brush my fingers up her bare legs, savouring the smoothness of her skin and nipping at her underwear.

She shivers with my touch.

I continue up her body—her arms, her breasts, her lips. I am as tender as the gentlest of lovers as I steal her breath, closing my mouth over hers, and tasting alcohol on her tongue.

She moves briefly, as if to pull away, yet obligingly remains within my embrace, and I watch her eyes close.

I know they won't open again.

I pull her deeper, down into my colder layers, the ocean claiming another soul.

K.B. Elijah is a fantasy author living in Brisbane, Australia with her husband and three cockatiels. A lawyer by day, and a writer by...also day, because she needs her solid nine hours of sleep per night (not that the cockatiels let her sleep past 6am). K.B. writes for various international anthologies, and her work features in dozens of collections about the mysterious, the magical and the macabre. Her own books of short fantasy novellas with twists, The Empty Sky and Out of the Nowhere, are available on paperback and Kindle now.
Website: www.kbelijah.com
Instagram: k.b.elijah

Food for Thought
by Kaitlyn Arnett

There is a creature down there, and Ainsley knew this was fact. Its name was ancient, lost in the legends and myths surrounding it, but everything had to have a calling. *Aegean* was what she settled on calling it, her monster of the deep.

Because they've barely begun to explore the oceans, and all of those myths had to be based in fact. They always were.

Miles below the surface, the ancient beast stirred. It heard her thoughts, taking them. Bit by bit, day by day. *Food for thought,* as the saying goes.

And the creature awoke from its slumber.

Kaitlyn Arnett is a teen author who has been writing for five years. She focuses on the fantasy and thriller genres, specifically drabbles and short stories.

Beneath
by J. Dorden

The waters rose, coming over the bow of the ships, carrying those who were unlucky enough to get caught in its grasp off the ship. Bells and whistles and shouts of men overboard could barely be heard above the crashing waves and roaring winds. The lighting speared and cracked upon the masts. Little fires start, but quickly put out by the rain pouring down upon the poor unfortunate souls trapped in the tempest. The ocean's anger could be felt as it pulled the ships and the men into the dark depths below. The ancient beast beneath, forever hungry and waiting.

J. Dorden is a writer/author with a self-published science fiction book, currently working on the second. She is 28 years old, was born in Georgia but raised in Florida and recently moved to Maryland. Hobbies include writing, crochet, and video games.
Twitter: @DordenJessica

She Loves Me
by Cassandra Angler

It's unlike anything we've ever seen. Scales black and neon green, and its face too humanoid for comfort. I heard the scientist speculating that this is the first of a hybrid breed, or a mutation from an oil spill. Its eyes watch my every movement through the glass of its tank. I can hear it in my head, begging me. Its eyes shift between me and the scalpel beside the examination table. I nod, bringing a smile to the creature's lips. One by one, I slit the throats of the lab's occupants. I return to her, bloody. She loves me.

Cassandra Angler is a married mother of four who lives in the State of Ohio in the USA. When she isn't busy caring for her family, Cassandra works on her upcoming novel due out in November of 2020 titled Contaminated. Cassandra has three short story publications as well as several flash fiction and drabble publications.

At a Reasonable Price
by Hannah Retallick

Come one, come all! Half-price tickets to the Ocean Aquarium. Tell your friends, your family, that guy in the office. Bring your kids – they'll be dying to visit! Here, take a brochure, sir. We have plenty to see today:

Plastic net lobsters, ring pull shrimps, drinking straw crabs, milk carton octopuses, carrier bag jellyfish, clingfilm sea dragons, crisp packet stingrays, pesticide whales, microfibre clownfish, and giant sewage squids.

Come one, come all! See for yourself, our glorious Ocean. Thank you, madam, I'll show you in. And the Underwater Café is open for business. Free bottled water for all who thirst.

Hannah Retallick is a twenty-six-year-old from Anglesey, North Wales. She was home educated and then studied with the Open University, graduating with a First-class honours degree, BA in Humanities with Creative Writing and Music, and is studying for an MA in Creative Writing. She is working on her second novel and writes short stories and a blog. She was shortlisted in the Writing Awards at the Scottish Mental Health Arts Festival 2019, the Cambridge Short Story Prize, and the Henshaw Short Story Competition June 2019.
Website: ihaveanideablog.wordpress.com

The Octopus' Garden
by McKenzie Richardson

The diving expedition started well enough.

Inside the underwater cave Kas had stumbled across, their flashlights lit up rock formations and seaweed. Ren blushed when he was momentarily shaken by a rock pile that looked almost human. He illuminated it with his light, hoping Kas would fall for the same trick, then stopped abruptly.

He hadn't been mistaken; it *was* human, an open-mouthed corpse, ankles tied with twisted seagrass, anchored to a rock. He swung around, realising the cave was littered with similarly-bound bloated bodies.

Then eight huge, suction-cupped tentacles wrapped around his mask, and all the light faded out.

McKenzie Richardson lives in Milwaukee, WI. Her horror stories have been featured in various anthologies including Evil Lurks, Pandemic, and After: Undead Wars. She has also published a variety of poems and flash fiction pieces.
Facebook: mckenzielrichardson
Blog: www.craft-cycle.com

The Leviathan
by Zoey Xolton

God looked down upon Earth and saw the destruction that his creations of clay and water had wrought. Earth was always intended to be Eden—the Garden had been just the beginning—but his children had failed him; and continued to do so for generations beyond memory.

It was time.

They'd had their chance.

Deep within the ocean, wrapped around the warm, magma core of the planet, the slumbering Harbinger of Doom uncoiled itself, answering its master's summons. The seven seas boiled and ran red. The mantle of the world itself, shattered.

The sea serpent's awakening obliterated all of humanity.

Zoey Xolton is an Australian Speculative Fiction writer, primarily of Dark Fantasy, Paranormal Romance and Horror. She is also a proud mother of two and is married to her soul mate. Outside of her family, writing is her greatest passion. She is especially fond of short fiction and is working on releasing her own themed collections in future.
Website: www.zoeyxolton.com

The Cold Heart of the Ocean
by R.J. Meldrum

No-one was there to witness the last mountain top being engulfed by the rising ocean. Humanity was confined to floating rafts, at the mercy of the wind and current. They weren't worried. The ocean would feed them. They were still the masters of the planet.

Weeks passed with nothing being caught in the nets. Food began to run out.

Suddenly grey shapes were seen below the rafts.

"Whales!"

"We can hunt them!"

"We're saved!"

The humans celebrated their good fortune, but they were premature. One by one, the whales capsized the rafts. Their revenge, long overdue, was being served cold.

R.J. Meldrum is an author and academic. Born in Scotland, he moved to Ontario, Canada in 2010. He has had stories published by Horrified Press, the Infernal Clock, Trembling with Fear, Darkhouse Books, Smoking Pen Press, and James Ward Kirk Fiction. He also has had stories published in The Sirens Call e-zine, the Horror Zine and Drabblez Magazine. He is an Affiliate Member of the Horror Writers Association.
Twitter: @RichardJMeldru1
Facebook: richard.meldrum.79

Lost City
by G. Allen Wilbanks

The sonar imagery proved correct. 800 meters down in the southern Atlantic Ocean, Professor Bellamy and two fellow researchers guided the diving bell through the majestic structures of a long-lost city.

Bellamy steered the underwater craft closer to the rounded peaks of what appeared to be multi-levelled buildings. An eerie bioluminescence provided enough light to see.

"Oh, my god," muttered Bellamy.

"What is it?" asked one of the researchers.

Bellamy just shook his head. The extreme depths were messing with his eyes. For an instant, he thought he'd seen a face staring back at him from one of the windows.

G. Allen Wilbanks is a member of the Horror Writers Association (HWA) and has published over 100 short stories in various magazines and on-line venues. He is the author of two short story collections, and the novel, When Darkness Comes.
Website: www.gallenwilbanks.com
Blog: DeepDarkThoughts.com

Cold North Sea
by Will Christian

Waves crash and erupt spume and foam. The white horses that don't exist.

A mighty frigate that fought the horses, now plunges to meet Davy Jones. A feast for us, those brave seafarers. Forever trapped souls, no sun to see.

Fathoms below, it's becalmed: no light to shine our way. The weeds and rocks we hide amongst don't give up secrets, they just hold them forever and a day.

We move by senses honed and refined by eons of hunting for food. If you dare visit, we will lock you with us forever. Lost souls entombed in the eternal dark.

Will Christian is a father of two writers and a husband to his beautiful wife (who paid him to write that). With a sense of humour that his eldest daughter calls "adorable and groan-worthy dad jokes with surprising creativity", Will can usually be found wandering the local beaches, writing poetry and drabbles, and wistfully daydreaming about the boat that his girls haven't yet agreed to buy him.

Drifting Off
by Steven Lord

Has it really been three nights? Three nights clinging to flotsam, nothing but dark ocean stretching from horizon to horizon, sky a black quilt overhead. So many stars.

Optimism will keep you alive, they had said. I didn't pay attention. Survival training was for pessimists. I was going to live forever.

It's hard to maintain hope in the face of an uncaring infinity of time and space. Every lonely second an eternity. Every glittering star an unkept promise.

The sky looks beautiful tonight. And I'm so tired. The water is lovely, dark and deep. Time to slip off, I think.

Steven Lord is a debut author based in the south of England. He is currently attempting to cram writing in alongside a busy day job, with varying levels of success. While his long-term aspiration is to get a novel published, at present he would be pretty pleased with a drabble or two.

BLACK HARE PRESS

Water Damage
by Jasmine Jarvis

The water trickles in at first through the gaps in my bedroom door and window. Slowly it builds in intensity, the bedroom door bowing under the strain of sea water pushing against it. I close my eyes and tell myself this is just a dream, but still the water continues to rise. I thrash and struggle to no avail, and soon I am pinned to my bed under the weight of the ocean. My bedroom door gives way to monstrous tentacles unfurling. Searching for food. It finds me. Its tentacles squeeze me tight, snatching me up to be devoured alive.

Jasmine Jarvis is a teller of tales and scribbler of scribbles. She lives in Brisbane, Australia with her husband Michael, their two children, Tilly and Mish; Ripley, their German Shepherd, and indoor fat cat, Dwight K. Shrute.

Men and the Sea
by E.L. Giles

Thirsty for conquest and glory, they braved the wildest waters. For wealth and supremacy, they crossed the seas, seeking to appease their basest instincts of violence and their desire for dominion.

Aboard their machines of destruction, they decimated, mile by mile, the fragile harmony that reigned over the unfathomable depths of the world below. Wherever their ships went, a hecatomb followed in their wakes.

They contemplated the blood oozing from the harpoon wounds and running over the murky water, satisfied. Their eyes followed, as they departed, the spectacle of the floating carcasses that starving seabirds and opportunist sharks alike refused.

E.L. Giles is a dreamer, passionate about art, a restless worker and a bit of a weird human. He started his artistic journey as a music composer until the need to put his thoughts and stories down on paper grew too strong for him to resist it any longer. He lives in the French Province of Quebec, Canada, with his girlfriend and two boys.
Facebook: elgilesauthor
Website: www.elgilesauthor.com

Lay Down to Perish
by Crystal L. Kirkham

Monstrous waves threw us upon the ice.

Stuck. Helpless. Waiting for rescue.

Torrential rains and heavy fog.

We held tightly to a tenuous string of hope.

Days passed. We waited. The water slowly filled the boat.

Shivering, starving.

We knew that we would not return.

Our wives might never know the fate of those for whom they wait.

As they stand with candles upon the shore.

So we wrote our names upon a gaff.

Our hands shook from the cold.

Our last goodbye barely legible.

Unwillingly, we lay down to perish.

As the cold and the sea took us away.

OCEANS

Crystal L. Kirkham is a multi-genre speculative fiction author. She has published novels across several genres including her fantasy adventure Feathers and Fae (October 2019 from Kyanite Publishing) and her self-published urban fantasy series, Saints & Sinners. She is also a contributing author to multiple best-selling anthologies. Hailing from the wilds of Canada, she is an avid outdoors person, unrepentant coffee addict, part-time foodie, servant to a wonderful feline, and companion to three delightfully hilarious canines - Treble and Freddie the Standard Poodles, and Nahni the Australian Shepherd.
Website: www.crystallkirkham.com

The Statue of Atlantis
by D.J. Elton

After the typhoon unleashed its fury on several thousand small islands, a colossal statue poked up through the angry seas. Not seen until now, the ancient art lay hidden in Atlantis for centuries. And who has seen Atlantis anyway?

Island people sang, played music, and brought offerings to this giant rock woman, now facing calmly across their bays. Her arms broken, breasts chipped and cracked, belly half missing, yet a face intact.

Eyes of clean crystal, a curved smile, a shattered nose.

Some called her a witch. Others, insightfully, called her a goddess, and blessed the ocean for sending her.

D.J. Elton is a writer living in Melbourne's west. As a child she came from England to Australia, on the last boat down the Suez Canal, where she underwent a sacrificial dunking ritual in the court of King Neptune, and has never looked back. She likes creating speculative micro fiction and short stories, as well as random essays. Her work has been published in several anthologies, and she has written a historical fantasy novella, 'The Merlin Girl.' When not playing with a pen, she likes most of all to go to the green country.

The Breathing Hole
by V.A. Vazquez

The restaurant was serving seal-meat dishes.

She didn't care about the protesters; her family had hunted here for generations. And they needed the money.

She sat on a milk crate, spear in-hand. The wind whistled past her icebox-ears, as she tugged the drawstring on her hood. She heard a sound under the ice, a *scritch-scritch-scritch* that didn't sound like a seal. She knelt down on the pack ice, squinting into the bottomless black water of the breathing hole.

She heard it again: *Scritch-scritch-scritch.*

Finally, she lifted the milk crate.

Fingernails, so long they twisted like twigs, scratched against the ice.

V.A. Vazquez writes urban fantasy and paranormal romance. She currently lives in Glasgow, Scotland with her husband and small doggo.
Website: www.vavazquez.com

The Watching Waves
by S.N. Graves

My fiancé was gone when I woke on the beach. His towel remained, gold watch tossed haphazardly in its folds, the late hour a sallow, digital pulse on its face. I thought perhaps he'd gone for another dip in the water. But he'd chosen this spot for seclusion; the lights from the nearest pier—nearest anything—were a mile down the shore. No one would swim in the ocean in total darkness. That's what made the hordes of shining green eyes staring back at me—like punched holes in the black screen of roaring waves and starless sky—so unsettling.

S.N. Graves was born in the South and can't see calling anyplace without a Waffle House home. She earned her M.F.A. in Popular Fiction from Seton Hill University in 2014 and was a senior editor at Loose Id LLC. She is twenty-three years happily married to the self-proclaimed victim of Stockholm syndrome, Brian David Graves, and enjoys duct taping her two adult sons to a chair and forcing them to read all the ugly first drafts of her books. Graves also freelance edits and creates art, including book covers.
Website: www.sngraves.com
Facebook: Shannon.N.Graves

The Ocean
by Musaab Sultan

I loved the ocean; the sparkling waves, the cool winds and the smell of saltwater and sand. The ocean brought peace to my mind, gave me new life and something to look forward to. Those waters were my haven and my heart. They were my source of joy and solace.

That is until the first body washed ashore, then the second, and before I knew what was happening, my symbol of peace and joy—the place that gave me life— then became the stuff that nightmares were made of. I once loved the ocean, now it was my greatest dread.

Musaab Sultan is a 22 year old university student and aspiring writer from Karachi Pakistan who spends his time buried in fictional universes, books and animes when not battling to keep his grades afloat.

287

That Sinking Feeling
by Henry Snider

"Sinking," Terrance gasped. "We're really fucking sinking."

He smacked the cracked remote for what felt like the fiftieth time.

A muffled boom reverberated through the cruise ship, and without warning, it listed starboard. The growl of water rushing away from steerage was music to his ears.

He threw the door open and slid across the hall's drenched floor.

Lights dimmed to a muddy glow.

"No," was the only word he managed.

The remote fell to the floor. Terrance stared at the sticker on its back as a wall of water rushed to meet him.

TIME TRAVEL TOURS: RIDE THE TITANIC!

For over two decades, **Henry Snider** has dedicated his time to helping others tighten their writing through critique groups, classes, lectures, prison prose programs, and high school fiction contests. He co-founded Fiction Foundry (fictionfoundry.org est. 2012) and the award-winning Colorado Springs Fiction Writers Group (1996-2013). While still reserving enough time to pursue his own fiction aspirations, he continues to be active in the writing community through classes, media work, editing services, and advice. Henry lives in Colorado with his wife, fellow author and editor Hollie Snider, and numerous neurotic animals, including, of course, Fizzgig, the token black cat.

Website: _fictionfoundry.org/members/henry-snider_

Unlikely Compassion
by Eddie D. Moore

Sailors scattered as the Kraken wrapped large tentacles around the ship. Several men jabbed fruitlessly at the monster with spears while others tried to load passengers onto life rafts. The ship threatened to roll as boards creaked and cracked under the weight of the beast.

Ada braced herself against the cabin door frame with her right arm as she stepped onto the deck. She held her newborn daughter against her breast with her left. A giant eye broke the surface of the water and stared at her for several long seconds before releasing the ship and vanishing into the depths.

Eddie D. Moore travels hundreds of hours a year, and he fills that time by listening to audiobooks. When he isn't playing with his grandchildren, he writes his own stories. You can find a list of his publications on his blog or by visiting his Amazon Author Page. While you're there, be sure to pick up a copy of his mini-anthology Misfits & Oddities.
Website: eddiedmoore.wordpress.com
Amazon: amazon.com/author/eddiedmoore

Sea of Revenge
by Harry J. Canis

Within the dark forest, my body sways with the kelp stems, which endlessly reach for the light above. The creatures get little nourishment from my decomposed corpse, as my tormented spirit awaits release. Revenge will come, so I wait.

People swim from the pier above, their bodies just out of reach. I wait for the day my husband forgets his betrayal and plays here with his prefect replacement family. On that day of our reunion, I will grasp for him, hold him in an eternal cold embrace until his life dwindles and the eels have new organs to feed upon.

Harry J. Canis is a writer based in the beautiful English Lake District. You can often find him running or hiking within the area and being immersed in nature. His genre is Fantasy/Sci-Fi/Horror, with strong environmental and natural survival themes. Within his writing, he tries to bring an understanding that our planet is precious and needs our care and respect. Website: harryjcanis.com

Melisande
by Cecelia Hopkins-Drewer

Melisande licked the salt off her lips and glanced around. Yellow sand, blue sky, darker water. She had always loved the beach.

The only thing that spoiled her pleasure was the occasional stinger broken from a jellyfish, forcing Melisande to monitor her footsteps carefully.

What large fragments had been washed up today…if the tentacles are that long, how immense might the actual creature be?

A bulbous head rose from the water, its amorphous, bluish form disguised by the waves. The monster floated lazily in the ocean, waiting for the girl to bathe. Even partially immersed, its deadly reach was impressive.

Cecelia Hopkins-Drewer lives in Adelaide, South Australia. She has written a Masters paper on H.P. Lovecraft, and her weird poetry has been published in THE MENTOR (edited by Ron Clarke), and SPECTRAL REALMS (edited by S.T. Joshi). Her novels include a teenage vampire series commencing with MYSTIC EVERMORE. Short stories have been published in WORLDS, ANGELS & MONSTERS, BEYOND, STORMING AREA 51, and UNRAVEL. (Dark Drabbles anthologies edited by Dean Kershaw).
Amazon: amazon.com/Cecelia-Hopkins-Drewer/e/B071G968NM
Website: chopkin39.wixsite.com/website

The Rescue
by Maxine Churchman

"Closer," Brian shouted above the wind's roar.

He hefted the rope in his wet hands. On the third attempt, the loop snagged a jagged edge and held. Carefully, he used the rope to reach the rock and haul himself up.

As he approached, he saw the figure was a naked girl with long hair; her skin seemed impossibly blue. He touched her icy shoulder and she spun round, her face splitting wide, exposing rows of needle-sharp teeth. Brian's scream was cut short as she ripped out his throat before diving into the water with a flash of her iridescent tail.

Maxine Churchman lives in Essex UK and has recently started writing poetry and short stories to share. Her interests include learning to improve her writing, reading, knitting, walking and teaching yoga. She is also planning a novel.

Beach Trip
by V. Mylynne Smith

My daughter and I lived in beautiful, sunny California. We made frequent trips to the beach where she built sandcastles, squealing with joy when the tide came in and nipped her feet. I'd never loved anything quite as much as I adored her.

My late husband liked to hit us, and I finally got sick of it. We made another trip to the beach and dropped him off in the water. The cement block tied to his feet sent him hurtling into the depths.

"Bye-bye," I said, waving as he sank. "Let's see how long he can hold his breath."

V. Mylynne Smith primarily writes thrillers, but sometimes dips a toe into horror. Her love of psychology helps her craft malicious characters with the worst intentions. She aims to create twists and turns that keep the reader guessing until the end. Smith is an Oklahoman that moved to Northwest Arkansas after meeting her husband. The pair live together in a cozy house with two pets: a pitbull named Renegade and a feisty cat named Bandit. When Smith isn't stringing words together, you can find her in front of a mirror with make-up in hand or baking something delicious and fattening.

Floating
by Regina Kenney

"A mermaid!" I squealed, scooting closer to the edge of our dinghy.

Another boy mermaid. I thought mermaids were always girls, but father explained more boy mermaids come to the top to help carry sailors to shore. That's why they're always near broken ships.

There were loads of mermaids when we left the big boat.

"Why do they float with their heads facing down?" I asked.

My father frowned. "Because they can't breathe air, so they have to keep their heads in the water."

I said that I wanted to be a mermaid someday and my father started to cry.

*Originally from Minnesota, **Regina Kenney** brought her irrational fears to the empty alleys of Chicago, the foggy streets of London and to the dank and dark pubs in her new home, Dublin. Her first horror story was published in the 2019 Hamthology collection and her stories have been accepted to nine more horror anthologies to be published in 2020.*

PSI
by Drew Starling

How am I on air? Let's check the regulator.

300 psi. Wait. 300 psi?? Should be over 1000! Uh oh. How far down is this dive? Twenty meters? Oh shit.

Oh SHIT. 250. MY TANK IS BROKEN. Oh God. Okay, gotta surface. Now.

GAHHH! My lung! Oh fuck! It. Ah. It must have collapsed. Oh God. The pain. I can't breathe. I'm not. I can't. I have to surface. The boat.

Made it up. Okay. But this PAIN. Every inhale like a knife.

The boat. It's. FUCK. It's so far. And the pain. GULP. Breathing water. Pain. I'm sinking.

I—

Drew Starling is an author of horror and dark fiction. His short stories have been published in over a dozen anthologies and his collaborative novel "Storming Area 51: Horror at the Gate" spent time ranked as Amazon's #1 Sci-Fi Anthology. His only rule of writing is the dog never dies.
Website: www.drewstarling.com
Twitter: @ScaryStarling

Rising Up
by Mikko Rauhala

I open the hatch and launch upward, an oxygen tank in one hand and the black box in another. The sound of crushing metal reverberates in my ears. Screw the bends. I inflate my vest to speed me along.

After an eternity of kicking upward, I burst through the surface. The black box glows a green light. Signal detected, distress call made, transmitting data. My body aches all over. Nitrogen bubbles in my veins.

At least the data's out. At least they'll know.

Something wraps around my ankle and pulls me under. I inhale the water to make it quick.

Mikko Rauhala is a Finnish author of speculative fiction with a national Atorox award nomination under his belt. Informed by his master's degree in intelligent systems, Rauhala is most at home in hard science fiction settings, though he's not exclusive and likes to cross genres. Rauhala has dabbled in editing flash fiction for The Self-Inflicted Relative anthology, and some of his English science fiction can be found in the Infinite Metropolis short story and audio drama collection, co-authored with Edmund Schluessel.
Blog: <u>rauhala.org</u>
Podcast: <u>infinitemetropolis.com</u>

Creature as Red as Blood
by Matthew M. Montelione

Uncle Jim insisted that we take his boat out off the Long Island coast. I'm prone to becoming sea-sick, so I wasn't too enthusiastic about the venture. But Uncle Jim was excited and promised not to go far out.

After ten minutes of cruising, he stopped the boat. "Here's a nice spot for a swim, Zack!"

It was really hot out; I dived right into the cool, refreshing ocean.

Suddenly my uncle yelled something.

The head of a human-like creature as red as blood appeared above the dark water. Quickly it submerged, then slimy claws gripped my ankles and tugged.

Matthew M. Montelione is a horror writer born and raised on Long Island in New York. His work has been published in many titles, including MONSTERS: A Horror Microfiction Anthology, Mother Ghost's Grimm, and Quoth the Raven: A Contemporary Reimagining of the Works of Edgar Allan Poe. Matthew lives with his wife in New York.
Website: maybeevils.com
Facebook: maybeevils

Strawkling
by Kelly Matsuura

"Okay, Strawklers. Who's gonna collect the most trash today?!" The peppy guide blew his whistle.

"Isn't this awesome?" Holly asked, wading in.

I feigned excitement. "Sure is!"

We dived down, collected plastic, filled the floating buckets. Repeated.

I reached for something shiny on the ocean floor. A gold medallion! Jackpot!

As I pulled my treasure free, a coral-and-algae covered corpse rose from the seabed with it—an old woman with tangled hair and pointed teeth. She grabbed my face and exhaled her dark soul into my mouth….

***

"It's so rewarding to help the ocean," Holly said.

"Yes. *Very* rewarding."

Kelly Matsuura writes diverse YA, fantasy, and literary fiction. She is the Creator of The Insignia Series' anthologies (Asian fantasy themed) and has had stories published with Ink & Locket Press, A Murder of Storytellers, Crushing Hearts & Black Butterfly, and many more. Kelly lives in Nagoya, Japan with her geeky husband. She loves traveling, knitting, cooking, and of course, reading.
Website: www.blackwingsandwhitepaper.com

One Missed Catch
by Nerisha Kemraj

Her scales shimmered under the pale moonlight as Coral swam through the vast expanse of blue.

She stopped, noticing the boat.

Humans.

They were animatedly trying to pull their net onto their vessel. A big catch.

Coral's heart sank, seeing Ian's magnificent, greyish-blue tail bleeding as it surfaced, the net wound tightly around him.

In a matter of minutes, they'd see he was a merman, and she couldn't allow their discovery.

A signal from Coral, and her friend—the blue whale—jumped up, capsizing the boat as the startled men fell overboard.

Coral grabbed a lifeless Ian and disappeared underwater.

Nerisha Kemraj *resides in Durban, South Africa with her husband and two mischievous daughters. Writing since 2017, she has had over 100 short stories and poems published in various publications, both print and online. She has also received an Honourable Mention Award for her tanka in the Fujisan Taisho 2019 Tanka Contest. She holds a Bachelor's degree in Communication Science, and a Post Graduate Certificate in Education from University of South Africa.*
Amazon: amazon.com/author/nerisha_kemraj
Facebook: Nerishakemrajwriter

Deep Sea Dying
by N.M. Brown

My girlfriend's chain broke when we were boating one day, slipping into the ocean. She was devastated.

I decided to attempt the impossible and take my boat out to try to find it myself. Deep sea diving wasn't a new experience for me, and I had all the proper equipment.

As I made my descent into the depths of the waters, the ocean floor started to materialise. Almost a dozen cinder blocks lay abandoned against the sand. The chain glinted underneath the aquiferous sun, snagged under a block.

The blocks were chained to bloated bodies in various stages of decay.

Since **N.M. Brown** made her first post to a popular Internet forum, she's taken the horror community by storm. Her ability to create, terrify, and drive home her stories is insurmountable. N.M. Brown's published works can be found in multiple anthologies for all to read, but be forewarned, if you do... you may want to call your therapist after, her stories are terrifying, disturbing and devilishly unsettling. She is not only a fright visually, but also has a creepy tentacle in horror podcasting as well. Sinister Sweetheart writes, voice acts and is the media director of the Scarecrow Tales podcast.
Website: Sinistersweetheart.wixsite.com/sinistersweetheart
Facebook: NMBrownStories

My Ancestor's Tears
by J.M. Meyer

Swept up in the comforting rhythm of the azure waves, I sat on the beach where David and I met. I believed I could make this sad man's dreams come true. Learning that David dreamed of money and power, not love, left me lost. I am going home to follow my own desire. I disrobe. Savouring the feel of the sand beneath my feet, I wade into the sea. I will not drown in this divine liquid left from my ancestor's tears. My sisters are there to greet me. We rejoice as my legs transform back to my silvery fin.

J.M. Meyer is a writer, artist and small business owner living in New York, where she received her master's degree from Teachers College, Columbia University. Jacqueline enjoys writing speculative fiction and mysteries. Her favorite author is Alice Munro and her favorite film…is…anything horror related. Jacqueline also enjoys hiking with her dog Molly and the company of her husband Bruce and daughters; Julia, Emma and Lauren. Jacqueline's Mantra lately; there's no such thing as failing, it's called learning.
Website: jmoranmeyer.net
Amazon: www.amazon.com/author/jacquelinemoranmeyer

Maritime Nightmare
by K.C. Clarke

In the still of the night, a torpedo hit our starboard bow, igniting a pillar of fire soaring several hundred feet into the moonlit sky. It took twelve eternal minutes for the ship's corpse to rest peacefully on the ocean floor.

Their white fins were invisible among the white swells and murky depths. We never saw them coming, but they found us with little effort. Devoured us with even less. Blood stained the ocean's verdant waters crimson as bodies disappeared, one by one.

Nine hundred men made it into the water alive.

Only one hundred and fifty survived the night.

K.C. Clarke is a new author working on her debut novel, Little Black Dress, due out early 2020. She's been published in a handful of anthologies under various pen names. When she isn't writing, she spends her days with her husband and two girls in Toronto, watching movies and playing the piano. She's also a fur mama to two rescue dogs. She loves to write romance, but her true love is fantasy, stemming from her love of JRR Tolkien and Neil Gaiman. She's a self-diagnosed caffeine and pickle addict, an ailment for which she does not wish to seek treatment.

The Siren's Call
by A.R. Dean

Since the creation of the seas, I have been into being. Man is a horrid blight to my world; they only know destruction. I drag as many as I can to the watery doom. My ocean floor is covered in their bones.

I hear the men on their harbinger of death. I will sing them to the rocks. Any that wish to cling to small boats; I will yank down with my own talons. I enjoy taking them to the final darkness. My smile grows wicked as the human sounds grow quieter in the creaking ship. It is my time.

A.R. Dean is a dark and twisted soul. Dean has spent their whole life spreading fear with the tales from their head. Best known for stories that terrify and show the evilest side of human nature. So, look for Dean haunting your local cemetery or under your bed, because they're here to spread the fear. Turn off your lights and enjoy a scare. Dean is being published in Black Hare Press's Beyond and Unravel Anthologies. Keep a lookout for more stories.

Facebook: *A.R. Dean Author & Ghoul*

Ophelia

by Stacey Jaine McIntosh

I had never put much thought into how I would die, but the breeze off the ocean ruffled my skirt. It had been a long time since I had smelled the salt air. Just a few more steps and I would be home.

It was different than I remembered. The waves crashed louder. The roar was deafening to my ears, and as the waves lapped at my ankles, I waded further into the water embracing the cold. Sinking until the water rose over my head, until all I could see was blue. Even the fish disappeared with each passing moment.

Stacey Jaine McIntosh was born in Perth, Western Australia where she still resides with her husband and their four children. Although her first love has always been writing, she once toyed with being a Cartographer and subsequently holds a Diploma in Spatial Information Services. Since 2011, she has had a vast number of stories and a few poems published online as well as in various anthologies. Stacey is also the author of Solstice, Morrighan, Lost and Le Fay and she is currently working on several other projects simultaneously. When not with her family or writing she enjoys reading, photography, genealogy, history, Arthurian myths and witchcraft.
Website: www.staceyjainemcintosh.com

The Sea Witch
by Paula R.C. Readman

On many other occasions, Maggie had watched the boats come in, but this was the first time she'd caught Callum's eye.

She took pleasure in seeing the strength of his back, the curve of his lips, and the arch of his brow as he winked at her.

She knew from the numerous tales the fisherfolk told that he was a dangerous catch.

Maggie baited her hook with a flash of her ankle and a glint in her eye,

Days later, Callum's boat was a no-show.

The tearful fisherwomen gathered at the harbour to lament another loss to the sea witch.

Paula R.C. Readman learnt 'How to Write' from books which her husband purchased from eBay. After 250 purchases, he finally told her 'just to get on with the writing'. Since 2010, she's had 34 stories published.
Blog: paulareadman1.wordpress.com

The Ocean's Thief
by Patricia Elliott

Dead...alive...what does it matter? Twenty days at sea with salt-caked hair. No hope left. Wet and alone. Swollen sores across my skin. Giant swells rock the orange raft. Dark clouds thicken. Another storm is rising. I know what's waiting for me. I see the shadows beneath the surface. They already took my sweet husband, Jeff. I can hear him calling me.

"Ashley, come home."

Waves reach out for me, like a hand. I hold tightly to the yellow rope, my lifeline. My god of safety, but tis not meant to be. The water god steals my beating heart.

Patricia Elliott lives in beautiful British Columbia with her family. Now that her lovely kids are all teenagers, she has decided to actively pursue her passion for the written word.
When she was a youngster, she spent the majority of her time writing fan-fiction and poetry to avoid the harsh reality of bullying. Writing allowed her to escape into another world, even if temporarily; a world in which she could be anyone or anything, even a mermaid. Dreams really can come true. If you believe it, you can achieve it!
Website: patriciaelliottromance.com

Murky Waters
by Destiny Eve Pifer

Deep into the darkness it dragged her. An invisible force that had gripped her ankles and was now pulling her into the dark murky ocean waters. She wanted to scream but had foolishly chosen to swim alone. Now here she was, being attacked by something she knew nothing about. She tried to wiggle free, but it was no use. Whatever had her wasn't about to let go until it reached the bottom. She could feel her lungs starting to ache, she could taste the salt water as it ran down the back of her throat. This was her final day.

Destiny Eve Pifer is a published author whose work has appeared in numerous anthologies and magazines. Her stories have been featured in FATE Magazine, True Confessions, Spotlight on Recovery and Country Magazine. A lover of all things supernatural and spooky she resides in Punxsutawney, Pennsylvania with her son Dartanyan.

Shortcut
by A.S. Charly

The cracking of the hull was audible even through the music filling the Manta. Water accumulated and dropped into Ian's cockpit. With a sigh, he geared down, left the current and opted for one of the submarine canyon shortcuts to head back for a repair.

Steering through a narrow passage, he didn't notice the hungry eyes following him.

The unexpected blow sent his ship spinning against the wall, and everything turned black.

Soaked, he regained consciousness. With awe he watched the battle of two enormous beasts, illuminated by his green, flickering emergency lights, as the Manta sank deeper and deeper.

A.S. Charly loves to lose herself in fantastical worlds far away between the stars, filled with magic and wonder. She also writes and draws when her head is not stuck in the clouds. Her writing has been published in various anthologies and online publications.
Facebook: A.S.Charlydreams
Amazon: www.amazon.com/author/a.s.charly

Beneath the Surface
by Paul Eric Carberry

He descended into the black, frigid water, blackness greater than the vacuum of space threatening to pull him under, asphyxiating. Regret degenerated into terror. Trapped for eternity. Unknown terrors awaited in the depths. Monsters with rows of razor-sharp teeth like a torrent of razor blades prowled in the shadows. Pain radiated from his chest, his heart thumping so rapidly he couldn't distinguish when one beat ended and the next began. Fear assaulted his rational mind, giving the ice-cold waters entry to his lungs. Unable to tell if his eyes were open or shut, entombed in darkness. Filled with dreadful thoughts.

Paul Eric Carberry is the author of the Zombies on the Rock series. His tales of the zombie apocalypse in Newfoundland are inspired by George A. Romero's Living Dead series. He has also published several short stories over three "from the Rock" anthologies including "Halloween Mummers", "The Light of Cabot Tower", "Into the Forrest" and "Harmon Field". His Zombies on the Rock series currently has three novels, "Outbreak", "The Viking Trail" and "The Republic of Newfound" and is currently working on the fourth novel "Extinction". Paul is from Newfoundland and is currently living in Shearwater, Nova Scotia.
Website: engenbooks.com/zombies-on-the-rock

Wolves of the Sea
by Evan Baughfman

The group of swimsuit models appeared out of nowhere to join the bachelor party's afternoon yacht excursion. The women had brought their own booze, too.

Guys got sufficiently wasted. Lost track of time.

Eventually, the models insisted on skinny-dipping under the full moon's light. Men didn't need much convincing.

Once in the water, however, the partygoers lost sight of their companions.

Where had the beauties gone?

The men screamed as they soon discovered themselves surrounded by a group of killer whales.

Too late they realised: they'd been duped by a pack of hungry orcanthropes, the legendary wolves of the sea.

Evan Baughfman works in a very scary place: a middle school! He writes all genres, but horror is where he's most comfortable. Much of his writing success has been as a playwright. He's had many different plays produced across the globe. Heuer Publishing has published his Poe adaptation, "A Taste of Amontillado". Additionally, Evan has adapted a number of his short stories into screenplays, of which "The Emaciated Man" and "The Creaky Door" have won awards in various film festival competitions. Evan's "Just Plants" was recently published in Soteira Press's horror anthology, The Monsters We Forgot - Volume 1.

The Fury Within
by J.W. Garrett

Wind whipped, churning the ocean, its surface normally a smooth pulse, now angry as it slammed against the shore.

The last islanders evacuated, those remaining were isolated, facing the storm's wrath.

The house shuddered, groaning under the water and wind. The walls collapsed, with it the roof and windows.

Swept away by the crushing wind, the man clung to a piece of debris. Remnants of his life floated by: a chair, cracked frame, yesterday's newspaper…

He held tight.

Squinting, surrounded by sea, he drifted as the sun bit his skin and his muscles turned to mush.

The water inched higher.

J.W. Garrett *has been writing in one form or another since she was a teenager. She currently lives in Florida with her family but loves the mountains of Virginia where she was born. Her writings include YA fantasy as well as short stories. Since completing Remeon's Quest-Earth Year 1930, the prequel in her YA fantasy series, Realms of Chaos, she has been hard at work on the next in the series, scheduled to release August 2020. When she's not hanging out with her characters, her favourite activities are reading, running and spending time with family.*
Website: www.jwgarrett.com
BHC Press: www.bhcpress.com/Author_JW_Garrett.html

Escape
by Maxine Churchman

The ship pulled out of the dock, and I breathed a sigh of relief; safe at last. He wouldn't find me now.

Beneath my feet, the floor thrummed with the power of the engines. Every second propelled me further away from my tormenter and towards a new life across the ocean. I was free to start again.

It would not be easy; I had used most of my money on the ticket. I looked around the shared cabin. There were no frills down here in 3rd Class. The name *Titanic*, however, filled me with hope; such a strong, promising name.

Maxine Churchman lives in Essex UK and has recently started writing poetry and short stories to share. Her interests include learning to improve her writing, reading, knitting, walking and teaching yoga. She is also planning a novel.

Leave No Wake
by Jesse Highsmith

Traci could not believe her eyes. A moment of dancing had transcended into a journey deep underwater, surrounded by tropical fish and other bioluminescent wonderments. She looked at the wisps of red prom dress that now hovered around her body with the same rhythm as her auburn coloured hair. Just then, an electrical tremor shot through her as Chase's voice flooded her eardrums.

"Wake up! Oh, God, please wake up!"

"Get back!" an EMT said, charging his defibrillator once again.

"She didn't take that much, I swear!" her friend yelled, panicked.

No, Traci thought calmly. "I don't want to leave."

Jesse Highsmith is an adventurous wordsmith, musician, podcast enthusiast, and internet jokester from Central Florida, U.S. His specialty is short form flash fiction written within the confines of a large pesticide truck. However, he is currently writing his first novel, an otherworldly dive into death, acceptance, sacrifice, and redemption. He is also hard at work on his first foray into children's books with former Infectious Magazine editor Sami Marshall, a project due to be completed very soon. They live in a rural countryside with his son Logan, dog Snowy, and a shadow-chasing cat dubbed Sir Liam Frederick, Duke of Cuteness.

Superstition
by Renée K. Reeves

In the middle of a navigation lesson, the midshipman lowered his sextant. "Sometimes, sir," he began, "I think the figurehead smiles at me."

The captain frowned. "Is that so?"

The boy nodded. "Her teeth are quite sharp, you know. And when her hair slips, I tuck it back behind her ears."

When confronted, the bosun shrugged. "It's bound to happen. Seawater is harsh and it's been months since we had her shellacked."

The captain sipped cold coffee and consulted a chart. "Fix her before we cross the northern sea," he finally said. "We'll perish if her sisters hear her sing."

Renée K. Reeves enjoys folk music and morbid history, ideally combined. She's a tall ship sailor and science educator who writes speculative fiction on her days off. Renée's work has appeared in Friday Flash Fiction, Scribendi, 101 Words, and elsewhere.

Scotland
by Kevin J. Kennedy

Scotland was the birthplace of most mythological creatures. Now, only few survive. Selkies such as I have been here since the beginning of time. Created and favoured by the old gods. Able to switch between our seal-like self and human form. Nessie is also real to but there are far more at sea than there are in Loch Ness. Just one trapped there with no other to breed with. Other cryptids existed. Humans called them Bigfoot, griffins, Centaurs and unicorns, all hunted to extinction aeon's ago by the plague called humankind, but the sea is ours and we will remain.

Kevin J. Kennedy is a horror author & editor from Scotland. He is the co-author of You Only Get One Shot & Screechers, and the publisher of several best selling anthology series; Collected Horror Shorts, 100 Word Horrors & The Horror Collection, as well as the stand alone anthology Carnival of Horror. His stories have been featured in many other notable books in the horror genre. He is an active member of the Horror Writers Association. He lives in a small town in Scotland, with his wife and his two little cats, Carlito and Ariel.
Website: www.kevinjkennedy.co.uk
Amazon: : amazon.com/Kevin-J.-Kennedy/e/B016V0NA7M

Medusa Rising
by Freddy Iryss

The world at three thousand feet below the sea's surface is alien and full of things I've never seen: plastic bottles from last century, fishing lines, a boat propeller. A jellyfish floats past, with a yellowtail and a brim swimming—alive and well—in its see-through guts.

"What are the fish doing in the belly of that jellyfish?"

"Surviving, of course," said my travel companion who, like me and a thousand others, had taken to the water to escape the raging fires on land.

A giant jellyfish, well-fed in these rising temperatures, grabs me with its tentacles and swallows me.

*To impress her older brother, **Freddy Iryss** read her way through his collection of Isaac Asimov's books of SciFi at the tender age of ten. She pretended that she understood what was going on in those futuristic worlds, while deep down she found them disturbing her peace of mind. Who and what was out there? Iryss' non-fiction writing includes themes on identity, the postcolonial and post-national. Her fiction evolves around the concept of the anthropocene. Writing SciFi is to imagine the world of our reality without bounds.*
Website: freddyiryss.blogspot.com
Twitter: @FreddyIryss

Going Down
by A.R. Johnston

They were going down and there was nothing that could be done. They had hit something in the middle of the night. Now the boat was slowly leaking, and the storm was getting worse.

"Are they going to rescue us in time?" She spoke loudly over the howling wind, the waves crashing against the boat.

"I hope so. I'm sure I saw something circling out in the water. I don't think it's just waves hitting the boat."

"What?"

Then it didn't matter, something crashed harder into the boat. Water rose. Then she saw the fin in the water. She screamed.

A.R. Johnston is a small-town girl from Nova Scotia, Canada. She is known to write mostly urban fantasy, though she goes where the muses lead her and you never know where that may be. She is a lover of coffee, good tv shows, horror flicks, and a reader of good books. She pretends to be a writer when real life doesn't get in the way. Pesky full-time job and adulting!
Facebook: <u>arjohnstonauthor</u>
Website: <u>arjohnstonauthor.wordpress.com</u>

Captain's Knowledge
by Radar DeBoard

Captain Nadal stood at the helm of the ship. His wise eyes looked out over the vast ocean they currently sailed upon.

His years of sailing had brought him experiences that could not be simply taught. He knew the wind picking up as well as the waves climbing in height meant a storm was coming.

Nadal knew from their current position that if they sank, no one would be able to save them.

That also meant that no one would be able to hear the screams of the sailors down below as his crew and him tortured and killed them.

Radar DeBoard is a horror movie and novel enthusiast who resides in the small town of Goddard, Kansas. He occasionally dabbles in writing, and enjoys to make dark tales for people to enjoy. He has had drabbles and short stories published in various electronic magazines and anthologies.
Facebook: WriterRadarDeBoard

Satisfy the Hunger
by Brandi Hicks

I swim fathoms below the surface, but I'm starved, and fish don't fill my gut. Not even the sharks help to stave the hunger. I need more. It's an unrelenting pain, I have to eat more. The creatures stumbling into the water are filled with a liquid that curbs the ache. Now I long for it.

I can sense it now that I've had it. I can feel it coursing through the water, like it's searching just for me. Thump, thump. Thump, thump. The hunger grows, the ache rages. I see it and I want it.

So I take it.

*Growing up in West Virginia, **Brandi Hicks** loved to have her nose in a book, her eyes toward the night sky and putting a pen to paper. Her imagination was always sparked by her grandfather and her mom taking her to new places and teaching her about the unusual. She loves fantasy, sci-fi, and learning about science and history. She has two beautiful children, and hopes to instill creativity and a love of reading in them. Finding new crafts to try keeps her busy when not playing with her kids or working.*

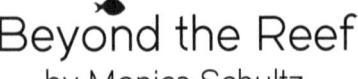

Beyond the Reef
by Monica Schultz

It sees him. Mark doesn't know what it is, but it knows him. He shivers, even as the sunshine warms him and dances across the clear water.

No one else has frozen. Mark's family still bobs on gentle swells, crossing the rift without hesitation; eager to reach the shipwreck.

The guide warned them, but he still glances down. A gaping maw splits the reef in two. Night slumbers beneath his dangling feet. Mark clutches his floatie, but it's too late. Their eyes have met.

It reaches for him; the pressure crushing his bones. Devouring him. The depths silence Mark's screams.

Monica Schultz is a full-time Mathematics and History teacher from Ipswich, Australia, with a passion for writing fantasy. When she isn't busy finding 'x' in the latest equation, you can find her curled up with a young adult book and a cat on her lap.
Website: https://monicaschultzauthor.weebly.com/
Instagram: @monicaschultzauthor

A Sailor's Sacrifice
by A.R. Dean

The waves rock gently below my boat. I grunt as I drag the struggling parcel to the boat's edge.

"Hush. It's only the sea." I pet the girl's hair.

She struggles around her gag.

"No one can hear you," I gently remind her. "Not where we are."

I tie the irons around her wrists as she cries. With a shake of my head I toss her overboard and into the waves. She disappears quickly to a watery grave.

I hum a sailor's tune as I head back to shore. If Neptune enjoyed my gift, tomorrow the nets will be full.

A.R. Dean *is a dark and twisted soul. Dean has spent their whole life spreading fear with the tales from their head. Best known for stories that terrify and show the evilest side of human nature. So, look for Dean haunting your local cemetery or under your bed, because they're here to spread the fear. Turn off your lights and enjoy a scare. Dean is being published in Black Hare Press's Beyond and Unravel Anthologies. Keep a lookout for more stories.*
Facebook: A.R. Dean Author & Ghoul

Swims with the Fishes
by Sean P. Chatterton

Every bridge support column on the Trans-Atlantic Bridge has a low density patch the size of a human body. The mafia owned the companies that built it. Any contractors, or union people who caused problems were given a choice of swimming with the fishes or becoming an upstanding citizen.

Those that chose to swim were given concrete boots and dropped off the bridge. If they survived the drop, they had plenty of time to drown, long before they reached the sea bed hundreds of metres below.

As for the others: Well, they will now be upstanding for hundreds of years.

Sean P. Chatterton has been a reader of Science Fiction and Fantasy since he could read. Being introduced at a young age to Tolkien's middle earth, E. E. "Doc" Smith's Lensman series, and Asimov's robots, amongst countless others, gave Sean an active imagination and a yearning for something more. Like the world famous grandfather of modern SF, Arthur C. Clarke, his first published short story was of a teleporter accident. This was sheer coincidence but one that Sean is very proud of. He now produces short stories on a regular basis and has had over twenty published stories to his credit..
Website: www.seanpchatterton.co.uk/bio.htm
Facebook: sean.p.chatterton

The Thing Underwater
by E.L. Giles

"Did you hear it?" said Second Officer Smith, his eyes glinting. "Her voice. She's singing. I need to see her."

Taking Captain Trumbull unaware, Smith started to run across the deck, unexpectedly jumping overboard into the fathomless and icy black water.

"Smith!" cried Trumbull, feverishly searching the murky waters. "Man overboard!"

Turning, Trumbull found an almost empty deck. The few men remaining were in the process of jumping overboard as well.

Just as Trumbull turned to stop the last man from diving in, he heard it, her voice—soothing, melodious, simply intoxicating. Only one thought remained: *I must join her.*

E.L. Giles is a dreamer, passionate about art, a restless worker and a bit of a weird human. He started his artistic journey as a music composer until the need to put his thoughts and stories down on paper grew too strong for him to resist it any longer. He lives in the French Province of Quebec, Canada, with his girlfriend and two boys.
Facebook: elgilesauthor
Website: www.elgilesauthor.com

Siren Song
by Jo Mularczyk

"Mum I'm bored!" she moaned.

"Where's your new toy?" her mother answered.

Lorelai glanced at the man lying listless on a nearby rock. He sensed her gaze and tried to rise. His arm flopped into the water.

"It's all worn out," she cried disgustedly.

"Then find something else to do." Her mother was unsurprisingly distracted by the effort of staying perched upon her human float, who was somehow managing to swim and simper simultaneously.

"Fine," Lorelai huffed. She swam towards the boat routes and waited for her moment. Then she tilted her head back, opened her mouth and sang…

Jo Mularczyk's stories and poems appear in magazines and anthologies including - The School Magazine's Blast Off and Touchdown; Zinewest 2017, 2018, 2019; Short and Twisted 2017; Open House 2 and 3; Short Tales 4 and 5; Christmas Tales 4; Wonderment; an upcoming Bloomsbury UK book of poems for children; fourW thirty; and several upcoming publications. Jo mentors gifted and talented students' writing groups, runs junior writing workshops and is a co-author with the student literacy program, Littlescribe. Through Littlescribe Jo provides writing tips and story starters for students to complete as co-authors. Jo lives in Australia with her husband and three children.

Website: www.jomularczyk.com

Facebook: jo.mularczyk.author

Cousin Joe

by Cecelia Hopkins-Drewer

My cousin, Joe, was holidaying from the East Coast. (If you have heard the tales, you might know some coastal folk share DNA with us ocean dwellers.) He admired the tube worm encrusted buildings and was astounded by the giant spider crab and vampire squid.

When we encountered the frilled shark, he remarked that it looked strangely like me. I was proud to receive the compliment and opened my mouth to display rows of trident shaped teeth.

"Yeuch!"

"Come back, Joe!"

Fully intending to comfort my relative, I gave chase. Unfortunately, Joe swam away and refused to visit ever again.

Cecelia Hopkins-Drewer lives in Adelaide, South Australia. She has written a Masters paper on H.P. Lovecraft, and her weird poetry has been published in THE MENTOR (edited by Ron Clarke), and SPECTRAL REALMS (edited by S.T. Joshi). Her novels include a teenage vampire series commencing with MYSTIC EVERMORE. Short stories have been published in WORLDS, ANGELS & MONSTERS, BEYOND, STORMING AREA 51, and UNRAVEL. (Dark Drabbles anthologies edited by Dean Kershaw).
Amazon: amazon.com/Cecelia-Hopkins-Drewer/e/B071G968NM
Website: chopkin39.wixsite.com/website

Molinere Underwater Sculpture Park

by Vonnie Winslow Crist

Facing into the ocean currents, Jason deCaires Taylor's concrete people gave Liam the heebbie-jeebbies. Still, he took selfies with his friends.

Created from life-casts of Grenadians, the sculptures covering the seafloor had already been colonised by corals. Liam knew eventually, their features would be erased like the identities of slaves tossed overboard during the journey from West Africa to the Americas. A journey which included these waters.

The circle of children holding hands bothered Liam the most. Especially when one turned its concrete head to stare into his eyes.

They're haunted, thought Liam.

Heart racing, he swam for the surface.

Vonnie Winslow Crist is author of The Enchanted Dagger, Owl Light, The Greener Forest, Murder on Marawa Prime, and other award-winning books. Her fiction is included in "Amazing Stories," "Cast of Wonders," "Outposts of Beyond," Killing It Softly 2, Defending the Future - Dogs of War, Midnight Masquerade, Chaos of Hard Clay, and elsewhere. A cloverhand who has found so many four-leafed clovers she keeps them in jars, Vonnie strives to celebrate the power of myth in her writing.
Website: www.vonniewinslowcrist.com*

O Captain
by Henry Herz

O Captain! My Captain! Our hunting trip is done.

The ship has gathered mermaids all, the captives sought are won.

The port is near, the cheers I hear, their Sunday best a'wearing.

While follow eyes our bloody prow, our vessel grim and scaring.

From ruthless trip the victor ship returns with bullion sought,

'Though now our craft is anchor'd, the lesson dearly bought.

My Captain does not answer, his lips are pale and still,

My master does not feel my arm, he has no pulse nor will,

Upon the deck my Captain lies red,

My skipper fallen cold and dead.

Henry Herz *edited BEYOND THE PALE, featuring stories by Peter Beagle, Heather Brewer, Jim Butcher, Rachel Caine, Kami Garcia, Nancy Holder, and Jane Yolen. He authored the short stories Gluttony (CLASSICS REMIXED anthology), Zombie Sonnet 43 (MONSTERS anthology), Ghost Father (BEYOND anthology), Sins & Virtues (ANGELS anthology), and Pay the Piper (Highlights Magazine). He authored the books: MONSTER GOOSE NURSERY RHYMES, WHEN YOU GIVE AN IMP A PENNY, MABEL & THE QUEEN OF DREAMS, CAP'N REX & HIS CLEVER CREW, HOW THE SQUID GOT TWO LONG ARMS, ALICE'S MAGIC GARDEN, 2 PIRATES + 1 ROBOT, THE MAGIC SPATULA.*
www.henryherz.com

The Leviathan
by Jim Bates

In the deepest part of the ocean, the Mariana Trench, there lives a huge beast scientists call the Leviathan. Two men in a research bathyscaphe led a scientific exploration of the trench in the early sixties. The only known photo of the beast was taken at that time, just before radio contact was lost. The image is of the oesophagus of the creature as the vessel was swallowed whole. The screams of the two scientists to this day still haunts those who heard it. The tragedy has been kept secret. Can you image what would happen if word got out?

Jim Bates lives in a small town twenty miles west of Minneapolis, Minnesota. His stories have appeared online in CafeLit, The Writers' Cafe Magazine, Cabinet of Heed, Paragraph Planet, Nailpolish Stories, Ariel Chart, Potato Soup Journal, Literary Yard, Spillwords (Dec, 2019, Author of the Month), The Drabble, The Academy of the Heart and Mind and World of Myth Magazine. In print publications: A Million Ways, Mused Literary Journal, Gleam Flash Fiction Anthology #2, the Portal Anthology and the Glamour Anthology by Clarendon House Publishing, The Best of CafeLit 8 by Chapeltown Publishing, the Nativity Anthology by Bridge House Publishing and Gold Dust Magazine.
Website: www.theviewfromlonglake.wordpress.com

A Mother's Rage
by Kaitlyn Arnett

Rubbish filled her precious waters, touched her children, yet the people feigned surprise that their planet grew ill.

But she was done. She was sick of watching her children suffer, sick of the trash loitering amongst the waves, sick of crying salty tears.

On January 1st, she struck.

Waves crashed against every shore, every state, every country, dragging people out to sea.

January 2nd, her reach extended further. Floods raced inland, reclaiming everything the humans had stolen from her.

By January 3rd, more than half the world had fallen into her salty depths.

This was the price for their ignorance.

Kaitlyn Arnett is a teen author who has been writing for five years. She focuses on the fantasy and thriller genres, specifically drabbles and short stories.

Toes in the Water
by Raymond Johnson

Sandy had loved the ocean ever since she was a child. She recalled inhaling the briny sea air and the taste of salt on her lips when she'd climbed from the warm water; watching crabs scuttle and building castles with a bucket.

Today, she found herself sitting idly with her toes kicking ocean water as her legs dangled over a ledge of stone, and she ate the last bit of her sandwich. She hadn't expected to find herself on the sea front, but she was glad that she had been climbing Pikes Peak when the ocean rushed in from nowhere.

Raymond Johnson is a funeral director in central Ohio who basically writes horror and Litrpg stories in the little spare time he has. He has five children, a wife, a dog, and a cat and for fun he does a YouTube show called the Litrpg Audiobook Podcast.

Piss on It
by Dawn DeBraal

"Ouch, I've been stung!" shouted Olivia.

"Wait, I'll piss on it. That's supposed to take the sting out," said Margaret, who squatted over her friend.

"That did nothing. It still hurts like hell. Are you sure that's what you're supposed to do with a horsefly bite?' Oliva asked.

"Horsefly? I thought you were stung by a jellyfish. You're killing me!" Margaret laughed at her friend, who had just suffered one of the most embarrassing moments of her life. "I'm in pain from laughing so hard!" cried Margaret.

Oliva found a large stone and put Margaret out of her misery.

Dawn DeBraal lives in rural Wisconsin with her husband Red, two rat terriers, and a cat. She has discovered that her love of telling a good story can be written. Published stories with Palm-sized press, Spillwords, Mercurial Stories, Potato Soup Journal, Edify Fiction, Zimbell House Publishing, Clarendon House Publishing, Blood Song Books, Black Hare Press, Fantasia Divinity, Cafelit, Reanimated Writers, Guilty Pleasures, Unholy Trinity, The World of Myth, Dastaan World, Vamp Cat, Runcible Spoon, Dark Christmas, Siren's Call, Iron Horse Publishing, Falling Star Magazine 2019 Pushcart Nominee.
Amazon: _amazon.com/Dawn-DeBraal/e/B07STL8DLX_

Beneath the Surface
by Carys Crossen

Sometimes the sea moaned.

Deep, strange moans belched from the blackest, deepest recesses of the ocean. Recording devices—belonging to oceanographers, fishing vessels, amateur monster hunters—documented them, transmuted them.

Speculation raged about what kind of creature made them. A disfigured whale, or a strange beast, unknown to science. The Kraken, even.

Scientists discredited them all. It's the ice in Antarctica, they repeated. One ice shelf grinding against another.

Now the ice was melting.

"What do we tell people?" the scientist responsible for suppressing information about the moans asked the secretly convened council of world leaders.

None of them answered.

Carys Crossen has been writing stories since she was nine years old and shows no signs of stopping. Her monograph The Nature of the Beast has been published by University of Wales Press and her fiction has been published by Mother's Milk Books, Ink and Sword Magazine, Riggwelter, Dear Damsels, Honey and Lime Lit and others. When she's not writing she's walking dogs/contemplating nature/living in Manchester UK with her husband.

Best Laid Plans
by J.W. Garrett

Jason strayed from his underwater adventure group.

I paid to see the sunken ship, and that's what I'll do.

Ducking behind the coral reef and clumps of seaweed, he headed for the wreckage. The instructor said it was unstable. On the ocean floor? How could that be?

After checking his oxygen levels, Jason swam through a hole in the side. Inside, the ship burst with colourful sea life. Fish, stingrays, jellyfish, even a seahorse meandered by.

I'm good. A few more minutes...

He tugged at a fallen door.

A long tentacle dragged him inside.

Another one shut the door again.

J.W. Garrett *has been writing in one form or another since she was a teenager. She currently lives in Florida with her family but loves the mountains of Virginia where she was born. Her writings include YA fantasy as well as short stories. Since completing Remeon's Quest-Earth Year 1930, the prequel in her YA fantasy series, Realms of Chaos, she has been hard at work on the next in the series, scheduled to release August 2020. When she's not hanging out with her characters, her favourite activities are reading, running and spending time with family.*
Website: www.jwgarrett.com
BHC Press: www.bhcpress.com/Author_JW_Garrett.html

Late Night Swim
by Mark Mackey

Elizabeth McGraven, strapped to a hard steel operating bed, cried in intense pain as a scalpel was cut into her stomach. It caused blood to escape, which was collected into metallic vials. She was being experimented on, deep beneath the ocean.

She'd been captured by one of the extra-terrestrial races called the Filercane during a late night swim at McClernan Beach. It was beyond terrifying—a Grey, but with tentacles connected to its torso. Dragged quick as a flash down into its ovalish silver craft, it then cut into her throat, and she closed her eyes for the last time.

Mark Mackey is a speculative fiction writer who now resides in Rockford Illinois after spending an abundance of time in Chicago. The author's stories can be found in various anthologies, some charity, some not, including some belonging to Australian publisher, Black Hare Pres, and Suicide House Publishing, now known as Nocturnal Sirens Publishing, headed by Natalie Brown.

Barry drowns his feelings
by D.J. Elton

Barry's emotions cool completely as he sinks into the sea.

That fierce madness haunting him whenever he sees his father is gone. Whispered far away when he touches the water wall. Feet in water. Legs sliding. Cold. Comforting.

Confronting those feelings head on, he greets the ocean as he sinks down.

It's cold, clean. Clears his tight heart. Soothes his mad, bad head where pain gets stuck. Hot, horrible.

Yet here he can sink down in pleasure. There's no need to worry. To think. To reflect. It's all null and void here. Barry loves the ocean. It has power. Magic.

D.J. Elton is a writer living in Melbourne's west. As a child she came from England to Australia, on the last boat down the Suez Canal, where she underwent a sacrificial dunking ritual in the court of King Neptune, and has never looked back. She likes creating speculative micro fiction and short stories, as well as random essays. Her work has been published in several anthologies, and she has written a historical fantasy novella, 'The Merlin Girl.' When not playing with a pen, she likes most of all to go to the green country.

Wave Goodbye
by D.M. Burdett

My lungs burned and my head pounded, but she watched from afar as I floundered.

Breathe.

Her dark eyes—ebony pools—pleaded, but her smile was wide, sharp teeth glinting, as I slipped below the surface.

I reached out, movements slow and tortured, but she dodged and dived.

Breathe, she whispered without words from close behind, just as darkness began to curl at the edges of my world.

Breathe, she bellowed, her face close to mine, and I sucked in a great lungful of salty water.

And as I closed my eyes for the last time, she finally kissed me.

D.M. Burdett initially roamed as an army brat, but now lives in Australia where she spends her days avoiding drop bears and killer spiders. She has published a Sci-Fi series, has short stories in various anthologies, and has published two children's series. She is currently working on the first book in a dystopian series.
Website: www.dmburdett.com
Facebook: DMBurdett

Live Raft
by Dawn DeBraal

Floating in the ocean for weeks, two thin men aboard a crumbling raft.

"I found something," shouted Zeb as he reached into the water.

"Is it edible?" Bob asked hungrily.

"I don't know, let me pull it off." Zeb reached into the water, grunting as he brought up the creature.

"Oh, my God! It's a giant shipworm!" Bob cried, putting his head in his hands.

"Shipworm? Is that bad? There's a whole bunch of them on the underside of the raft."

"You idiot, they eat wood!"

A piece of the raft floated away.

"We'll be ok, that piece got away."

Dawn DeBraal lives in rural Wisconsin with her husband Red, two rat terriers, and a cat. She has discovered that her love of telling a good story can be written. Published stories with Palm-sized press, Spillwords, Mercurial Stories, Potato Soup Journal, Edify Fiction, Zimbell House Publishing, Clarendon House Publishing, Blood Song Books, Black Hare Press, Fantasia Divinity, Cafelit, Reanimated Writers, Guilty Pleasures, Unholy Trinity, The World of Myth, Dastaan World, Vamp Cat, Runcible Spoon, Dark Christmas, Siren's Call, Iron Horse Publishing, Falling Star Magazine 2019 Pushcart Nominee.
Amazon: amazon.com/Dawn-DeBraal/e/B07STL8DLX

The Harrow's Last Sail
by Ali House

Deep beneath the dark waters lay *The Harrow*. The ship was preserved by the cold, intact except for a large crack in the middle, almost splitting it in two.

Tales of her demise had spread quickly, and although many assumed she lay at the bottom of the ocean, nobody knew where.

Some said she was taken by a rogue wave, others by mutiny, and others by a fierce battle. But if one were to look at her now, they would see a large octopus-like tentacle wrapped around her, and if they could read thoughts, they'd hear one simple word:

"Mine."

Ali House is the author of sci-fi/fantasy novels *The Six Elemental* and *The Fifth Queen*, along with various short stories in the *"From the Rock"* series published by Engen Books. She is a traveller, baker, and fan of the Oxford comma. *Website:* engenbooks.com/tag/house-blog/

Into the Arctic
by C.L. Williams

I am in the ocean, doing my usual hobby of scuba diving, when a current takes me out of my spot in the ocean. The current knocked me out as I float along the waves and into uncharted waters. The sound of my oxygen tank running low wakes me up, I'm now low on oxygen, and I'm freezing.

I see the icebergs below, and that is when I realise the current sent me south. I'm now in the Arctic Ocean. Ice barriers build around me, and now I question what will kill me first; the ice or lack of oxygen.

C.L. Williams is an international best-selling author currently living in central Virginia. He has written eight poetry books, four novellas, one novel, and a contributor to a multitude of anthologies and magazines. His most recent anthology appearance ANGELS: Dark Drabbles #2 from Black Hare Press became a number one in hot new releases. C.L. Williams is currently working on his second novel and a new poetry book.
Facebook: writer434
Twitter: @writer_434

Prey

by Dawn DeBraal

Sam searched the rocks, looking for crabs, away from everyone else. Finding many of the small creatures, he plucked them from the water and put them in his bag. There would be good eating tonight.

Excitedly, he leaped across a small crevice. His foot slid down the wet stone, becoming wedged. He tried pulling up the stones around his crushed foot; tugging, he prayed his foot didn't break.

While Sam was preoccupied, trying to set himself free, a creature in the rocks watched its prey and waited for the rising tide to take Sam. There would be good eating tonight.

Dawn DeBraal lives in rural Wisconsin with her husband Red, two rat terriers, and a cat. She has discovered that her love of telling a good story can be written. Published stories with Palm-sized press, Spillwords, Mercurial Stories, Potato Soup Journal, Edify Fiction, Zimbell House Publishing, Clarendon House Publishing, Blood Song Books, Black Hare Press, Fantasia Divinity, Cafelit, Reanimated Writers, Guilty Pleasures, Unholy Trinity, The World of Myth, Dastaan World, Vamp Cat, Runcible Spoon, Dark Christmas, Siren's Call, Iron Horse Publishing, Falling Star Magazine 2019 Pushcart Nominee.
Amazon: amazon.com/Dawn-DeBraal/e/B07STL8DLX

Resting Place
by N.M. Brown

The October sun sparkled off my wife, Annie's, eyes the day we got married. We got married with ocean waves licking our feet. High tide came faster than expected, soaking her dress as she laughed with joy.

As we ride into the sunset on our boat, I think back to that day. Decades have passed since then, taking more of Annie's health with each passing year.

She passed away this morning.

I decided it's my time too. The medicine I've taken will stop my heart by the time we reach bottom; eternally resting in the ocean we got married at.

*Since **N.M. Brown** made her first post to a popular Internet forum, she's taken the horror community by storm. Her ability to create, terrify, and drive home her stories is insurmountable. N.M. Brown's published works can be found in multiple anthologies for all to read, but be forewarned, if you do... you may want to call your therapist after, her stories are terrifying, disturbing and devilishly unsettling. She is not only a fright visually, but also has a creepy tentacle in horror podcasting as well. Sinister Sweetheart writes, voice acts and is the media director of the Scarecrow Tales podcast.*
Website: Sinistersweetheart.wixsite.com/sinistersweetheart
Facebook: NMBrownStories

Never Fall in Love with a Mermaid

by Wondra Vanian

Cartoons make mermaids look all cute and adorable but, truth is, they're just jerks. Which was why Dave hunted them.

One of the reasons, anyway.

There was also the fact that Margaux broke his heart and dove back into the sea without a backward glance. Dave had taken his revenge on many merfolk since then, but never Margaux.

Until now.

She was surprisingly calm with a harpoon pointed at her heart.

"What do you have to say for yourself?" Dave demanded.

"You humans," she sneered, haughty as ever. "Stories make you sound all fun and exotic, but you're just jerks..."

Wondra Vanian is an American living in the United Kingdom with her Welsh husband and their army of fur babies. A writer first, Wondra is also an avid gamer, photographer, cinephile, and blogger. She has music in her blood, sleeps with the lights on, and has been known to dance naked in the moonlight. Wondra was a multiple Top-Ten finisher in the 2017 and 2018 Preditors and Editors Reader's Poll, including the Best Author category. Her story, "Halloween Night," was named a Notable Contender for the Bristol Short Story Prize in 2015.
Website: www.wondravanian.com

The Sea Maiden
by McKenzie Richardson

Her underwater home was decorated with the skulls of drowned sailors, phosphorescent algae adorning their empty spaces so they glowed like ghastly jack-o'-lanterns. She fingered a jewelled ring from her collected treasures on the table, rubbing at the dried blood that marred its surface.

Through the porthole of the shipwreck, the waters darkened momentarily before resuming their usual luminance. She peered out to see the receding shadow of a boat overhead. Glancing in the mirror, she picked a bit of meat from between her knife-edged teeth and smiled.

Then silently, she swam up to the unsuspecting boat, prepared to feast.

McKenzie Richardson lives in Milwaukee, WI. Her horror stories have been featured in various anthologies including Evil Lurks, Pandemic, and After: Undead Wars. She has also published a variety of poems and flash fiction pieces.
Facebook: mckenzielrichardson
Blog: www.craft-cycle.com

Call of the Siren
by Emma K. Leadley

"I ain't no witch!"

"Throw her overboard!"

The sailors grabbed the screaming cabin girl, binding her arms and legs. They threw her over the side and jeered as she disappeared downwards until just a few bubbles remained. Beneath the waves, Lizzie's lungs weighed like iron, and her vision faded. She was near dead when the mermaids approached. They kissed her on the mouth, breathing life back into her body.

"One of us," they chanted, untying her limbs.

Lizzie swam back to the ship and sang the most beautiful song, watching the sailors fling themselves to their deaths at her call.

Emma K. Leadley is a UK-based writer, creative geek, and devourer of words, images and ideas. She began writing both fiction and creative non-fiction as an outlet for her busy brain, and quickly realised scrawling words on a page is wired into her DNA.
Website: emmaleadley.co.uk
Twitter: @autoerraticism

His Very own Mermaid
by Carole de Monclin

He visited the sheltered cove almost every day, plunging below the surface with anticipation.

When the tide was just right, light streamed through and illuminated his love.

She looked even more beautiful than she had on land. The ocean had made her its own, transforming her delicate body.

And she belonged only to him.

Thinner chain bracelets should be gracing her ankles, but they were necessary to anchor her among the jagged rocks. Her hollow ribcage sheltered fish and octopuses. Sadly, some of her smaller bones had drifted away.

Even when she didn't, he'd known she belonged amid the waves.

Carole de Monclin *travels both the real world and imaginary ones. She's lived in France, Australia, and the USA; visited 25+ countries; and explored Mars, Ceres, and many distant planets. She writes to invite people on a journey. Her stories can be found in The Arcanist, The Deep Space Anthology, and every volume of the Dark Drabbles series.*
Website: CaroledeMonclin.com
Twitter: @CaroledeMonclin

Webbed

by Cassandra Angler

The sound of scraping against the side of the boat woke us, concerns of icebergs raced through our minds. We rushed to the bow and froze in awe. She stood over six feet, pointed fins at her side. The face was sunken and skeletal. We backed away, unsure. She hissed and spat green goo at our feet. It ate away the wood of the ship to its core; the wood dropping away like liquid fire. We scattered, and it chased, webbed feet shaking the ship with every step. Water filled the boat, most jumped overboard. I was the only survivor.

Cassandra Angler is a married mother of four who lives in the State of Ohio in the USA. When she isn't busy caring for her family, Cassandra works on her upcoming novel due out in November of 2020 titled Contaminated. Cassandra has three short story publications as well as several flash fiction and drabble publications.

The Cecaelias of Kepler 62f
by Vonnie Winslow Crist

Archie navigated the mini-sub through Kepler 62f's ocean. Usually, the exoplanetary research vessel was packed with team members arguing about evolution. But today, he was speeding to Outpost Two alone.

Without warning, a translucent alien flung herself onto the sub's windshield. Archie saw her lower half was tentacled, while her upper portion appeared humanoid.

The word Cecaelia came to mind, but before he could whisper the name of the mythological siren, others of her kind latched onto the windshield. They were all singing.

Enraptured by their voices, Archie closed his eyes and let his vessel drift to the ocean's floor.

Vonnie Winslow Crist is author of The Enchanted Dagger, Owl Light, The Greener Forest, Murder on Marawa Prime, and other award-winning books. Her fiction is included in "Amazing Stories," "Cast of Wonders," "Outposts of Beyond," Killing It Softly 2, Defending the Future - Dogs of War, Midnight Masquerade, Chaos of Hard Clay, and elsewhere. A cloverhand who has found so many four-leafed clovers she keeps them in jars, Vonnie strives to celebrate the power of myth in her writing.
Website: www.vonniewinslowcrist.com

The Call
by Eddie D. Moore

Brandon walked on a sandy beach under a majestic night sky. It was the perfect night for a romantic stroll. Unfortunately, his fiancé hadn't shown up yet. His phone chimed, and after checking the message, he sighed and shook his head.

A feminine voice gently called Brandon's name from the water, and when he searched the waves, he caught a glimpse of a naked woman between the swells.

"Who's there?"

"Come to me, my love. A night like this shouldn't be spent alone."

Brandon's eyes lost focus, and he followed the seductive call until a dozen hands pulled him under.

Eddie D. Moore travels hundreds of hours a year, and he fills that time by listening to audiobooks. When he isn't playing with his grandchildren, he writes his own stories. You can find a list of his publications on his blog or by visiting his Amazon Author Page. While you're there, be sure to pick up a copy of his mini-anthology Misfits & Oddities.
Website: eddiedmoore.wordpress.com
Amazon: amazon.com/author/eddiedmoore

Deep Blue Fear
by Thomas Sturgeon Jr.

I've always had a fear of being in this ocean; so full of deep water; creatures along with sharks and squid. My friends had wanted me to come along with them out on a cruise ship. I told them that I didn't want to go out into the ocean. I became angered with them when they jumped into the shark infested waters while I stayed onboard.

I had to face my fears. I saw my friends were in danger after I noticed a huge fin come out of the water.

Without warning, a huge snake had swallowed my friends whole.

Thomas Sturgeon Jr. began writing at 13 years old. He loves to read and spend time with his family and friends. He loves horror movies and fiction. He currently lives in Chatsworth, Georgia and wants more out of life. He's been published before in Weird Mask magazine and by Deadman's Tome. His short stories that were published were "The Dead City" and "Disturbed Valentine". He currently is at work on a Horror short story collection and he is loved by his family and friends. Despite being told by his teachers that he would never be published, he has proved them wrong.

Deep Dive
by Shelly Jarvis

I am an explorer. I'm seeing something no one else has.

Sometimes it helps when I think this; makes me braver. Today it does not.

It was easier when I was watching through the HOV's cameras. I could pretend I was somewhere else, safe. But staring out this porthole, seeing these things with my own eyes…

I shudder, unable to suppress the fear coursing through me. I pick up the radio again, but there's still no response. I need someone to hear me, a *person*.

The things gnashing against my ship—they hear me. But they are far from human.

Shelly Jarvis is a speculative fiction author from West Virginia, US. She found a life-long love of sci-fi and fantasy in the 3rd grade when she found Madeleine L'Engle's "A Wrinkle in Time." Shelly is an avid reader, a Whovian, the ideal viewer of dog rescue videos, and undoubtedly Ravenclaw. She currently has three YA sci-fi books available for purchase on Amazon. Website: www.ShellyJarvis.com

A Quizzers' Guide to Geography
by Hannah Retallick

Arctic: Smallest–The one that's also the coldest. Pretty pathetic, I know.

Southern: Small–The one that's sometimes known as the Antarctic Ocean. Also cold.

Indian: Medium–The one that's the warmest. Cocooned by Africa, Asia, and sunny Australia.

Atlantic: Big–The one that's sometimes called The Pond. Home of the mystic Bermuda Triangle.

Pacific: Bigger–The one that's known as the biggest. You might have to take another look.

World: Biggest–The one that's growing yearly, growing uncontrollably, while humans sleep. The one that ends us.

*Please refer to Note 13 at the back for further Oceans quiz trivia.

Hannah Retallick *is a twenty-six-year-old from Anglesey, North Wales. She was home educated and then studied with the Open University, graduating with a First-class honours degree, BA in Humanities with Creative Writing and Music, and is studying for an MA in Creative Writing. She was shortlisted in the Writing Awards at the Scottish Mental Health Arts Festival 2019, the Cambridge Short Story Prize, the Henshaw Short Story Competition June 2019, and the Bedford International Writing Competition 2019*
Website: *ihaveanideablog.wordpress.com*

The Prize
by Lynne Phillips

Julian donned his snorkel and mask, grabbed the net bag and dived.

Deeper and deeper he went, his eyes darting everywhere, seeking the prize that would make him rich.

The abalone clung tightly to the rock. Julian worked quickly to lever them off and fill his net. He smiled and kicked off, but something had hold of his ankle.

The giant squid held fast. Julian frantically tried to pull the suckers off, but the squid held firmer. It pulled him towards its cave. Out of breath, Julian let go of the net. His precious prize scattered on the ocean floor.

Lynne Phillips, a retired teacher, lives in the beautiful Northern Rivers Region of New South Wales Australia. Her stories, across all genres, have been published in anthologies and various online magazines. Her priority is spending time with her family. Her passions are reading, writing and keeping fit.

Way Downtown, NY
by Shawn M. Klimek

Captain Omar withdrew a bouquet of flowers from the ice cooler and began wiring them to a lead weight. Sweat dripped from his brow. "This heat," he complained.

"It's the humidity," Felix countered sagely.

"December wasn't always like this."

Ahead, waves broke against a rusting, ruined radio tower, jutting like a periscope leaning into a headwind.

"Shut engines, and moor us to that," Omar commanded. "Time to pay our respects."

"Here, sir? But we can still make New York by nightfall. I can already see the skyline."

"That's *New* New York ashore," Omar corrected. "New York is thirty fathoms down."

Shawn M. Klimek is an internationally best-selling short-story writer and poet, and author of Hungry Thing. More than 150 of his works have been published online or in such anthologies as BHP's Deep Space, Eerie Christmas, Bad Romance, Jibbernocky, and every book in the Dark Drabbles series.
Website: jotinthedark.blogspot.com
Facebook: shawnmklimekauthor

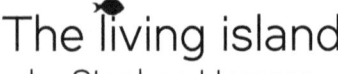

The living island
by Stephen Herczeg

I slept. My boat drifted peacefully, on a calm and still ocean, beneath a dark and moonless night. Safe I had assumed.

I was wrong.

Crunch. We struck solid ground. Staggering to the deck, I was thrown overboard, the boat lurching suddenly.

My breath burst out as I landed on solid ground.

Through blurry eyes, my boat was crushed and disappeared without trace.

I stood on a small barren island of some strange spongy rock.

As the morning sun beat down, a long, low moan erupted all around. The ground shifted beneath my feet.

The island moved.

It was alive.

Stephen Herczeg is an IT Geek based in Canberra Australia. He has been writing for over twenty years and has completed a couple of dodgy novels, sixteen feature length screenplays and numerous short stories and scripts. His horror work has featured in Sproutlings, Hells Bells, Below the Stairs, Trickster's Treats #1 and #2, Shades of Santa, Behind the Mask, Beyond the Infinite; The Body Horror Book, Anemone Enemy, Petrified Punks and Beginnings. He has also had numerous Sherlock Holmes stories published through the Belanger Books - Sherlock Holmes anthologies.
Amazon: amazon.com/-/e/B07916SQQS
Facebook: stephenherczegauthor

Fishing

by Gabriella Balcom

Aaron cast his line, watching it soar through the air, landing in the ocean with a plop.

Time passed and he got no bites, eventually giving up on fishing. Shucking his clothing down to his boxers, he dived off the boat, his body slicing through the water.

An enormous shark suddenly launched itself at Aaron, mouth gaping wide, revealing dozens of wicked teeth, and he shrieked.

It yanked him under, biting his leg. Searing agony shot through him, and he surfaced screaming.

The nightmare creature ripped away part of his chest. Blood bubbled from his lips, and everything went black.

Gabriella Balcom lives in Texas with her family, loves reading and writing, and thinks she was born with a book in her hands. She works in a mental health field, and writes fantasy, horror/thriller, romance, children's stories, and sci-fi. She likes travelling, music, good shows, photography, history, interesting tales, and animals. Gabriella says she's a sucker for a great story and loves forests, mountains, and back roads which might lead who knows where. She has a weakness for lasagne, garlic bread, tacos, cheese, and chocolate, but not necessarily in that order.
Facebook: GabriellaBalcom.lonestarauthor

New Treasures
by Liam Hogan

The beach had been closed since the storm.

Grim-faced police in protective clothing traipsed up the slipway, carrying tarpaulin-covered stretchers. Bodies of migrants, so went the rumour. A dilapidated fishing boat overloaded with those seeking a better life.

Emily snuck down anyway, in the dying light of the fifth day. Storms always brought new treasures, and she could no longer resist.

There wasn't much to see. She walked the waterline, picked up a shell. She recalled her grandfather, a beachcomber before her, telling her if you held it to your ear, you'd hear the ocean.

All Emily heard were screams.

Liam Hogan is a London based short story writer, the host of Liars' League, and a Ministry of Stories mentor. His story "Ana", appears in Best of British Science Fiction 2016 (NewCon Press) and his twisted fantasy collection, "Happy Ending Not Guaranteed", is published by Arachne Press.

The Show Must Go On
by Lyndsey Ellis-Holloway

Waves crashed against the shore, in time to the music inside her head, her movement as fluid and graceful as the tide itself.

Debris gathered by her feet. The dancer remained unperturbed, even when a cold, dead hand brushed against her bare leg.

Tears ran down her bloodstained face, leaving white tracks along her cheeks.

The sea was an unforgiving mistress, and it tore apart the cruise liner with ease. Ripping it asunder, as though it were paper not steel.

Mid-performance, she was thrown overboard, alongside her audience, into unforgiving waters.

Still, she danced amongst the waves for the dead.

Lyndsey Ellis-Holloway is a writer from Knaresborough, UK. She writes fantasy, sci-fi, horror and dystopian stories, focussing on compelling characters and layering in myth and legend at every opportunity. Her mind is somewhat dark and twisted, and she lives in perpetual hope of owning her own Dragon someday, but for now she writes about them to fill the void... and to stop her from murdering people who annoy her. When she's not writing she spends time with her husband, her dogs and her friends enjoying activities such as walking, movies, conventions and of course writing for fun as well! Website: theprose.com/LyndseyEH

The Dark Dive
by Rickey Rivers Jr.

Daniel came up from the dive and coughed.

"Tough time?" asked Andy, holding a handcrafted weapon.

"Yeah."

"Sorry, had to be night. See the chest?"

"Nah."

Andy scanned the ocean, looking for any semblance. "She's resting."

Daniel coughed again. A straight blackness hit the sand.

"You sick?" said Andy.

The blackness became solid and flopped around.

Andy pulled Daniel to his feet. "That's a bad sign."

The ocean began to vibrate and emit a low hum. Then she rose. Her tail illuminated by moonlight.

Daniel fell.

"Hey! What wrong? What happened down there?"

But Daniel couldn't breathe on land anymore.

Rickey Rivers Jr. *was born and raised in Alabama. He is a writer and cancer survivor. He has been previously published with Fabula Argentea, Cabinet of Heed, Back Patio Press, (among other publications).*
Website: storiesyoumightlike.wordpress.com.
Twitter: @storiesyoumight

When Oceanus Comes Calling
by Susanne Thomas

Tradition and promises could be stretched too far, Dana thought. The boat rocked violently, and she could hear the pots and pans clattering from their cabinets. The crashes and rumbles of them were just a part of the world around her. The salt of the sea assailed her nose and was cut by a stronger, rancid odour.

Dana knew what waited for her out on the deck of the boat. An unbreakable compact sealed her fate. She shuddered and wiped the tears from her cheeks before opening the upper hatch. It was time to become the bride of a Titan.

Susanne Thomas reads, writes, parents, and teaches from the windy west in Wyoming. She's an MFA graduate of the University of Arkansas at Monticello Creative Writing Program and she loves fantasy, science fiction, speculative fiction, poetry, children's books, science, coffee, and puns.
Website: www.themightierpenn.com

Sinking Ship
by Liz Feldman

The giant squid had been having a normal Tuesday up to this point. Swimming along, it now watched as a colossal cruise ship sank into the ocean depths. The squid caught up to a porthole and peered inside. A woman struggled, wrestling to open her cabin door against the rising water. With a final desperate heave, she pulled it open—and stared aghast at a single, roving tentacle as water gushed through a neighbouring porthole. The woman screamed and flailed, clawing her way backwards, thrashing about for some kind of protection. The tentacle followed and gently stroked her face.

Dinner.

Liz Feldman is a writer and speaker in the Virginia Beach, VA area. She won her first writing award in elementary school and has loved dreaming up characters ever since. She enjoys writing short stories and speculative fiction of all kinds, as well as academic nonfiction. When not writing, she works as a Kids Director and enjoys hiking with her husband, young son, and dog.

The Dare
by Jim Bates

"I dare you," Ronny said. "Bet you're afraid."

Ben rolled out of the two-man kayak and started swimming for shore. "Piece of cake," he said over his shoulder. "No sweat."

Only a quarter of a mile and the ocean was calm. Easy.

But he'd forgotten about the seaweed. Long tendrils grabbed his legs like slimy, grasping fingers, twisting around his calves, tightening the more he struggled until they began to pull him under. He panicked, taking in water.

"Here, I've got you," Ronny called, reaching for him.

Ben pushed his friend's tentacle like hands away. "No," he yelled, terrified. "Get away!"

Jim Bates lives in a small town twenty miles west of Minneapolis, Minnesota. His stories have appeared online in CafeLit, The Writers' Cafe Magazine, Cabinet of Heed, Paragraph Planet, Nailpolish Stories, Ariel Chart, Potato Soup Journal, Literary Yard, Spillwords (Dec, 2019, Author of the Month), The Drabble, The Academy of the Heart and Mind and World of Myth Magazine. In print publications: A Million Ways, Mused Literary Journal, Gleam Flash Fiction Anthology #2, the Portal Anthology and the Glamour Anthology by Clarendon House Publishing, The Best of CafeLit 8 by Chapeltown Publishing, the Nativity Anthology by Bridge House Publishing and Gold Dust Magazine.
Website: www.theviewfromlonglake.wordpress.com

Float

by Beth W. Patterson

"Why are they called floats if they stay at the bottom of the ocean?" The boy was inquisitive on the submarine tour of the underwater city once known as New Orleans.

The tour guide smiled. "They were once used for parades, not for the bottom of the sea. Only a few survived…" She trailed off as the passengers saw a gargantuan jester head detach itself and float upward toward the submarine. The grinning mouth split open, revealing a maw large enough to engulf the craft.

The craft gave a violent lurch, and water poured into the hull.

Beth W. Patterson was a full-time musician for over two decades before diving into the world of writing, a process she describes as "fleeing the circus to join the zoo". She is the author of the books Mongrels and Misfits, and The Wild Harmonic, and a contributing writer to twenty anthologies. Patterson has performed in eighteen countries, expanding her perspective as she goes. Her playing appears on over a hundred and sixty albums, soundtracks, videos, commercials, and voice-overs (including seven solo albums of her own). She lives in New Orleans, Louisiana with her husband Josh Paxton, jazz pianist extraordinaire.
Website: www.bethpattersonmusic.com
Facebook: bethodist

Rising Tide
by Raven Corinn Carluk

Cordelia stood at the research vessel's bow, waiting for the test to complete. The North Wind skirled around her, biting her face and tearing her clothes, but she remained steadfast.

Mankind's disregard for nature steadily undid Marduk's crime.

The human scientists knew the Arctic ice melted, shrinking by the day. They worried about the fresh water mixing with the salt and changing the currents.

Her machine dinged and Cordelia turned. As she read the results, the ancient priestess let a smile crawl across her face.

The mortals finally had something to worry about: the blood of Tiamat was finally free.

Raven Corinn Carluk writes dark fantasy, paranormal romance, and anything else that catches her interest. She's authored five novels, where she explores themes of love and acceptance. Her shorter pieces, usually from her darker side, can be found in Black Hare Press anthologies, at Detritus Online, and through Alban Lake Publishers.
Twitter: @ravencorinn
Website: www.ravencorinncarluk.com

An Ocean of Despair
by Sabetha Danes

Unbeknownst to the surface dwellers, leagues beneath the ocean, a blood curdling scream escapes a lone survivor. No one hears it, and the isolation is deafening. The current rips the scream from its owner's lips, dragging it deeper into the ocean. A single soul has awoken to nothingness in a once jubilant place. Crumpled on the floor, a hollow void overtakes naïve eyes. Pain from the sudden abandonment rampages through every thought, depositing seeds of despair. They take root and blossom into irate emotions, turns to revenge. In time happiness will be fought for, but in this single moment—disillusionment.

Sabetha Danes is an eccentric introvert located in Central Texas, in a Stars Hollow-esque small town. Her default language is sarcasm, and is fueled by coffee. As a lifelong bibliophile, she reads and edits all genres but specializes in fantasy and cozy mysteries. Her degree in interpersonal communication helps her over-analyze characters that are only found in stories. She spends her days with her daughter and dude walking trails and drinking coffee. Did we mention she enjoys a great cup of coffee?
Website: aconitecafe.com

Nightfall
by J. Scott Hill

There hadn't been a ship in decades, but I took the job watching the lighthouse. The old caretaker turned with a warning, "Night falls you hit that light. You hear? Only thing 'tween them and the ones you love is that there light."

I nodded nervously, looking out over the beach. I didn't believe the old man and his stories, but night was falling.

I waited, then switched on the light. The beach illuminated in a bright flash, and there I saw and heard the crawling horrors screaming. Sunken things before the dawn of humankind, slinking back to the deep.

J. Scott Hill is a sometimes writer, avid gamer and IT professional in his spare time. He lives with his wife and two furry kids in Columbia, MO. He once received a Silver Honorable Mention for a short story, The Black Grave, entered in the L. Ron Hubbard Writers of the Future contest.

Jelly Head
by Nicola Currie

When I jumped off the cliffs and hit the water below, I didn't expect to be here, beneath the surface, weeks later, trapped in an eddy, twirling, smashing from rock to rock. At least it doesn't hurt. Pain stopped with my heart, my breath.

It's annoying though, boring even, to feel my body break slowly apart as it is washing-machined with each ebb and surge.

I sigh with relief as the final crack to my head opens my skull like an oyster. The gel-like remains of my brain ooze away as I am released, death welcomed like a cool swim.

Nicola Currie is from Cambridge, UK where she works in educational publishing. She has published poetry in literary magazines, including Mslexia and Sarasvati, and short stories in various anthologies. She has also completed her first novel, which was longlisted for the Bath Children's Novel Award. Website: writeitandweep.home.blog

Slipping Away
by Thomas Baker

Eli's hands were wet, and he was losing his grip on the side of his small boat. The waves rocked the tiny vessel violently as dark circles swarmed the water below. He cried out as he tried with all of his might to pull himself back into the boat. He could feel his strength depleting with every attempted lunge. An intense tug, followed by sharp pain, caused his chest to tighten in panic as blood began to fill the water around him. Eli trembled as he fought back tears just before another powerful tug pulled him beneath the ocean's surface.

__Thomas Baker__ is a lover of all things horror with a heavy emphasis on zombies, paranormal and things of the slasher variety! He aims to keep his writing fast paced and fun. Thomas has several stories featured in different anthologies but he is best known for his co-written "Outbreak Series" with his good friend and writing partner Robert Wagner. The series has reached trilogy status! You can follow him on his 6K Press page on both Facebook and Twitter to stay up to date on the latest shenanigans that are afoot! Be warned, some parental advisory required!

Lost Beneath the Waves
by Stuart Conover

Liam had been diving for years.

However, his childhood joy had become an obsession.

It was said Captain Dermuta's ship had sunk nearby.

Below its decks, the greatest treasure to ever be lost.

Liam knew that finding it was as realistic as the curse on all that gold.

Yet here he was.

Thirty-nine and chasing down shipwrecks.

Sinking beneath the waves, he knew it was worth it.

Before him lay Dermuta's ship.

On its deck, the remains of a solitary figure.

The captain himself.

Liam swam to greet the pirate lord.

Only, he hadn't expected Dermuta to greet him back.

Stuart Conover is a father, husband, rescue dog owner, published author, blogger, journalist, horror enthusiast, comic book geek, science fiction junkie, and IT professional. With all of that to cram in daily, we have no idea if or when he sleeps or how he gets writing done! (We suspect it has to do with having evil clones.) Stuart is a Chicago native and runs the author resource Horror Tree.

Group(er) Think
by Sara L. Uckelman

Tib stood on the edge of the sea, watching the boats unloading their fish. The fisher grinned a gap-toothed grin as the grouper slid and tumbled over each other in shining, shimmering piles, watching Tib watching her. "Strange fish, they are," she said. "Did you know that they are born women and become men when they grow up?"

The hunger Tib felt for the fish had nothing to do with her stomach. She pushed her way through the boats, dived into the water, and swam and swam her way into the depths of the sea, until the groupers surrounded him.

Sara L. Uckelman is an assistant professor of logic and philosophy of language at Durham University by day and a writer of speculative fiction by night. Her short stories are published or forthcoming in Manawaker Studio Flash Fiction Podcast, Pilcrow & Dagger, Story Seed Vault, and The Martian Wave, and anthologies published by Exterus, Flame Tree Publishing, Hic Dragones, Jayhenge Publications, QueerSciFi, and WolfSinger Publications. She is also the co-founder of the reviews site SFFReviews.com.

Slime of the Ancient Mariner
by Beth W. Patterson

The currents had swept us closer to hell, and "a sea of bodies" was no metaphor. From the crow's nest, I watched in numb disbelief as the churning ocean curdled, revealing the millions of bodies of which it was composed.

Maelstroms of viscous reanimated, spinning and smashing into one another, thrashed in a grisly ecstasy, if corpses could feel frenzied joy.

Rising from the water was the gargantuan lord of undead whirlpools, drawing our ship nearer to our final, eternal fate. His skinless face, taut with muscles, drew back his lips into a hungry rictus. Hallowed be his name: Eddy.

Beth W. Patterson was a full-time musician for over two decades before diving into the world of writing, a process she describes as "fleeing the circus to join the zoo". She is the author of the books Mongrels and Misfits, and The Wild Harmonic, and a contributing writer to twenty anthologies. Patterson has performed in eighteen countries, expanding her perspective as she goes. Her playing appears on over a hundred and sixty albums, soundtracks, videos, commercials, and voice-overs (including seven solo albums of her own). She lives in New Orleans, Louisiana with her husband Josh Paxton, jazz pianist extraordinaire.
Website: www.bethpattersonmusic.com
Facebook: bethodist

Mother of Pearl
by Kelly Matsuura

Kaoru tucked her hair under her hood and adjusted the heavy package on her back.

Taking a deep breath, she dropped into the cold ocean.

She found 'Mother' quickly. No time to waste, she unwrapped her offering.

It was always a male torso—no head or limbs, but genitals intact. Kaoru didn't ask where they came from, but every month, she delivered Mother her favourite meal.

The monstrous oyster opened wide and swallowed the torso in one mouthful.

Duty done, Kaoru returned home. She'd be back with her *Ama* sisters to collect the rarest, most valuable pearls found in Japan.

Kelly Matsuura writes diverse YA, fantasy, and literary fiction. She is the Creator of The Insignia Series' anthologies (Asian fantasy themed) and has had stories published with Ink & Locket Press, A Murder of Storytellers, Crushing Hearts & Black Butterfly, and many more. Kelly lives in Nagoya, Japan with her geeky husband. She loves traveling, knitting, cooking, and of course, reading.
Website: www.blackwingsandwhitepaper.com

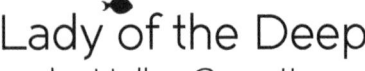

Lady of the Deep
by Holley Cornetto

Waves surged and spilled over the deck. The old wood creaked and moaned, begging mercy from the storm. The gale had blown in from nowhere. The ship rocked perilously over the unforgiving deep. Legend was true; she was cursed.

"Go, cut her loose!" the captain commanded.

"Sir?"

"Now!"

The sailor found the woman with the fishtail in the ship's hold. He cut the bonds and carried her above deck.

"Toss her back!"

When the mermaid hit the water, the storm cleared. In the quiet of the storm's aftermath, he thought he heard a woman's voice, singing, calling him to sea.

Holley Cornetto was born and raised in Alabama, but now lives in New Jersey. To indulge her love of books and stories, she became a librarian. She is also a writer, because the only thing better than being surrounded by stories is to create them herself.
Twitter: @HLCornetto

The Box Beside the Bed
by Sara L. Uckelman

Charlie kept an ocean in the box beside his bed. At night, he'd open the box and whisper in his secrets to the gently lapping waves. Sometimes the weather was rough, and the water would splash over the edge onto his pillow. But by morning, the droplets would be dry, leaving only salt behind.

Some nights the secrets were small, sometimes they were big. As he grew older, and he put more of his secrets in, the ocean grew bigger and he had to open the box wider and wider, until one day it swelled out and washed him away.

Sara L. Uckelman is an assistant professor of logic and philosophy of language at Durham University by day and a writer of speculative fiction by night. Her short stories are published or forthcoming in Manawaker Studio Flash Fiction Podcast, Pilcrow & Dagger, Story Seed Vault, and The Martian Wave, and anthologies published by Exterus, Flame Tree Publishing, Hic Dragones, Jayhenge Publications, QueerSciFi, and WolfSinger Publications. She is also the co-founder of the reviews site SFFReviews.com.

Solitude & Fate

by Sabetha Danes

Bump…

I know my fate. He waits, lackadaisical yet calculated. The turbulent ocean sealed my solitude days ago. With no hope for rescue, I will greet death like an old friend…

Bump…

Jolted awake from poetic delusions, I can't recall my purpose. One last bargain attempt—no answer. Will I be remembered?

Bump…

The rhythmic sway of the boat soothes my anxious nerves and lulls me into a false comfort. Death draws closer, awakening me each time I slip into sleep from dehydration.

Splash.

Sharp teeth puncture tender flesh, pulling me down to my watery grave. Don't forget me…

Sabetha Danes is an eccentric introvert located in Central Texas, in a Stars Hollow-esque small town. Her default language is sarcasm, and is fueled by coffee. As a lifelong bibliophile, she reads and edits all genres but specializes in fantasy and cozy mysteries. Her degree in interpersonal communication helps her over-analyze characters that are only found in stories. She spends her days with her daughter and dude walking trails and drinking coffee. Did we mention she enjoys a great cup of coffee?

Website: aconitecafe.com

383

Sunk
by Dawn DeBraal

The yellow life raft bobbed in the water. Rafe and Tom had been afloat since their boat capsized two weeks ago. They sat in an inch of water—uncomfortable, but the only freshwater anywhere, so they withstood the discomfort. As sharks circled the raft, things were looking bleak. Rafe took out his knife, suddenly cutting Tom's arm.

"What did you do that for?" Tom shouted.

"Sharks, I'm saving myself. Sorry," Rafe said. The angered Tom then lifted his knife and pierced the raft, sinking it with an escaping rush of air. While underwater, the sought-after rescue ship passed over them.

Dawn DeBraal lives in rural Wisconsin with her husband Red, two rat terriers, and a cat. She has discovered that her love of telling a good story can be written. Published stories with Palm-sized press, Spillwords, Mercurial Stories, Potato Soup Journal, Edify Fiction, Zimbell House Publishing, Clarendon House Publishing, Blood Song Books, Black Hare Press, Fantasia Divinity, Cafelit, Reanimated Writers, Guilty Pleasures, Unholy Trinity, The World of Myth, Dastaan World, Vamp Cat, Runcible Spoon, Dark Christmas, Siren's Call, Iron Horse Publishing, Falling Star Magazine 2019 Pushcart Nominee.
Amazon: amazon.com/Dawn-DeBraal/e/B07STL8DLX

A Discovery at Sea
by Ronnie Scissom

"Captain Draughn, the beast is alive," a rain soaked first mate says.

The captain stares out into the darkness through the starboard window. A flash of lightning exposes giant tentacles reaching out of the waves near the ship.

"Save as many as you can," the weary captain says.

"Yes, Captain," the first mate replies.

The captain hits the intercom switch on the control panel.

"Passengers and staff of the *Discovery*. May I have your attention. The object we struck is alive. Another attack is imminent. Please take emergency precautions now. May God be with us."

The ship is struck again.

Ronnie Scissom hails from Gruetli-Laager. When not working or writing, he likes to explore the beauty of the Cumberland Plateau. He dabbles in acting and has had background roles in several hit television series and motion pictures.

The Sinking of Port Royal
by Paul Benkendorfer

The streets of Port Royal were a bustle; brimming with spices, gold, harlots and ale. Just another day in paradise.

The world shook. Brick buildings rose and fell. The townsfolk collapsed to their knees. Solid ground turned to bubbling sludge; cobblestone streets sank beneath ooze. Some poor unfortunate souls were dragged in as well. Most remained only half buried in the quicksand.

The quaking gave way to the sound of roaring thunder. A tsunami, stretching to the heavens, came barrelling down, consuming Port Royal: its buildings, its inhabitants, and all its treasures. Dragging all to the bottom of the sea.

Paul Benkendorfer is an English and history teacher from Scottsdale Arizona who mainly writes historical fiction, poetry, non-fiction. He is currently working on his novel A Bridge Outside of Limerick based on the events of his great-grandfather who fought in the Irish Revolution of 1916. Paul has nearly 15 years experience working with at-risk youth and children with special needs and continues to primarily work with them to this day. In 2014 Paul received a Bachelors in Creative Writing from the University of Arizona and is currently process of obtaining his Masters in Teaching Writing from Johns Hopkins University.
Twitter: @PBenkendorfer

A Watery Collision Course
by John H. Dromey

During their frequent holidays on the shore of the Pacific Ocean, Tommy's mum told him to stay in the shallows where he'd be safe from great white sharks.

In her own way, Mother Nature encouraged healthy whales to stay out of the shallows so they would not become dehydrated while beached or, worse yet, create a publicity nightmare by accidently squashing a youngster looking for seashells.

The beneficial effects of both those powerful well-intentioned maternal instincts were wiped out in an instant by a thoughtless fifty-seven-foot-high tidal wave.

Nobody tells a tsunami what to do. They go their own way.

John H. Dromey was born in northeast Missouri, USA. He enjoys reading—mysteries in particular—and writing in a variety of genres. In addition to contributing to the Black Hare Press series of Dark Drabbles anthologies, he's had short fiction published in Alfred Hitchcock's Mystery Magazine, Martian Magazine, Mystery Weekly, Stupefying Stories Showcase, Thriller Magazine, Unfit Magazine, and elsewhere, as well as in numerous anthologies, including Chilling Horror Short Stories (Flame Tree Publishing, 2015).

The Hamptons Are Nice
by Nikki DeKeuster

The machine whirred to life, sending rumbles across the black expanse of ocean.

A severed foot danced between the twirling blades of the shredder tethered to the rear of the fisherman's ship. Sprays of fine red mist settled over a frenzy of churning grey fins.

Legs, arms, and a swollen, eyeless human head disappeared into the grinder, taking their places at the fathomless dinner table.

In life, the bastard had fancied himself a shark among minnows. In death, he'd become part of them.

The fisherman untethered the shredder, kicking it into the sea, and turned to chart a new course.

Nikki DeKeuster devours souls. She spits them onto her glowing screen and toys with their lives for your amusement. Reading this story makes you an accomplice to their suffering. You're welcome. A storyteller with decades of experience crafting tales with her friends, she's bound some of them to bring into the wider world. The stories, not her friends. She enjoys throwing stones into Lake Michigan with her daughter and keeping her husband up past his bedtime with her ramblings. The first novel in her horror series will claw its way out of the earth in 2020.
Website: NJDeKeuster.com

Christ of the Abyss
by Vonnie Winslow Crist

When Claire insisted they snorkel on the seaward side of Key Largo Dry Rocks to view Christ of the Abyss, Bob reluctantly agreed. She was the dive-enthusiast. He explored the oceans to please her.

As they swam around the site, Claire pointed at corals, snappers, grunts, and groupers.

Bob's eyes were locked on rays swimming like wide-winged angels around the figure of Christ. Third statue from Guido Galletti's mould, Christ's head was tilted back and his arms reached up.

Enthralled, Bob failed to notice a nurse shark until it sank teeth and his blood floated heavenward like a scarlet prayer.

Vonnie Winslow Crist is author of The Enchanted Dagger, Owl Light, The Greener Forest, Murder on Marawa Prime, and other award-winning books. Her fiction is included in "Amazing Stories," "Cast of Wonders," "Outposts of Beyond," Killing It Softly 2, Defending the Future - Dogs of War, Midnight Masquerade, Chaos of Hard Clay, and elsewhere. A cloverhand who has found so many four-leafed clovers she keeps them in jars, Vonnie strives to celebrate the power of myth in her writing.
Website: www.vonniewinslowcrist.com

The Custom of the Sea
by R.A. Goli

Sweat streamed down Gunter's face as he waited. Shipwrecked for weeks with no sign of rescue. Men were starving, but none dead yet. The captain had to make the decision; it was his burden alone. One to save many.

The captain walked the line of men, closed fist presented as sailors pulled straw after straw. A flood of relief washed over Gunter as the man beside him pulled the short straw. The captain held his hand towards him, and Gunter's heart dropped to the pit of his stomach.

The second shortest straw. Gunter would act as butcher for the sacrifice.

R.A. Goli is an Australian writer of horror, fantasy, and speculative short stories. In addition to writing, her interests include reading, gaming, the occasional walk, and annoying her dog, two cats, and husband. You can check out her numerous publications including her fantasy novella, The Eighth Dwarf, and her collection of short stories, Unfettered on her website and sign up to her newsletter for free short stories, updates and other fun stuff.
Website: ragoliauthor.wordpress.com/
Facebook: RAGoliAuthor

Grendel's Grottoes
by John A. McColley

"Grendel's Grottoes?" she asked.

"Nobody really knows where Grendel and his mother lived. It's just what they're called. It's just words." The innkeeper stoked the fireplace to fight back the storm. The wind rose again, screeching through the roof tiles, backed by a soul-shuddering wail.

"It's just words," she repeated to herself.

"The howling is just the wind. Don't you have weather where you come from?"

"Of course, just words. Wind." Despite herself, she peered out into the dark. The clouds broke. Moonlight ignited the surf far below. A figure, there. On that rock. A giant man with one arm.

John A. McColley writes from the woods of New Hampshire, caught between millennia and a thousand shades and hues of reality. He's accompanied by his wonderfully creative wife, three small children, three cats, and apparently this cricket. Despite all challenges to his writing time, he's turned out four novels in various stages of repair, published a few dozen SFFH short stories, and become an associate member of the SFWA
Twitter: @JohnAMcColley
Patreon: www.patreon.com/JohnAMcColley

Last Call of the Siren
by Leedine Lah

I know you're thirsty—drink.

Swelling, sloshing, the temptation alluring,

waves that caress the tongue.

How does my undulating foam frighten?

Drop your heavy anchor and dive down into the depths.

There is quiet here, immersed back into the womb.

Float, suspended in deliverance.

You've wrung yourself dry, your soul parched,

desiccated by life.

I can quiet the noise, still that pounding heart of yours.

I'm anaesthesia for the disdain, respite from the self-righteous.

Don't let the briny taste sway you, I'm liquid and cool.

Fill your belly, fill your lungs,

I won't spit you back out into the world.

Leedine Lah lives a nomadic life having sold all her worldly possessions to roam the planet in search of experiences. "Home-free" since 2017, Leedine is currently in Toronto, Ontario, Canada as she finishes her first novel. Previous careers in music, acting, and medicine provide much fodder for her tales.
Instagram: ecstatictraveller

Shrine of Apophis
by P.C. Darkcliff

The archaeologist moored her powerboat by a barren islet, waded ashore, then entered a ruined shrine. She gasped when her flashlight lit fading frescoes of the scaly body of Apophis, the Egyptian snake-god of chaos.

Through puddles of seawater, she crossed the prayer room.

Behind the altar, a gurgle came from a blowhole that connected the shrine with the sea. A salty geyser drenched her face. She screamed when a giant snake poked its head out of the blowhole.

A tidal wave swept over the islet as she ran to the exit. Weeks later, the empty powerboat reached mainland Egypt.

P.C. Darkcliff is the author of two novels, Deception of the Damned and The Priest of Orpagus. In September 2020, he's going to launch Celts and the Mad Goddess, the first installment of The Deathless Chronicle.
Social Media: plu.us/p.c.darkcliff
Reader List: mailchi.mp/c5550d315607/pcdarkcliff

Unabashed Self-Promotion
by Shawn M. Klimek

"Does this mean I'm first mate now?"

Captain Donner regarded her second mate with a disapproving scowl. Leach was the senior most sailor aboard, and she looked it. Decades of exposure to the sun, cold and briny wind had given her face the look of old driftwood. She might have been promoted far sooner if not for her criminal record. "McKay's body isn't even cold yet, you heartless crab," the captain said at last. "Grab her legs and help me toss her over. Once she's away, we can discuss your future."

As they heaved, Leach decided to simply become captain.

Shawn M. Klimek is an internationally best-selling short-story writer and poet, and author of Hungry Thing. More than 150 of his works have been published online or in such anthologies as BHP's Deep Space, Eerie Christmas, Bad Romance, Jibbernocky, and every book in the Dark Drabbles series.
Website: jotinthedark.blogspot.com
Facebook: shawnmklimekauthor

The Monster
by Jim Bates

Stay away from the Great Pacific Garbage Patch. It's south of Guam and roughly three times the size of France. It's bounded by an enormous spinning gyre of ocean currents that pull sea trash to the centre creating an immense garbage vortex. That's just fine for the monster that lives there. Its hulking mass grows more immense every day as it feeds on the refuge of humanity, mostly plastic. One wonders what will happen when it has eaten its fill and ventures out into the greater ocean. If it develops a taste for cruise ships, things could get ugly. Fast.

Jim Bates lives in a small town twenty miles west of Minneapolis, Minnesota. His stories have appeared online in CafeLit, The Writers' Cafe Magazine, Cabinet of Heed, Paragraph Planet, Nailpolish Stories, Ariel Chart, Potato Soup Journal, Literary Yard, Spillwords (Dec, 2019, Author of the Month), The Drabble, The Academy of the Heart and Mind and World of Myth Magazine. In print publications: A Million Ways, Mused Literary Journal, Gleam Flash Fiction Anthology #2, the Portal Anthology and the Glamour Anthology by Clarendon House Publishing, The Best of CafeLit 8 by Chapeltown Publishing, the Nativity Anthology by Bridge House Publishing and Gold Dust Magazine.
Website: www.theviewfromlonglake.wordpress.com

Dragon Treasure
by Cecelia Hopkins-Drewer

We didn't know the treasure was cursed. We loaded the chest onto the boat and set sail for the homelands. A few knots out to sea, the sailor on watch spotted something flying after us. A speck in the sky at first, it grew and grew.

A gigantic dragon had been disturbed and was being drawn ever onwards by that cursed gold. We tried to outrun the beast. Futile!

The creature opened its mouth and huffed, breathing flame all over the boat. The cloth sails caught on fire. The second puff ignited the deck.

We threw ourselves into the water.

Cecelia Hopkins-Drewer lives in Adelaide, South Australia. She has written a Masters paper on H.P. Lovecraft, and her weird poetry has been published in THE MENTOR (edited by Ron Clarke), and SPECTRAL REALMS (edited by S.T. Joshi). Her novels include a teenage vampire series commencing with MYSTIC EVERMORE. Short stories have been published in WORLDS, ANGELS & MONSTERS, BEYOND, STORMING AREA 51, and UNRAVEL. (Dark Drabbles anthologies edited by Dean Kershaw).
Amazon: amazon.com/Cecelia-Hopkins-Drewer/e/B071G968NM
Website: chopkin39.wixsite.com/website

The Pull
by Jennifer Hatfield

While scuba diving, Bethany discovered coral in the brightest rainbow of colours. Awed by its beauty, she lingered a little longer than she should've.

Something slimy seized her ankles, pulling her to a depth she was unprepared for. She struggled to break free, while being dragged through a cave and released.

Surrounded by darkness, and gem-like sparkles above her, she swam, frantic to find a way out, until exhaustion took over.

Pulling herself onto a ledge, her heart sank seeing piles of bones. When a human skull flew out of the water beside Bethany, her screams echoed throughout her grave.

Jennifer Hatfield *spent a large portion of her life being a dedicated mother and wife. She managed her epilepsy diagnosis, and handled the loss of her husband. Grateful to find comfort in the ability to write in an effort to express her feelings, thoughts, and struggles. She's published 5 poems.*

Ocean Eyes
by Zoey Xolton

Sun-baked, lacerated and wind-burned, the sailor lay sprawled atop the floating debris, his body wracked with endless pain. Long blonde hair matted with salt, parched lips cracked and bleeding—he could no longer trust his sea-blind vision.

From the gently lapping waves, eyes like the ocean regarded him thoughtfully.

"Are you here to end my suffering?" he asked, raising his head from the wooden boards, a heart-rending note of hope in his voice.

"Would you like that?"

"Very much."

A flash of silver fins and they were face to face.

"Kiss me," she said, her eyes mesmerising, "and know peace."

Zoey Xolton is an Australian Speculative Fiction writer, primarily of Dark Fantasy, Paranormal Romance and Horror. She is also a proud mother of two and is married to her soul mate. Outside of her family, writing is her greatest passion. She is especially fond of short fiction and is working on releasing her own themed collections in future.
Website: www.zoeyxolton.com

Sargasso Sea
by N.M. Brown

Legend states to never, under any circumstances, be on the Sargasso Sea under a full moon.

Some things sadly can't be helped though, can they? Brody Pierce found himself on that very same sea on such a night.

He started to feel effects as the moon reached its apex in the sky. The skin from his limbs sloughed off like the wisps of a dandelion's fluff. His hair receded from his scalp, taking all of the flesh with it.

But Brody didn't die, not even close. He remained a skeletal figure, destined to torment and float forever on the sea.

*Since **N.M. Brown** made her first post to a popular Internet forum, she's taken the horror community by storm. Her ability to create, terrify, and drive home her stories is insurmountable. N.M. Brown's published works can be found in multiple anthologies for all to read, but be forewarned, if you do... you may want to call your therapist after, her stories are terrifying, disturbing and devilishly unsettling. She is not only a fright visually, but also has a creepy tentacle in horror podcasting as well. Sinister Sweetheart writes, voice acts and is the media director of the Scarecrow Tales podcast.*
Website: Sinistersweetheart.wixsite.com/sinistersweetheart
Facebook: NMBrownStories

The Fish Don't Sing
by Jesse Highsmith

"Where's the coke?" Jimmy Scantalone asked, pulling the remainder of the heavy line into the boat. "There's just an anchor at the end of this."

"This is not that kind of *drop*," Dom said as he grabbed his accomplice from the back. "This line's for *you*."

Just then, Jimmy's face slammed into the railing he was leaning over. *Bam!* Using hair like a handle, Dom forced Scantalone's head over the shimmering salt water and held it there.

"We know you snitched."

Jimmy's faint cry became gurgling as a knife's searing kiss poured his throat's contents toward his wavering reflection below.

Jesse Highsmith is an adventurous wordsmith, musician, podcast enthusiast, and internet jokester from Central Florida, U.S. His specialty is short form flash fiction written within the confines of a large pesticide truck. However, he is currently writing his first novel, an otherworldly dive into death, acceptance, sacrifice, and redemption. He is also hard at work on his first foray into children's books with former Infectious Magazine editor Sami Marshall, a project due to be completed very soon. They live in a rural countryside with his son Logan, dog Snowy, and a shadow-chasing cat dubbed Sir Liam Frederick, Duke of Cuteness.

A Deeper Shade of Blues
by Shawn M. Klimek

In the final chapter of "50 Shades of Blue," the novel's heroine watched her tears fall into the ocean before leaping dramatically to her death at sunset. Suicidally inspired, Evelynn Dorsey booked the same cruise. As the sky dimmed on the fateful evening, however, a lingering passenger spoiled her solitude. Frustrated, Evelynn approached.

"Could I be alone, please?" she begged. "This is my final sunset."

The stranger's eyes lit up. "I loved that quote," she said, whipping her own copy of the novel. "Suddenly, I don't feel so alone."

"In that case, can I give you a boost?" asked Evelynn.

*Shawn M. Klimek is an internationally best-selling short-story writer and poet, and author of Hungry Thing. More than 150 of his works have been published online or in such anthologies as BHP's Deep Space, Eerie Christmas, Bad Romance, Jibbernocky, and every book in the Dark Drabbles series.
Website: jotinthedark.blogspot.com
Facebook: shawnmklimekauthor*

A Shocking Development
by John H. Dromey

An inquest was held following the loss of three crewmembers in an ill-fated dive on the wreck of a Spanish galleon.

The captain was a no-show.

The jury foreman questioned the first mate.

"The captain's log shows lined-out names of the sailors lost at sea and indicates a cause of death. The first remark—*shark*—is self-explanatory. The second—*bends*—I take to mean the diver returned to the surface without properly decompressing."

"That's correct."

"I'm puzzled by the third explanation—*depth charge*. Did you encounter unexploded ordnance from World War II?"

"No, sir. Jenkins was attacked by electric eels."

John H. Dromey was born in northeast Missouri, USA. He enjoys reading—mysteries in particular—and writing in a variety of genres. In addition to contributing to the Black Hare Press series of Dark Drabbles anthologies, he's had short fiction published in Alfred Hitchcock's Mystery Magazine, Martian Magazine, Mystery Weekly, Stupefying Stories Showcase, Thriller Magazine, Unfit Magazine, and elsewhere, as well as in numerous anthologies, including Chilling Horror Short Stories (Flame Tree Publishing, 2015).

Captain Dancing Dan
by J.B. Wocoski

Captain Dancing Dan, in every port of call, lured many a man aboard his pirate ship. He swore they would set sail over the seven seas to do as they pleased.

He did not promise his crew heaven, instead, lots of treasure with loads of fun and a fair amount of rum. He bragged about how smart he was and all the raping and pillaging they would do with impunity.

Dancing Dan broke the code and stole their treasure. When found, Dan hung around. After a quick drop, he did a mid-air jig dancing from the end of a jib.

J.B. Wocoski is the author and narrator of the shortstorypodcast.com with three flash fiction short story books published in the last three years. He is currently working on book 4 "Short Story Podcast 2019." He writes mostly science fiction, fantasy, and horror stories. He won the 2016 Little Tokyo Short Story Writing Contest with his short story "The Last Master of Go"
Website: shortstorypodcast.com

The Pyre
by Daniel J. Brown

The king's pyre glided across the moonlit sea, leaving a shimmering reflection in its wake. Hundreds arrived to see off the monarch, and the masses sang a song of morning as the vessel drifted further and further away. The king's family clasped hands and offered prayers to their gods for safe passage into the afterlife. But far too soon, it was time.

The king's son waded knee deep into the frigid water, solemnly drew his bow, lit an arrow, and fired true at the pyre. It was soon ablaze, and the roar of the inferno drowned out the king's screams.

Daniel J. Brown is a graduate of Furman University in Greenville, South Carolina. He currently resides in Alexandria, Virginia with his wife Stephanie. When not reading or writing, Daniel enjoys boxing, chess, video games, and theatre.

For the Love of Money and Girls

by J.W. Garrett

The sun's rays beat down on him. Even in the morning it was hot as hell. He waited for the lifeguard to count down his certification test. After eight weeks, he was ready. A quarter mile swim separated him from the money and girls; his with the lifeguarding job after passing his swim test.

Ready. Set. Go!

Instructions streamed in his head as he beat out a rhythm with his arms and feet. Breathe. Repeat. Past the breaking waves to smoother water.

A burn seared his foot, his arm, his face.

Jellyfish…

His throat swelled.

Pass on girls, money.

Air!

J.W. Garrett *has been writing in one form or another since she was a teenager. She currently lives in Florida with her family but loves the mountains of Virginia where she was born. Her writings include YA fantasy as well as short stories. Since completing Remeon's Quest-Earth Year 1930, the prequel in her YA fantasy series, Realms of Chaos, she has been hard at work on the next in the series, scheduled to release August 2020. When she's not hanging out with her characters, her favourite activities are reading, running and spending time with family.*

Website: www.jwgarrett.com
BHC Press: www.bhcpress.com/Author_JW_Garrett.html

My Sister, the Ocean
by Kaitlyn Arnett

Frigid water, cold enough to *burn*, was all that Maren knew. Her cries were lost, echoes of nothing amongst the water rushing past her body. She wanted to *scream*, to rage against those who had wronged her, those who tossed her aside because of superstition.

The sea wrapped her in its charge, and slowly, her dying form began to change.

Air drained from her lungs, replaced with saltwater as she was reborn. Scales replaced her skin, and she smiled.

The ocean was her sister, Maren knew that now.

Swim, it whispered, and so she did, hunting those who drowned her.

Kaitlyn Arnett is a teen author who has been writing for five years. She focuses on the fantasy and thriller genres, specifically drabbles and short stories.

Hungry for Love
by Rich Rurshell

The muscles in his back rippled as he rowed towards me. I could see when he was stood on the cliff that he was a strong, handsome man.

I sang louder and he rowed harder. Faster. With renewed purpose.

As his boat splintered on the rocks where I sat, he turned and looked me in the eyes. He climbed out of the sinking boat towards me. He kissed my neck as I sang, unconcerned, with my tail between his legs. Unconcerned as my teeth sank into his throat. Totally enthralled as I dragged him under the waves to his demise.

Rich Rurshell is a short story writer from Suffolk, England. Rich writes Horror, Sci-Fi, and Fantasy, and his stories can be found in various short story anthologies and magazines. Most recently, his story "Subject: Galilee" was published in World War Four from Zombie Pirate Publishing, and "Life Choices" was published in Salty Tales from Stormy Island Publishing. When Rich is not writing stories, he likes to write and perform music.
Facebook: richrurshellauthor

Isn't the Water Lovely!
by Hannah Retallick

It really is, my love.

Yes, a little longer, but I don't want you getting tired. And the reservation's at 7. And you need to remember your medication.

Grown man? I'll be the judge of that.

Seventy years isn't enough for most men and certainly isn't for you.

Silly boy.

Let go, my love, people are starting to stare!

I care.

Oh, fine. Hehe. Get away with you now.

Don't go out too far, please.

Fine, have it your way. Mind the wave!

Silly boy.

What are you doing?

My love, please don't mess around, you're scaring me.

John?

John!

Hannah Retallick is a twenty-six-year-old from Anglesey, North Wales. She was home educated and then studied with the Open University, graduating with a First-class honours degree, BA in Humanities with Creative Writing and Music, and is studying for an MA in Creative Writing. She is working on her second novel and writes short stories and a blog. She was shortlisted in the Writing Awards at the Scottish Mental Health Arts Festival 2019, the Cambridge Short Story Prize, and the Henshaw Short Story Competition June 2019.
Website: *ihaveanideablog.wordpress.com*

Vacation Dreams
by A.R. Dean

The Hawaiian vacation is a dream come true. I lay back on the warm sand, the sun bursting over blue water. My children giggle as the waves crash at their feet.

My daughter, Arya, comes running up. "Mommy, why is the water red?"

"Oceans are blue," I tell her, not looking up from my book.

"Not anymore."

I glance up to see the crimson waves. My son is screaming hysterically at the edge. I drop my book and rush towards him, pulling him into my arms. "Where's your father?" I ask him as he points out to the red spot.

A.R. Dean is a dark and twisted soul. Dean has spent their whole life spreading fear with the tales from their head. Best known for stories that terrify and show the evilest side of human nature. So, look for Dean haunting your local cemetery or under your bed, because they're here to spread the fear. Turn off your lights and enjoy a scare. Dean is being published in Black Hare Press's Beyond and Unravel Anthologies. Keep a lookout for more stories.
Facebook: A.R. Dean Author & Ghoul

The Same Deep Water as You
by Antonia Rachel Ward

We ran down to the water's edge, laughing, hand in hand. Night swimming. It was your idea; I took some persuading.

"Why not?" you said. "Nobody's looking."

So I followed you. Trusted you. But the water was cold as ice. When I tried to turn back, you gripped my arm tighter, pulling me in until the ocean was up to my knees. My thighs. My waist. You wrapped your arms around me like a lover, dragging me under. A watery kiss filled my mouth, forcing itself into my lungs.

The last thing I saw was the darkness in your eyes.

Antonia Rachel Ward is a writer of Gothic, horror, and futuristic fiction based in Cambridgeshire, UK. She holds an MA in English Literature with a specialism in Eighteenth-Century Gothic, and is currently working on her first novel.

Day Jobs
by Shelly Jarvis

I sidle up to my spot, stretching until my neck gives a satisfying pop. I nod to the girl beside me, hoping she doesn't greet me. I'm not a morning siren and prefer not to get chatty before sunrise.

But of course, she *must* talk to me, because my voice makes me a local celebrity. "Eglimornae, how's it going?"

I shrug, "Eh, you know, same ocean, different sailors."

I turn to the sea before she can say anything else, letting out a sweet song. In the distance, a ship turns our way. I smile for real, fangs ready for flesh.

Shelly Jarvis is a speculative fiction author from West Virginia, US. She found a life-long love of sci-fi and fantasy in the 3rd grade when she found Madeleine L'Engle's "A Wrinkle in Time." Shelly is an avid reader, a Whovian, the ideal viewer of dog rescue videos, and undoubtedly Ravenclaw. She currently has three YA sci-fi books available for purchase on Amazon. Website: www.ShellyJarvis.com

Cold Shower
by V.A. Vazquez

She cranked the faucet hard to the left and took a step backwards, reaching for the shampoo. But her foot didn't settle on the acrylic floor. It plunged down into nothingness and took the rest of her along with it. Ice-needles punctured her lungs as she sank into the arctic breathing hole that had opened up in her shower.

She struggled to swim upwards, the fluorescent light trembling just above the water's surface, her mother's knocking on the bathroom door muffled. Something wrapped around her ankle—hard and brittle, like keratin—and tugged her down into the bottomless black water.

V.A. Vazquez writes urban fantasy and paranormal romance. She currently lives in Glasgow, Scotland with her husband and small doggo.
Website: www.vavazquez.com

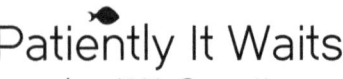

Patiently It Waits
by J.W. Garrett

Pieces of the gigantic glacier had been falling back into the ocean for decades. Now larger chunks were returning to the sea. The material encapsulated during the last ice age predated humanity.

Bones of animals long extinct escaped from their icy graves. With them, a prehistoric virus never exposed to mankind trickled through the water, searching for its next host.

Next victim.

Among others, fish, whales, birds, sea lions and clams ingested the pathogen. Stored now, it lurked, mutating, while it waited for more suitable, complex organisms to attack.

Defenceless against its unknown wrath, death for the people was certain.

J.W. Garrett has been writing in one form or another since she was a teenager. She currently lives in Florida with her family but loves the mountains of Virginia where she was born. Her writings include YA fantasy as well as short stories. Since completing Remeon's Quest-Earth Year 1930, the prequel in her YA fantasy series, Realms of Chaos, she has been hard at work on the next in the series, scheduled to release August 2020. When she's not hanging out with her characters, her favourite activities are reading, running and spending time with family.

Website: www.jwgarrett.com

BHC Press: www.bhcpress.com/Author_JW_Garrett.html

The Undertow
by Jim Bates

I watched as the guy and his girlfriend stopped walking along the shore and started yelling at each other. It was like the undertow was waiting for them. She threw up her hands and stormed into the raging surf, kicking at the waves until she lost her footing. It was then the undertow took hold and dragged her out to sea. The guy swam after but floundered close to where she struggled and he was swept past, their arms outstretched and grasping, their fingertips nearly touching. Then they were gone, and all I heard was the sound of something laughing.

Jim Bates lives in a small town twenty miles west of Minneapolis, Minnesota. His stories have appeared online in CafeLit, The Writers' Cafe Magazine, Cabinet of Heed, Paragraph Planet, Nailpolish Stories, Ariel Chart, Potato Soup Journal, Literary Yard, Spillwords (Dec, 2019, Author of the Month), The Drabble, The Academy of the Heart and Mind and World of Myth Magazine. In print publications: A Million Ways, Mused Literary Journal, Gleam Flash Fiction Anthology #2, the Portal Anthology and the Glamour Anthology by Clarendon House Publishing, The Best of CafeLit 8 by Chapeltown Publishing, the Nativity Anthology by Bridge House Publishing and Gold Dust Magazine.
Website: www.theviewfromlonglake.wordpress.com

Night Watch
by Alyson Faye

Fountain Reid perched in the crow's nest of *The Hesper,* on night watch. Senses straining. The whistling might have been the wind, but Reid knew different. He heard the wet slap of flesh on deck. He skimmed down the rigging, knife between his teeth.

Behind him a voice, sexless but sexual, whispered, "Man of water…join us." A tongue licked his neck. Slime dripped down his collar.

Hands snaked around his chest and Reid leant into the salt-stained embrace; letting go of loneliness.

Then whipping round, knife blade gleaming, he slashed.

The siren wailed her death song.

Alyson Faye lives in the UK; her fiction has been published widely both in print anthologies - DeadCades, Women in Horror Annual 2, Trembling with Fear 1 & 2, Stories from Stone and in ezines. Her Gothic story, Night of the Rider, is published by Demain in their Short Sharp Shocks! E book series, and Demain have just published her crime novella, Maggie of my Heart. Her work has been placed in several competitions, read in podcasts, and is available as downloads. She performs at open mics, teaches, edits and attends horror conventions. Website: alysonfayewordpress.wordpress.com Twitter: @AlysonFaye2

The Holy Sea
by Eddie D. Moore

A mist of salty water washed over Luca as he peered over the edge of the bow. A large unblinking eye just under the surface of the water stared back at him. Reverence kept Luca from looking away. He couldn't imagine how large the creature was or how it swam so fast.

Luca heard screams behind him as the ship came to a sudden stop, and momentum sent him over the guardrail and into the sea. He glanced back once at the tangle of tentacles that pulled the ship under and swam as he prayed fervently to his newfound god.

Eddie D. Moore travels hundreds of hours a year, and he fills that time by listening to audiobooks. When he isn't playing with his grandchildren, he writes his own stories. You can find a list of his publications on his blog or by visiting his Amazon Author Page. While you're there, be sure to pick up a copy of his mini-anthology Misfits & Oddities.
Website: eddiedmoore.wordpress.com
Amazon: amazon.com/author/eddiedmoore

An Ocean in Motion, the Emotion of Moana
by Steven Holding

I hadn't seen the sea (or maybe it had not seen me?).

Backs of postcards, holiday snap scrapbooks; ponds, muddy puddles, overflowing sinks.

None seemed to satiate my need. Stranded in the city, it felt beyond my reach.

To remedy this immediately, I set off in search of the beach; trudged to the edge where the land ceased to be.

My God! Such beauty! Flooding my vision, broadening my horizons, feasting my eyes upon its infinite magnificence.

Exhausted, I slept upon the sand.

Dreamt that the seven oceans simply disappeared.

Awoke to silence.

And remained afraid to open my eyes.

Steven Holding lives with his family in the United Kingdom. His stories have appeared both online and in print. Most recently his work has featured in the collections 'TREMBLING WITH FEAR YEAR TWO', 'SPLASH OF INK', and the anthologies 'MONSTERS', 'BEYOND' and 'DARK MOMENTS - YEAR ONE' from Black Hare Press. He is currently working upon further short fiction and a novel. Website: www.stevenholding.co.uk

Attack of the Sea Serpents
by Wondra Vanian

Take a cruise, they said. It'll be fun, they said.

Wrong.

Of course, they probably meant cruises that *weren't* under attack by enormous sea monsters.

Lorelle clutched her weapon (okay, steak knife—it was a *cruise*!) as one of the slimy creatures slammed into the locked door. A razor-sharp spike sliced through the cheap wood.

Somehow, Lorelle's wild flailing managed to nick the thing. Green blood oozed onto the floor. She celebrated a moment's victory before the thing reared back and charged again.

Next year, she thought, I'm going to the Grand Canyon.

Wood splintered.

If I live through this…

Wondra Vanian is an American living in the United Kingdom with her Welsh husband and their army of fur babies. A writer first, Wondra is also an avid gamer, photographer, cinephile, and blogger. She has music in her blood, sleeps with the lights on, and has been known to dance naked in the moonlight. Wondra was a multiple Top-Ten finisher in the 2017 and 2018 Preditors and Editors Reader's Poll, including the Best Author category. Her story, "Halloween Night," was named a Notable Contender for the Bristol Short Story Prize in 2015.
Website: www.wondravanian.com

A New Friend
by Wendy Roberts

Tracey didn't expect to find a friend at the bottom of the ocean. She also didn't expect her foot to be wedged between two rocks that shifted when the eel she took photos of swam past it. But here she is, stuck between a rock and a hard place as her oxygen hits that red line. Staring into the four eyes of a beast three times her size. Four of its tentacles shove the rock off her foot as another wraps around her waist. Tracey's hope that it'll swim up is shattered when it dives further into a dark hole.

Writing short stories and novels started as a past time for **Wendy Roberts** *and has now become a fully fledged passion. She posts short stories on her website and can be found most days on Twitter.*
Website: flippinscribbler.com
Twitter: @_WARoberts

Finding Closure
by Wendy Roberts

Everyone suggested that Tanya visit his grave. That it would help give her some sense of closure. So, here she is, over three thousand feet below sea level, staring at her father's corpse that's rotting in this wreckage. Tears roll down her face because she's not sure how this makes it any better. It's an image that will forever be seared into her brain, even as she reaches for the pocket watch with the photo of her parents placed inside. Sure, it's probably ruined, and sure, she shouldn't be taking from the dead. But she doesn't have anything left, so...

Writing short stories and novels started as a past time for ***Wendy Roberts*** *and has now become a fully fledged passion. She posts short stories on her website and can be found most days on Twitter.*
Website: flippinscribbler.com
Twitter: @_WARoberts

Death Wish
by A.R. Johnston

"You know it's dangerous to sit there?" a voice spoke from behind him.

"I do. But life is boring without that element of danger, don't you think?" came his reply as he continued to stare into the watery depths from a gangplank, watching as sharks did lazy circles beneath his feet.

"And if one of those sharks decides to jump and eat you?"

He laughed, standing up, a wobbly balance on the plank.

"All the better. But why don't I give them some sport?"

He winked and dived. Screaming, she raced to the railing.

"Damn shifter with a death wish."

A.R. Johnston is a small-town girl from Nova Scotia, Canada. She is known to write mostly urban fantasy, though she goes where the muses lead her and you never know where that may be. She is a lover of coffee, good tv shows, horror flicks, and a reader of good books. She pretends to be a writer when real life doesn't get in the way. Pesky full-time job and adulting!
Facebook: arjohnstonauthor
Website: arjohnstonauthor.wordpress.com

Sole Survivor
by Matthew A. Clarke

As I lie here on this sun-baked rock, brushing crusted salt from my arms, the bodies of young and old float lazily around me.

I know you might be thinking I should consider myself lucky, that I'm still alive. You're wrong.

My passengers, dead.

My crew mates, dead.

It returned for the few that had managed to get some distance in the life rafts, too.

At this point, death would be a mercy, but I'm too weak to do it myself.

A tremendous tentacle rises from the darkness to snatch another body.

Soon, it will be my turn.

Matthew A. Clarke is a new face in the world of horror. He has been writing short fiction as a hobby for two years and has decided to share his passion with likeminded people. Matthew loves all things that go bump in the night, having been introduced to slasher movies at a young age. He lives on the South Coast of England with his fiancé, Isabelle, and a little dachshund called Frank.
Facebook: matthewaclarkeauthor

The Decoy

by Amber M. Simpson

They found the girl, naked, knee-deep in the water, as they took their morning stroll.

"You okay?" called Kevin as they approached.

"Where're your parents, sweetie?" Nicole questioned, scanning the deserted beach.

The girl remained mute, staring out at the waves. With looks of concern, they waded towards her and draped a towel over her shoulders. Almost immediately, they felt in unison, a cold slimy grip around their ankles.

No time to react, they were jerked off their feet and dragged screaming beneath the water.

The decoy shuddered, the form losing its shape as it dissolved back into the ocean.

Amber M. Simpson *is a dark fiction writer from Northern Kentucky with a penchant for horror and fantasy. Her work has been published in multiple anthologies, as well as online. She assists with editing for Fantasia Divinity Magazine, where she's gotten to work with many talented authors from all over the world. While she loves to create dark worlds and diverse characters, her greatest creations of all are her sons, Max and Liam, who keep her feet on the ground even while her head is in the clouds.*

Website: <u>*ambermsimpson.com*</u>
Facebook: <u>*authorambermsimpson*</u>

Bermuda
by Jasmine Jarvis

The DSV slowly glides along the ocean floor collecting samples for scientific research.

Silt suddenly engulfs the DSV, obscuring the view from the pilot window. When it clears, the crew stare out in disbelief, for materialising before them is a graveyard of aircraft wreckages, the terrified faces of passengers visible in cabin windows.

A dark shadow descends over the DSV and its doomed crew within.

The captain nervously stands by on the ship's deck as the tech tries to regain comms with the DSV. A crackle breaks the silence followed by the terrified screams of the crew before cutting out.

Jasmine Jarvis is a teller of tales and scribbler of scribbles. She lives in Brisbane, Australia with her husband Michael, their two children, Tilly and Mish; Ripley, their German Shepherd, and indoor fat cat, Dwight K. Shrute.

Horse to the Water
by Andrew Anderson

Eirwen refused to stay in the field with the other horses at night, and no fence could be built which she didn't leap over with ease. She should have proven lucrative to Iain McColm, but she never bore a rider.

Little Shona was sent to find her each morning; Eirwen would be running along the black sand beach, chasing the waves, but exhausted and with salt encrusting her dripping white mane.

Shona offered to sleep beside her one night.

She became Eirwen's first and final rider, as she ran into the foam to join the other kelpies—they never returned.

Andrew Anderson is a spare-time writer of microfiction, flash fiction and short stories, from Bathgate, Scotland. His work has been published on FlashFlood and Re:Written, and published in Black Hare Press anthologies.
Twitter: <u>*soorploom*</u>

The Sight of the Kraken
by Clint Foster

"Haul to starboard, I see it there! Hooks and harpoons, all hands man the rails and steel your spines for the sight of the wrath of the seas. Look! See! It is coming as the sea boils. An eye the size of an island, a mouth as big as the sky. Stand! Stand with your strong arms ready and your salty hearts full, for Davy Jones accepts nary a coward to his crew. The time has come to pay the debt we all owe to the sea, for now, the kraken comes to the surface to do battle with us."

Clint Foster lives with his herd of four cats, beloved Basset, Zero, and wonderful wife, Nik. He loves to tell stories just as much as he loves to read them and is excited to share his work. A long-time consumer of media of all kinds, he enjoys giving back what he hopes everyone else thinks are good stories.
Facebook: ClintFosterAuthor

Lusana, Mermaid of the Deep
by Vonnie Winslow Crist

Lusana adjusted her costume, waited for the crowd to enter her tent. Parents were hard to find for a foundling suffering from *sirenomelia*, but Sheila and Butch of *Zamundi's Wonders* had adopted her. Lusana repaid them by starring in their sideshow.

"But I'm so lonely," she whispered.

At closing time, she climbed into her wheelchair. Rather than go home like usual, she rolled herself to pier's end, gazed at the ocean, wished to belong.

A merman appeared in the waves beneath her.

Eyes filled with tears, Lusana spread her arms, leaned forward, and dived into the waters of her birth.

Vonnie Winslow Crist is author of The Enchanted Dagger, Owl Light, The Greener Forest, Murder on Marawa Prime, and other award-winning books. Her fiction is included in "Amazing Stories," "Cast of Wonders," "Outposts of Beyond," Killing It Softly 2, Defending the Future - Dogs of War, Midnight Masquerade, Chaos of Hard Clay, and elsewhere. A cloverhand who has found so many four-leafed clovers she keeps them in jars, Vonnie strives to celebrate the power of myth in her writing.
Website: www.vonniewinslowcrist.com

Do Do Doo Do Do Doo

by Raven Corinn Carluk

Jessie clicked Rewatch, and everyone sang along. He was too stoned to make the motions, but Rachel and Allison continued to do so. Others on the yacht danced, drank, smoked, and used their devices to add to the view count.

"A billion!" Rachel screamed and refreshed the video. Weary, Jesse got to his feet to celebrate the achievement, nonetheless.

The sea stilled, the air turned to ice, and everyone stopped. The song played on, happy and unaware of the ominous change.

Bass growling joined in, a toothy maw breaking the surface. Everyone screamed in terrors as it sang. "Run away."

Raven Corinn Carluk writes dark fantasy, paranormal romance, and anything else that catches her interest. She's authored five novels, where she explores themes of love and acceptance. Her shorter pieces, usually from her darker side, can be found in Black Hare Press anthologies, at Detritus Online, and through Alban Lake Publishers.
Twitter: @ravencorinn
Website: www.ravencorinncarluk.com

The Affair
by Ximena Escobar

She didn't understand his coldness.
She didn't understand his restless murmur of here,
and away.
She didn't understand the cloud of his heart
Buried secrets she felt in her own bones,
cells stirring,
Searching.
She longed for his depth,
Overwhelming reflection of the sky,
Her smallness longed to disappear
in the immensity
of his strength.
He pushed her away,
He warned her with fury,
but
By then she had decided
she was nothing without him.
He got in the way of
Every conversation,
Every blank canvas
Any horizon,
Stretching

434

Swaying,

Pulling her

Until,

Her bones became one of his secrets.

Ximena Escobar *is writing stories and poetry. Originally from Chile, she is the author of a translation into Spanish of the Broadway Musical "The Wizard of Oz", and of an original adaptation of the same, "Navidad en Oz", both produced in her home country. Since 2018 she has published several short stories in various anthologies and online platforms, and is now slowly working on her own collection. Ximena has a degree in Arts & Communication Science and lives in Nottingham with her family.*
Facebook: Ximenautora
Twitter: @laximenin

Waking Up
by Steven Lord

The lapping of warm saltwater rouses me from the depths of slumber. I am alive.

I lift my head from the moist sand and look around. White beaches unfurl left and right. Lush jungle in front of me, sea behind.

I am alone. Hundreds set off into the vast ocean of the night, all in different directions. None will follow to this speck of dirt in the void.

I have been baptised, immersed in these foreign waters and born anew. I sit down on this alien shore and watch a second sun crest into the blood-red sky. I am home.

Steven Lord is a debut author based in the south of England. He is currently attempting to cram writing in alongside a busy day job, with varying levels of success. While his long-term aspiration is to get a novel published, at present he would be pretty pleased with a drabble or two.

Here There be Monsters
by G. Allen Wilbanks

The old maps used to carry the legend, "Here there be monsters," in the open uncharted regions of the open sea. It was a warning to all who travelled to be wary of the unknown.

But ancient superstitions were soon cast aside for logic and a thirst to explore the previously unexplored.

Sometimes the old ways were better, the captain thought. A little fear is a healthy thing.

A crack like a gunshot filled the air as the keel of the wooden hull broke in the jaws of the leviathan beneath them.

He cursed and prepared to meet the monster.

G. Allen Wilbanks is a member of the Horror Writers Association (HWA) and has published over 100 short stories in various magazines and on-line venues. He is the author of two short story collections, and the novel, When Darkness Comes.
Website: www.gallenwilbanks.com
Blog: DeepDarkThoughts.com

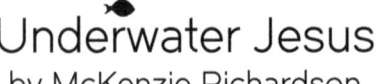

Underwater Jesus
by McKenzie Richardson

Jesus' arms were outstretched, his eyes gazing upward through the turbid waters to the rippling sunlight above. Divers circled the statue, in awe of the oddity resting on the ocean floor. Barnacles enveloped most of the statue's surface along with bits of sea plants, giving the entire scene an eerie feel.

Despite the warm waters, a shiver ran down one diver's spine. With a trail of bubbles rising in his wake, he approached the statue, a hand outstretched to touch Jesus' face.

What a story this would make back at the office.

As he brushed the statue's chin, Jesus blinked.

McKenzie Richardson lives in Milwaukee, WI. Her horror stories have been featured in various anthologies including Evil Lurks, Pandemic, and After: Undead Wars. She has also published a variety of poems and flash fiction pieces.
Facebook: mckenzielrichardson
Blog: www.craft-cycle.com

Treasure
by Cindar Harrell

I sit in my grotto, playing with my treasures. For centuries I have collected things discarded by sunken ships; what the humans forgot were now mine.

But there is one thing I am most excited to explore. A box made of a material I cannot identify fell from the ruins of an old world. Ships long crashed were buried there amongst the stone rubble. I had never seen it before until today. Of all the wonders there, though, this box spoke to me most.

I open it.

Screams fill my ears as every horror was unleashed.

What have I done?

Cindar Harrell loves fairy tales, especially ones with a dark twist. Her writing is often fairy tale inspired, but she also loves mystery and horror. Her stories can be found in various. Traveling is a passion for her as it inspires her imagination to run wild, especially in places that have a mystic presence in the air. She regularly moonlights as another human, but no matter who she is, she is always writing. Her novella inspired by The Snow Queen is set to release in 2020 as well as her debut novel, Lithium, and short story collection, Perchance to Dream.
Facebook: *CindarHarrell*

Blood Runs Deep
by Andrew Anderson

Skipper Tam was devastated.

He'd taken all possible precautions after last time: compulsory lifejackets; safety lines; relentless health and safety drills.

And yet Ben MacAskill was still lost at sea.

Avoiding a Man Overboard at all Costs: The Dangers of Cold Water Shock and Hypothermia.

Not this time—the safety line had been snapped, and a bloodied lifejacket had surfaced minutes after Ben went under.

Tam was at a loss: how to explain to Mrs MacAskill how Ben had died at sea, like his father, uncles and grandfather before him; that something had clearly developed a taste for this family.

Andrew Anderson is a spare-time writer of microfiction, flash fiction and short stories, from Bathgate, Scotland. His work has been published on FlashFlood and Re:Written, and published in Black Hare Press anthologies.
Twitter: <u>soorploom</u>

Tourist Trap
by Raven Corinn Carluk

"Look at the fishies!" The young women giggled, pointing at a passing shark. Half-dressed, toasty tans, they stood apart from the other tourists on the boat.

Loud, obnoxious, brash, Santiago could hear them all the way up on the deck. Only another ninety minutes until they were back in port.

"Come here, fishy."

"Go to the dentist, fishy."

They sounded like every other college girl down for Spring Break. He couldn't have told them apart; their faces simply blended together.

Made it easier to tell the police he didn't remember them. And the sharks never left much to be recognised.

Raven Corinn Carluk *writes dark fantasy, paranormal romance, and anything else that catches her interest. She's authored five novels, where she explores themes of love and acceptance. Her shorter pieces, usually from her darker side, can be found in Black Hare Press anthologies, at Detritus Online, and through Alban Lake Publishers.*
Twitter: @ravencorinn
Website: www.ravencorinncarluk.com

Repurposed Beauty
by Chris Bannor

The waters rose, and the oceans were filled with the refuse of a civilization that couldn't control itself. They built higher and wider, but never better. They made people too busy to realise they were happier without the noise and clamour of three devices, the ding of notifications.

When the cities sank, we took the castoffs and made them beautiful. Coral gardens filled once condemned buildings. Fish swam through the broken windows of long-dead cars.

They feared we might someday rise again, but we preferred to wait in the beauty of our water world.

They would destroy themselves soon enough.

Chris Bannor is a science fiction and fantasy writer who lives in Southern California. Chris learned her love of genre stories from her mother at an early age and has never veered far from that path. She also enjoys musical theater and road trips with her family but is a general homebody otherwise.
Facebook: chrisbannorauthor
Website: ChrisBannor.com

Deep See
by A.L. Paradiso

Here's another, down deep with his SCUBA. Is he one of the good ones who tries to befriend me, or one who wants to eat me? No way to communicate; how can he know I come from another planet, am smarter than humans, and can advance his race?

Spear gun! Bad human! Quick turn; shoot ink; dive deeper for deep see community entrance. I'll squeeze into covert again, four legs first, four follow. Happy no bones I have; his big bones can't follow. Foolish humans. When will they learn to come in peace as we did millennia ago? So sad.

A.L. Paradiso was born in Europe, English is his second language, following Italian—then Latin, Pig Latin, French and assorted computer languages. He lives in upstate NY with three cats. In college he took a dislike to writing of any kind and swore never to try that again. Some years later, influenced by Babylon 5's creator and his own pressure to write about two traumatic events, he turned to creative writing. As of Feb 2020, he has shared 130+ published stories with others online (> 4.6 million views), in eleven anthologies, DRAGON TALES COLLECTION, and two literary journals.
Amazon: www.tinyurl.com/Paradiso-dragons
Books2Read: books2read.com/ap/RWjj5e/AL-Paradiso

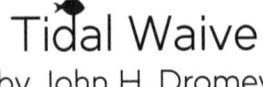

Tidal Waive
by John H. Dromey

"Have you heard? A ruthless lone-wolf pirate, armed only with a cutlass, hijacked a sailing ship. It was a bloodbath. Afterwards, he set down his gore-covered blade and climbed up the mast to display the Jolly Roger with its white skull and crossbones on black cloth. When he came back down, the police were there to arrest him."

"The *police*? Not the Coast Guard? I thought pirates operated on the high seas."

"Not this one. He has thalassaphobia, a fear of the ocean. The ship was in dry dock. A passing motorist recognised the pirate flag and called the cops."

John H. Dromey was born in northeast Missouri, USA. He enjoys reading—mysteries in particular—and writing in a variety of genres. In addition to contributing to the Black Hare Press series of Dark Drabbles anthologies, he's had short fiction published in Alfred Hitchcock's Mystery Magazine, Martian Magazine, Mystery Weekly, Stupefying Stories Showcase, Thriller Magazine, Unfit Magazine, and elsewhere, as well as in numerous anthologies, including Chilling Horror Short Stories (Flame Tree Publishing, 2015).

Explore the Depths
by A.R. Johnston

People have only searched the surface of the waters. There is so much more below the surface, where there is no light, and no air to breathe. Water is beautiful, but there are things to fear within. Things you have never seen before live in the water; gliding monsters. Be afraid of what you do not know. They will come, these monsters, the most beautiful ones with shimmering scales and teeth that will tear. Or if you're lucky, they will kiss you, and drag you down to a watery death.

Dark waters are a scary place. Will you go below?

A.R. Johnston is a small-town girl from Nova Scotia, Canada. She is known to write mostly urban fantasy, though she goes where the muses lead her and you never know where that may be. She is a lover of coffee, good tv shows, horror flicks, and a reader of good books. She pretends to be a writer when real life doesn't get in the way. Pesky full-time job and adulting!
Facebook: arjohnstonauthor
Website: arjohnstonauthor.wordpress.com

445

Elf

by Lesley Drane

I waited at the quayside whilst my husband negotiated the speedboat hire.

"This beauty is ours for two hours, Elf." His annoying nickname for me.

Terry jumped in and held out his hand. I was dubious, anxiety creeping along my bones. I couldn't swim.

"Come on, it's ok, the cove isn't far. Then we can finally get to the beach we could only see from the jeep."

The beach was empty, no boats nearby. Terry jumped into the water, then helped me. He kissed me.

"I love you, Elf, but love the million dollar life insurance more. Bye my sweet."

Lesley Drane is a widow, and lives with her two year old Cavalier King Charles spaniel, Stephanie. Lesley enjoys to write stories about the supernatural and murder mysteries. Lesley also makes book sculptures using preloved books.

The Key to a Profitable Fishing Trip

by Crystal L. Kirkham

"Thick as pea soup out there," the captain said as he joined me out on the deck.

"Good thing for GPS…" My voice trailed off at the sight of a figure striding across the water. "What the…?"

"Ah, that's just Davy Jones, come to collect what's owed." The captain grinned at me. "We filled the tanks with the best crab this trip."

"What?" I backed away as a skeletal hand gripped the railing and a creature stepped onto the ship, eyes fixed on me.

The captain said nothing as the creature wrapped its icy fingers around my throat and squeezed.

Crystal L. Kirkham is a multi-genre speculative fiction author. She has published novels across several genres including her fantasy adventure Feathers and Fae (October 2019 from Kyanite Publishing) and her self-published urban fantasy series, Saints & Sinners. She is also a contributing author to multiple best-selling anthologies. Hailing from the wilds of Canada, she is an avid outdoors person, unrepentant coffee addict, part-time foodie, servant to a wonderful feline, and companion to three delightfully hilarious canines - Treble and Freddie the Standard Poodles, and Nahni the Australian Shepherd.
Website: www.crystallkirkham.com

Chum

by Evan Baughfman

They became chums upon learning they shared a passion for deep-sea fishing.

Danny's father had left him a boat. Mikey's father had taught him how to catch marlin.

Both of their fathers—members of the Mob—had shown their sons how to solve problems "the family way." Over time, Danny and Mikey became seasoned problem-solvers.

Until Mikey had a kid. Got a conscience. Became the problem.

He swore he'd confess to all their sins.

So, Danny took care of Mikey the family way. Took Mikey on his father's boat.

Tossed his old chum by the bucketful to sharks circling below.

Evan Baughfman works in a very scary place: a middle school! He writes all genres, but horror is where he's most comfortable. Much of his writing success has been as a playwright. He's had many different plays produced across the globe. Heuer Publishing has published his Poe adaptation, "A Taste of Amontillado". Additionally, Evan has adapted a number of his short stories into screenplays, of which "The Emaciated Man" and "The Creaky Door" have won awards in various film festival competitions. Evan's "Just Plants" was recently published in Soteira Press's horror anthology, The Monsters We Forgot - Volume 1.

Deep Sea Joyride
by Shawn M. Klimek

Jules twisted the knob on the control panel which would dim the stolen submersible's interior lights.

"Hey!" Marcel objected. "I'm reading!"

Jules shook his head. "Just outside this view portal are exotic, deep sea creatures most humans have never seen, and your fool face is buried in that book!"

"It's the owner's manual," Marcel defended.

"Even more pathetic."

"James Cameron is Canadian."

"You win the trivia prize. So what?"

Marcel pointed at the depth gauge. "It means the maximum safe depth is listed in meters, not feet, fool! Now, turn on the lights, so I can find the ascent controls."

Shawn M. Klimek is an internationally best-selling short-story writer and poet, and author of Hungry Thing. More than 150 of his works have been published online or in such anthologies as BHP's Deep Space, Eerie Christmas, Bad Romance, Jibbernocky, and every book in the Dark Drabbles series.
Website: jotinthedark.blogspot.com
Facebook: shawnmklimekauthor

A Drink Before Dinner
by Mason Harold Hilden

Alone on a raft, starving and blistered, Todd had finally given up.

Having seen a shark hours earlier, he pondered ending it then, but being eaten alive stifled the thought. Todd decided on drowning. Hop in, go under, breath in— pain gone. Mustering up courage, he made peace with himself and took the plunge.

To his shock, Todd found his body would not let him drown. He thrashed and convulsed. His horror only intensified upon seeing a shape approaching from below, with its rows of razor sharp teeth. Todd screamed underwater, letting blessed water in just as teeth met flesh.

Mason H. Hilden is a Bluenoser, who currently resides in Saint John, New Brunswick, with his family. Over the last twenty years, he has written comic-books, including one professional work. He has also dabbled in mini-biographies, interviews, baseball articles, and animation scripting. Mason recently began writing fiction, and believes that BHP may have created a monster by accepting his submissions.

Cleaning Fish
by Vonnie Winslow Crist

Sitting on the beach, Corinn watched Granddad clean a monkfish. As he pulled the scaler across its body, the creature shivered and iridescent disks scattered on sand.

Corinn picked up a scale, imagined thousands stitched together to make a cloak. She knew mermaids wore such things.

Staring as Granddad lopped off the monkfish's head and tail, she sighed when he slit its belly.

Fishguts plopped out, glimmering like rubies, moonstones, and pearls. When their oceany scent stung her nostrils and flooded her mind, Corinn was unable to resist the salt in her blood.

She stood, then walked into the Atlantic.

Vonnie Winslow Crist is author of The Enchanted Dagger, Owl Light, The Greener Forest, Murder on Marawa Prime, and other award-winning books. Her fiction is included in "Amazing Stories," "Cast of Wonders," "Outposts of Beyond," Killing It Softly 2, Defending the Future - Dogs of War, Midnight Masquerade, Chaos of Hard Clay, and elsewhere. A cloverhand who has found so many four-leafed clovers she keeps them in jars, Vonnie strives to celebrate the power of myth in her writing.
Website: www.vonniewinslowcrist.com

Surf's Up
by Derek Dunn

The sun finally breaks. A handful of locals roam the beach, but no one gets in the water. I don't know why. I've never seen better waves; and, it looks like I'll have them all to myself.

I run towards the sea, surfboard in tow.

"Cuidado!" someone says. "No metas al agua."

I ignore him. The water's warmth bathes my skin. I glide over the waves. They rise higher, pushing me upward.

But they don't fall.

I soar higher until the beach dwindles beneath me. A massive tentacle has lifted me up. Monstrous jaws open wide.

And then I fall.

Derek Dunn is a film enthusiast and musician who writes primarily horror and mystery stories. After obtaining a degree in Media Arts Studies and dabbling in film production, he's turned his efforts to writing fiction. Several of his works have appeared in recent anthologies. He lives in the American northwest with his family, dog, and fish.
Twitter: <u>DerekTDunn</u>

May the Catch Be Good
by A.L. King

"What will happen?" the girl asked.

"The gods of the ocean will carry you to an eternity of splendour," said the father.

"Can I be a mermaid?"

"You can be anything you want," the mother said.

Fires lit onshore. Music started. The parents leapt out of the small boat and pushed it away before swimming back to shore. The tide would take her. She could only scream.

Her cries were drowned out by music and chanting by the time they rejoined their tribe on the beach.

"May the catch be good. May the catch be good."

The parents joined in.

A.L. King is an author of horror, fantasy, science fiction, and poetry. As an avid fan of dark subjects from an early age, his first influences included R.L. Stine, Edgar Allan Poe, and Stephen King. Later stylistic inspirations came from foreign horror films and media, particularly Japanese. He is a graduate of West Liberty University, has dabbled in journalism, and is actively involved in his community. Although his creativity leans toward darker genres, he has even written a children's book titled "Leif's First Fall." He was raised in the town of Sistersville, West Virginia, which he still proudly calls home.

Piracy
by Rich Rurshell

As the *Black Mare* pummelled the approaching galleon with cannonballs, Captain Morris could hear the cackling and whooping of its undead crew.

"Captain?"

"Prepare to fight, Mr. Donoghue."

Grinning corpses fearlessly boarded the *Black Mare* and made short work of Morris' crew. One charged at Morris with a long pike. Donoghue took its head clean off with his cutlass. The headless corpse continued its advance and pinned Morris to the mast.

With his dying breath, Morris saw the captain of the rotten galleon standing at the wheel of the *Black Mare*, pointing at him, laughing heartily into the night sky.

Rich Rurshell is a short story writer from Suffolk, England. Rich writes Horror, Sci-Fi, and Fantasy, and his stories can be found in various short story anthologies and magazines. Most recently, his story "Subject: Galilee" was published in World War Four from Zombie Pirate Publishing, and "Life Choices" was published in Salty Tales from Stormy Island Publishing. When Rich is not writing stories, he likes to write and perform music.
Facebook: richrurshellauthor

Deep See Covert
by A.L. Paradiso

Cousin Otto, I hear you and will close the covert entrance to our Deep See home as you enter. Welcome, cousin, to safety.

Greetings cousin squid. Prepare our defences; all citizens line up at vents and prepare to ink all humans who approach. Citizen jelly fish, prepare to sting and flee. You and our squid squad will lead them away, to our former home. Brother Octum, if needed, you will steal spear gun, ink him and lead him away.

I often wonder, Rex Otto, if we should just abandon them to their fates and return home.

No! Humans have value.

A.L. Paradiso *was born in Europe, English is his second language, following Italian—then Latin, Pig Latin, French and assorted computer languages. He lives in upstate NY with three cats. In college he took a dislike to writing of any kind and swore never to try that again. Some years later, influenced by Babylon 5's creator and his own pressure to write about two traumatic events, he turned to creative writing. As of Feb 2020, he has shared 130+ published stories with others online (> 4.6 million views), in eleven anthologies, DRAGON TALES COLLECTION, and two literary journals.*
Amazon: www.tinyurl.com/Paradiso-dragons
Books2Read: books2read.com/ap/RWjj5e/AL-Paradiso

The Seventh Sea
by Olivia Arieti

Seadog Hendrik knew it would be his final voyage; many were the oceans his vessel had sailed, but this was where it was doomed to sink, the inevitable epilogue to the pirate's wickedness.

"Beware of the seventh sea," cried the last victim forced to walk off the plank.

The glare was as haunting as the curse launched at him.

The depraved crew, unaware of the imminent punishment, were already drunken ghosts feasting over the chests full of gold and gems.

Roars and howls mingled into a satanic cacophony as the phantom ship approached and its bow penetrated their captain's heart.

Olivia Arieti has a degree from the University of Pisa and lives in Torre del Lago Puccini, Italy, with her family. Besides being a published playwright, she loves writing retellings of fairy tales, and at the same time is intrigued by supernatural and horror themes. Her stories appeared in several magazines and anthologies like Enchanted Conversations, Enchanted Tales Literary Magazine, Fantasia Divinity Magazine, Cliterature, Medieval Nightmares, Static Movement, 100 Doors To Madness Forgotten Tomb Press, Black Cats Horrified Press, Bloody Ghost Stories Full Moon Books, Death And Decorations Thirteen O'Clock Press, Infective Ink, Pandemonium Press, Pussy Magic Magazine.

Trench, Mariana Trench
by Frances Tate

Trieste sank slowly into the dark canyon. Hiding in the silt, we knew invasion wouldn't be long.

After the submersible left, the committee met; sought volunteers for training and experimentation.

Agents travelled far and wide. Brought back samples clogged in their intestines, their gills.

Every species we encountered is affected. Damned. We—

No!

Light and cables descend: Camera.

Our strike force isn't ready yet.

Caught in the open, I morph. Shed my claws, teeth, I mimic the *other* immortal jellyfish template.

The image of a drowned plastic bag, here, shames the world.

So many decoys. You'll never see us coming.

Frances Tate is a British self-published writer of vampires and drabbles who lives in the north west of England. She enjoys gardening, exploring historical sites, cinema, reading and travelling. She's taken pleasure in flight-planning a cabbage white butterfly approach to careers, preferring to generalise rather than specialise. She trained as an Economics high school teacher and has a private pilot's licence amongst other things. Currently she writes (very restrained) overhaul instructions for an engineering company.

Where's the Rum?
by Wendy Roberts

Okay, so sailing across the world in a rickety old boat probably wasn't Elle's best idea. Especially when that hurricane came up out of nowhere and capsized her whole boat. Yeah, Elle's really regretting that one. But she still can't stop from smiling at the moment because how many people can say they've been rescued by one of the largest sea turtles that is currently pulling her toward paradise?

Nah, it definitely wasn't the greatest idea ever, but she's feeling like the world's best pirate right now, and all she really wants to know is: where's all the rum gone?

Writing short stories and novels started as a past time for **Wendy Roberts** *and has now become a fully fledged passion. She posts short stories on her website and can be found most days on Twitter.*
Website: flippinscribbler.com
Twitter: @_WARoberts

Back
by Cassandra Angler

She climbed up onto the pier, sea water dripping from her hair. Half of her face rotted with decay. She shouldn't be here, I thought I had fastened the cement block tightly enough. Behind her, others emerge. In all different stages of decomposition, one being nothing but bone. They stagger toward the crowd, limping on their broken limbs. Beach goers scream and scramble, some falling under the weight of sea logged attackers, being bitten and ripped apart. Choking on the smell of mildew and rotten meat, turning to run. There she is, blocking my way. My wife, back from sea.

Cassandra Angler is a married mother of four who lives in the State of Ohio in the USA. When she isn't busy caring for her family, Cassandra works on her upcoming novel due out in November of 2020 titled Contaminated. Cassandra has three short story publications as well as several flash fiction and drabble publications.

BLACK HARE PRESS

ACKNOWLEDGEMENTS

When we embarked on DARK DRABBLES—the first set of anthologies from BHP—we never envisioned the huge support we'd get from the writing community. We have been truly humbled by the number of submissions (more than 500 for WORLDS alone!) and have loved reading every single one of them. So, to everyone who crafted a tiny tale just for us; we thank you from the bottom of our hearts.

To everyone who has helped us on the way—our families and friends, collaborators and random strangers who took pity—we couldn't have done it without you. Thank you all.

www.blackharepress.com

BLACK HARE PRESS

Stories of new worlds, new creatures, alien colonisation, humanity's new home, space accidents, alien snackcidents, evil planets, military mashups, alien autopsies, and much, much more.

Beatific angels, holy wars, kitty saviours, epic battles between good and evil, devils and demons, fallen angels and many more tantalising tiny tales.

Wendigos, vampires, things that go bump in the night or hide under the bed, witches, demons, upirs, kelpies, toad people, zombies, sirens and hundreds of other tiny terrifying tales.

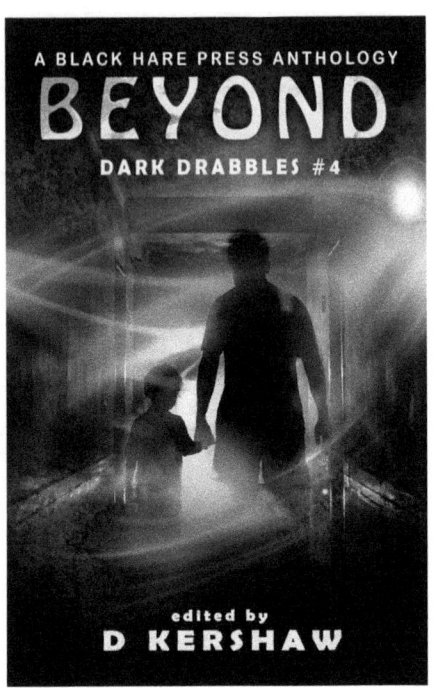

A BLACK HARE PRESS ANTHOLOGY

BEYOND

DARK DRABBLES #4

edited by

D KERSHAW

Micro myths of the paranormal;
poltergeists, spirit boards, ghosts
and ghouls, avenging apparitions
and horrifying hauntings.

Murder mysteries, criminal chronicles, whodunnits, revenge, suspicion, mayhem, intrigue, and lots more.

Lightning Source UK Ltd.
Milton Keynes UK
UKHW021214260420
362151UK00007B/161/J